# *But,*
# Even Now

A NOVEL

To Laura,
Happy reading!

*Jennifer* *Denaè*
**THOMAS** **JONES**

For those who are searching,
doubting,
and barely hanging on.
God's got your back.
Even now.

**But, Even Now**
Denae Jones and Jennifer Thomas



But, Even Now is historical fiction. The historical parts of But, Even Now are based on true stories from the gospels of Jesus Christ. Some locations change, and timelines were combined or condensed to fit the story. Artistic liberties were taken to tell backstories, and some characters or dialogue have been added. However, all context and artistic ingenuity support the true intention of the Scriptures. We encourage readers to explore the gospels of Luke and John, which contain different parts of the true story of Mary, Martha, and Lazarus and their relationship with Jesus.

Unless otherwise indicated, all the names, characters, places, events and incidents in the present-day parts of this book are either the product of the author's imagination or used in a fictitious manner. Any resemblance to actual persons, living or dead, or actual events is purely coincidental.



ISBN 979-8-9855200-9-5

**Table of Contents**

**Authors' note:**

For historical accuracy, we have attempted to use Jewish terms. These have been italicized. For clarity, you will find definitions for italicized, Jewish words in a glossary of terms at the back of the book, page 253.

**Special thanks to:**

Photo credits: Maggie Wickline-Jowers
Cover design: Matthew Postell at 5:13 Graphics and Media LLC

# *Prologue*

## Trista

October 14, 2017

The rest of my life was hanging in the balance of what would replace the three dots dancing across the message screen of my phone. We were finally at a place where I was texting questions, and he was answering them truthfully. I was so afraid to ask, but something in me told me the time was now. I needed to know. Seconds turned into minutes as I sat there on the corner of the couch, staring at the moving dots and hoping to see the answer pop up that I had been praying for.

He finally replied with a simple "no."

I texted back, "It sure seems like you were typing for a long time, as if you wrote another reply, then deleted it. The truth will come out, eventually." I then repeated the question, not knowing if I really even wanted the answer now.

The three little dots appeared on the screen again. Were they moving in slow motion, or was it just me? Time seemed to change to a sluggish pace all around me. I could hear nothing but the beat of my pounding heart.

"Please, God, NO!!!" I pleaded for the answer to remain no.

My fear was confirmed when the dots were replaced with his reply. "Yes, I'm so sorry."

# Chapter 1

## Adinah's Tears

31AD

Mary almost didn't hear the distant sobs.

Her mind was consumed with her own memories so acutely that the lines between past and present were blurred and confusing. She gripped the basket in her hand a little harder until she felt the vine press into her skin. It seemed strange that some days passed without thinking of her parents at all, and then there were days like today. For no particular reason, her *abba* and *aima* were so close in her memory that she could almost hear their voices. At one point, she felt their presence so strongly that she fully expected to see them standing behind her when she turned around. Yet, when she turned to look, all that lay behind her was the lonely trail of her own footprints. She didn't want to get used to the fact that her mother, her gentle *aima*, would never be by her side during the harvesting of dates again. Her heart could not fathom the thought of living the rest of her days without the love and guidance of her parents.

The swell of emotions made for another long morning, but at least she had a basket of dates to show for it. Her mother would be proud. Dust gathered around her feet as she walked. Their rhythmic beat lulled her imagination to a place where mere survival didn't consume every waking moment and their world didn't carry the stench of Roman rule.

From somewhere nearby, the resonance of heavy sobs yanked her back into the realization of the broken existence in which they lived. She instinctively walked toward the direction of the sorrowful sound, only to find her dear friend, Adinah, in a slumped heap behind some date palms just off the path. Absolutely despondent, her chest heaved with each crying breath.

Mary dropped the basket of dates she had just picked as she rushed to her friend's side. She could guess what was wrong, even before she asked. Adinah had been stricken with grief such as this many times, yet, releasing it never seemed to lift the sorrow. It wasn't the kind that hovered on the surface of a person's emotions. This kind ran deep into her very soul.

Hearing someone approaching, Adinah looked up, startled. She held her breath, waiting to see who it was. She didn't intend to draw attention to herself, and she was in no mood for company. Yet, when she realized it was Mary who had found her sitting there, it unleashed an unspoken permission to weep openly. She felt the arms of her friend fold in around her, and the two held one another, as Adinah's tears soaked through Mary's *tunic*.

Adinah was so weary with grief that her own basket had fallen to the ground when her knees buckled beneath her. It was as if her legs had hearts of their own that were breaking as well. She wasn't sure she could even muster the energy to speak, but she knew her dear friend would understand. Lifting her weary head off Mary's shoulder, she could hardly see. Tears, mixed with sweat, stung her eyes.

"Another season has passed. It has now been three years, Mary!" Adinah said. She began sobbing again, knowing that it needed no further explanation for her friend to understand, but felt the sudden urge to let the emotional floodgates release. "I don't understand! Since I was a child, I have followed the laws. I have honored my husband and been a good wife. I have obeyed the commandments. Why does He continue to punish me with a barren womb?" Her words were muffled and broken between deep gasps of air.

Mary hated the harsh realities of the world in which they lived. Her friend had to fight for everything. Right now, it seemed so unfair that she had to fight, even to breathe. Mary longed to be back in the safe harbor of her own imagination, where such things would never happen. There, she would see her father working alongside his friend, and he would walk out to meet her with a kiss on top of her head when she brought him a noonday meal. He would smile and wave to her as she turned to walk back home and share a story of his family with whoever he was working with that day. He was a skilled storyteller and always so proud of his family! Then, when she walked through the door of their home, the house would smell of fresh bread that her mother had just prepared. She would hum as she moved gracefully around the kitchen, preparing their meal as if it was instinctual. When she saw Mary, her face would light up in greeting, even though they had already spent the morning together. Her mother had that way about her. Her welcoming voice made everyone feel important. Mary often wondered how a person could be that excited to see the same people every day, but she always had been.

Adinah's sobs pulled Mary's attention back to the present. Sometimes their town of Bethany seemed all but forgotten by God. How was she to comfort her friend when she desperately needed comforting herself? Her mind raced to find the perfect story from the scrolls their father shared with them, but she didn't have an answer. Her heart broke for Adinah and her husband, Levik. Not being married herself, Mary couldn't truly understand the depth of her friend's pain. Her older sister, Martha, was so good with this sort of thing. Even without studying under a rabbi like the men could do, Martha's mind grasped the words from the scrolls that their father shared with them. She not only remembered the stories, but she applied them at the appropriate times so that the stories came to life and made sense. At times like this, Mary wished Martha was there to help console Adinah, because she would somehow know what to say. She always seemed to find the words that Mary lacked, and Mary envied that about her sister. Sometimes she wished they could sit at the feet of a rabbi and learn the way their brother, Lazarus, could. Maybe then she would be able to remember the stories better.

Knowing her words would come out jumbled, Mary did the only thing she knew to do and simply held her friend close. She allowed her to feel what she was feeling with no judgment or opinion. Sometimes words don't matter, anyway. You just need to know someone is there to go through the pain with you. She stroked Adinah's hair as she wept.

Mary thought of the last time her own mother had held her and gently smoothed her hair back in much the same way. She had no idea that she would never feel that kind of closeness with her mother again. Every now and then she wished she could go back to that moment, now knowing it would be the last, and soak up every second. Every touch. Every exchanged glance. Yet, other times, she was glad she was oblivious to the pain that was lying in wait. Mary remembered the day vividly. At the end of town, there was an abandoned home that had been turned into a refuge for the ill. Since Bethany was a short distance from Jerusalem, it was common for people who had been cast out of the city to wander down the road in their direction. The women of Bethany would take turns caring for them as best they could, and their mother helped as often as she was able. She was not a doctor, but knew how to use turmeric, garlic, flax, and milk thistle for basic ailments. She would bring the girls along with her as she offered comfort in the form of saying a prayer, sharing a story, or running an errand.

# But, Even Now

Unfortunately, most of the wanderers were so stricken with affliction by the time they reached Bethany that their days were few, so Mary's family didn't get to know many of them very well. However, one particular widow was there a bit longer and had grown quite fond of the girls. Young Mary and Martha had looked forward to their daily visits with such a gentle soul. They would stand outside of her window and listen as she told them stories of her home in Galilee. From the way she spoke of it, Galilee was a glorious place of peace, harmony, and bounty. Each new day, Mary and Martha couldn't wait to hear about the next adventure and delighted in walking with their mother to that converted home on the edge of town. The girls would pick flowers along the way, in anticipation of brightening the spirits of that sweet woman with gentle eyes. They hoped the bright colors and sweet smells would bring fond memories to their new friend and bring her back to her home in Galilee.

That particular day, the air had been unusually crisp for that time of year. The girls had dawdled in the wildflower patch longer than normal, and their mother hurried them along. She knew the old widow would be expecting them. Mary knew something was wrong when one of the women met their mother with whispers at the door and the girls were asked to wait outside. Why were they asked not to go near the window? The girls did as they were instructed and entertained themselves while the adults discussed whatever seemed so important. Mary and Martha looked for pretty rocks, then ran around and tried to step on each other's shadow as their mother sat at the bedside of her new friend. Unbeknownst to the girls, their mother was holding the old widow's hand and praying over her until she drew her last breath.

When their mother walked out into the sunshine, the somber expression on her face brought the joyful singing of the girls to a disconcerting halt. When she knelt down to tell them the news, Mary looked at the flowers she still held in her hand. Their vibrant beauty seemed to mock the tears welling up in her eyes. She threw them in the dust and buried her face in her mother's shoulder. Her *aima's* weathered hands felt soft as they stroked her hair back. It had brought such a sense of comfort and normalcy to a day that had just been shattered with unexpected sadness.

Now, as Mary sat in the dirt with Adinah, she stroked her hair back the same way her mother had done to her, hoping the same slight gesture would bring comfort to her friend. Adinah finally lifted her head and stared off somewhere in the distance, at nothing in particular. "I should be home, preparing for *Shabbat*, but I can't let Levik see my eyes swollen from tears yet again. He'll know why I was crying, and I'm sure he is tired of it." There was a long pause before she added, "Mary, I'm a disgrace! I have brought shame to my husband and to our home."

"You mustn't think like that, Adinah. You have brought no disgrace to Levik."

"It's so difficult to go back to a home that remains void of a child's voice. How many *Shabbats* will pass with just the two of us? How many years will we have the constant reminder that I was unable to provide him with an heir? How many stares must I avoid from those who sit in judgment, as if this is a punishment for sin? How long until I can prepare a meal for the descendants that my Levik deserves? How long until my barren womb drives him to the arms of another woman who can give him what I cannot?" The words came out with increasing volume and intensity.

One word stood out to Mary more than others. *How*? Mary wasn't sure of the answer. She expected Adinah had asked herself these questions a hundred times, and the lack of answers strangled any hope for peace in her heart.

Adinah moaned bitterly as she mumbled something into her arms that were now crossed over her knees. Mary leaned in, trying hard to understand what she was saying. She didn't want to ask Adinah to repeat something that was so difficult to say out loud in the first place. Yet, surely what she thought she just heard was not correct.

She got the answer as Adinah raised her eyes and spoke in a voice Mary barely recognized. "Levik keeps company with a woman who travels on the road from Jericho. I do not know her name, but I know what she looks like. He tells me he's meeting a group, but one day when my suspicions got the better of me, I followed him. As I suspected, it wasn't a group at all. It was only her. They walked off alone together, but I could not bring myself to follow any further. Part of me didn't want to see, because if I saw it with my own eyes, it would no longer be a suspicion. It would become a reality, and I cannot face yet another harsh reality. I cannot live with the fact that I am barren, and my husband may have gone astray. The image of them will forever be burned into my mind. I cannot live with looking him in the eye, knowing what he may be doing. So right now, I choose to keep telling myself it is just a suspicion."

Mary sat in stunned disbelief. It was no wonder Adinah was so overwhelmed with grief. Infertility and infidelity were heavy burdens to bear on their own, but she did not know how someone could straddle both issues at the same time and remain emotionally intact. There had been whispers of other men leading secret lives, but Levik was one of the most righteous people Mary knew. It was disappointing to think that even he was capable of such a thing.

Mary scanned the surrounding path to make sure nobody else had heard their conversation. If Adinah was right about Levik, that was no small accusation. Men got away with that sort of thing, but they had often stoned women for the same indiscretion. "Are you certain there is not another explanation? Maybe the other part of the group planned to go but had something come up that kept them from completing the trip?" Mary tried to offer hope.

Adinah looked Mary in the eyes for the first time since she sat down. "Is it possible? Yes. But is it likely? I do not think so. A woman knows her husband, Mary, and I can feel it in my gut. Every time he leaves our home, I am sick with suspicion. Do I follow him? Do I confront him? Or do I just trust that the words my husband says are true?"

Adinah's questions hung stagnant, like smoky air too thick to breathe. Mary hoped this was hypothetical and that she wasn't expecting actual answers. She wasn't even sure if there were any. Surely this wasn't God's plan for Adinah's life?

"I'm not sure what to say, Adinah." She knew she was treading on shaky ground and wanted to weigh her response carefully. She didn't want to say anything that would encourage Adinah's suspicions or risk her words causing a further divide in their marriage. What if she was wrong? But Mary would give her own life for her friend and wanted Adinah to know she had her complete love and support. She put her arm around Adinah's shoulders once more and drew her near. With a firm squeeze, she said, "You know we love you."

Mary's words caused Adinah to sob anew, but for a different reason. This time, her sorrow was mixed with tears of gratitude for being lucky enough to know genuine friendship.

They sat in silence until Adinah's chest stopped heaving and her breathing was back to a rhythm that matched her friend's. Although Mary wasn't sure how to make her feel better, she thought of something she could do to lighten her friend's load. Her voice sounded more spirited than she felt. "Adinah, we would love for you and Levik to have *Shabbat* dinner with us! Your company would be a welcome treat."

Adinah shook her head. "I'm afraid I would not be good company today."

"Nonsense! Our home is your home, and your tears are

our tears."

She didn't want to remind Adinah that their home, too, was void of voices. For Adinah, the missing voices were those of children. For Mary, Martha, and Lazarus, it was those of their parents. Perhaps the light-hearted conversation of friends would make the silence in both of their ears not seem so deafening.

Mary stood and reached out to clasp Adinah's hand. She helped her up, and the two stood, brushing off their *tunics*. They walked in silence for a while, arm in arm, until their village came into view. Mary glanced down and couldn't help but notice their dusty footprints, side by side, and it was a stark contrast to the ones she left on her own just a short time ago. Somehow, when you have a friend walking through the dirt with you, the world doesn't seem quite so broken.

Adinah's pace slowed almost to a stop as she spoke. "Mary, every fiber of my being wants to be someone's mother. I long to hear a small voice call me their *aima*."

With their parents gone, Martha and Mary had been the ones taking care of their brother, Lazarus. In many ways, she already felt like an *aima*. She knew children brought honor to a Jewish household, and they were a great blessing from God. But with all the cooking, cleaning, mending, washing, teaching and correcting she had done in caring for their brother, she didn't feel the same void that her friend felt. Although she loved her siblings more than life itself, her bones were weary from the responsibilities that had already fallen on them at such a young age, both at home and for the sick widows they continued to help in their village. She couldn't begin to imagine taking on another mouth to feed, even if it was a husband.

That's something else her sister was naturally good at. Much like their mother, Martha had such an instinctual servant's heart. She was a biological nurturer, and it was something Mary always admired. Sure, Mary did her part, but there wasn't anything that innately tugged her heartstrings to have a husband and children like most women. With marriages arranged by their parents, many of her friends had been paired with men they felt no love or affection for in any romantic sense. More often than not, they did not marry for romantic reasons; rather, it was out of necessity. As children came, many families couldn't afford to provide for all of them, so the oldest daughters were married off at a very young age to men who were good providers. That did not appeal to Mary in the least. She was told by other women that feeling would change in time, and perhaps they were right. For now, they were not hurting for money, and taking care of their home and caring for the sick who had been cast out of Jerusalem was challenging enough.

Mary looked into her friend's eyes, trying to make her own as soft and welcoming as possible. "Can we expect you and Levik this evening? Please, say yes."

Smiling through her pain, Adinah reluctantly answered. She nodded her head and said, "Friend, it would be an honor."

"Then it is decided. We will see you before sunset!"

The friends exchanged a knowing look before parting ways. Sometimes a look can speak words that the heart cannot yet express. Mary loved Adinah so much and wished more than anything that she could take her pain away. They embraced for a long moment, then each turned toward their own home.

"*Shabbat shalom*, Adinah!"

"*Shabbat shalom*, Mary."

As their home came into view, Mary could see Martha and a group of women from the village coming from the other direction. Each of them was carrying fresh water from the well. Oh no! She was supposed to be back to help Martha with the chores but got so caught up talking with Adinah that she had forgotten all about it. Sometimes her wandering mind was aggravating, even to herself. Mary had not purposely left her sister with more work, but the fact remained that it was too late to be of any help now. She wondered how many trips her sister had already made. Martha would make it clear soon enough.

Neighbors were rustling around, gathering what they needed to prepare their Sabbath meals before the heat of the day caught up with them. She saw a young mother walking with her daughters. Was it that long ago that she and Martha had walked through town with their own aima? She didn't know what it was about this day that made her miss her parents more than most. Sometimes it just seemed to sneak up on her for no apparent reason.

Their mother had been so patient with them as she taught them how to prepare fresh meals. Martha, being the oldest, learned to make things like goat cheese, bread, and lentil soup seasoned with cumin. Mary was younger, and would be in charge of more simple tasks, such as sorting the figs, dates, and olives into bowls, or picking flowers for the table. The preparation was sometimes daunting, but Mary always looked forward to the celebration and to the day of rest that followed.

*Shabbat* grew to be her favorite day of the week. On most days, everyone was scattered about, busy with their duties. And although her own family was among the more affluent of their village, they still worked to keep food on the table and taxes paid to Rome. Her father even secretly fed and paid debts for others as he saw the need. Mary wasn't supposed to know that information, as her father always did it in secret. She only put it together because she had overheard several people over the years thanking him profusely. Out of respect for him, she had never once mentioned this to another soul. She wondered if that had something to do with why he made so many trips to Jerusalem, which was but a short distance from their home. They always missed him when he was away, but on *Shabbat*, they were all home together. There were no exceptions. Mary liked the predictability.

She closed her eyes and allowed the memories of what she now called 'the golden years' to flood back into her mind. There were so many things that seemed small at the time, like a habit taken for granted. Now that they were taken away, they seemed like the biggest, most important things. One memory, for instance, was sitting in the window while her *aima* made final touches to the evening meal, as she watched the sky for the first stars to appear. Then she would peek to the side as the *Shabbat* prayers were said and see her family praising God together as one. It brought such joy to her heart, even at a young age. They always welcomed friends and even passersby who needed a place to rest and pray. Oh, how she missed those days! But she didn't have time to entertain those thoughts now. There was still so much work to be done, and Martha would be waiting for her. Then, from somewhere behind her, a gathering of men sounded as if they were quarreling, and she could recognize her brother's voice among them. *Lazarus, what are you getting yourself into now?* She could only imagine.

It wasn't a lady's place to be a part of such a discussion, but she had to make sure her brother wasn't getting himself into trouble again. After all, he was still walking with a limp after the last time Roman soldiers came to their village. Lazarus had a charm about him that made him beloved by anyone who took time to know him, but none of that mattered to Rome. The last time soldiers had barged into their town, it was to collect taxes a day earlier than expected. Her brother dared ask why they had come early, and a soldier moved so swiftly toward him that the girls were afraid he would be cut down right in front of them. Nobody dared speak without first being spoken to, especially if it was to question Rome's authority or agenda. They answered to nobody and looked for any reason to use an unorderly plebeian as an example.

As they watched the soldier face their brother, the girls

clung to one another. The Roman was so close that Lazarus could smell his foul breath and feel the heat of it on his skin. The man said nothing but stared intimidatingly into Lazarus' eyes, watching them fill with pain as he stepped on the boy's sandaled foot with hobnail *caligae* shoes. Lazarus, determined not to give the man the benefit of knowing he was in pain, stood with an unflinching, blank face. Not getting the agonizing cry he was looking for, the soldier gave his foot a twist before releasing it from the top of her brother's foot. There was an audible tearing of flesh, and Mary had to hold Martha back from running to their brother's side. Martha could tell from the look on Lazarus' face that the pain was intense, but he would pass out before he would give the soldier the satisfaction of hearing him cry out.

Now she listened from around the corner and hoped her brother's overly zealous opinions had nothing to do with the quarrel that seemed to start. Lazarus was old enough to be included but hadn't yet reached the age to be looked upon with the wisdom of elders like many of the others. He had won the hearts of the group after he stepped up in the absence of their dear father, so he got away with more than most, and seemed to enjoy taking advantage of it from time to time. He didn't mean to be brazen or speak out of turn, but he sometimes seemed overly comfortable expressing what others would choose to keep silent. Mary and Martha had discussed with him at length how they feared it would get him into trouble one day.

Quietly, to remain unnoticed, she slipped into the shadow of a stone wall and listened to the men voice their concerns one after another. Two of the voices she recognized as Chanoch and Yokim, who were both respected elders. There were others she did not know. At first, they were speaking in turn. However, it didn't take long before they started talking over one another, and the voices became louder and more intense. Mary could feel the tension grow, even from a distance. She listened closely, trying to decipher what they were saying without being accused of obvious eavesdropping.

"... How dare you make such claims, Chanoch! He is nothing but a charismatic mesmerist, at best." Mary couldn't see them, but from the sound of the words coming out of his mouth, she was sure he sent spittle toward his listeners.

"... I can understand why you might think that, Yokim, but you did not hear him! I heard him with my own ears. The last time I went to the temple in Jerusalem, he was teaching there as if he were a proficient rabbi, not a carpenter or a student. His teachings were flawless. One would think he had trained under the finest teachers of Jerusalem."

"Yet, you seem to forget that he has not had formal training! Just because a man speaks with a wise tongue does not mean his words are true. You seem to lean on what you hope for rather than what you know. We know he is from the northern district of Galilee, in Nazareth. We know his people and his family! They have visited Bethany many times and nothing about them seemed out of the ordinary. We know his trade. We know he is not a scholar of Jerusalem. So, if his teachings are like nothing you have ever heard, that should tell you something. The Pentateuch does not change, Chanoch. Men do. If he is preaching anything other than what the scrolls tell us, then all that proves to me is that he is a false teacher!"

There was a pause in the conversation, and Mary wanted so badly to peek around the corner to see what was going on, but she remained still, afraid to be spotted.

Chanoch breathed in heavily to calm himself before he spoke again. "Almost everything you have said is true, Yokim. Of course, we all agree that the scrolls are ancient and do not change." He gathered his thoughts before he began again. "But everything he said was also true. It is difficult to explain. New teachings did not come from him. He just taught the old things differently. He had a way of taking the ancient teachings and making them new again. Even the scribes and Pharisees were hanging on his words. Anytime you see him outside of the temple, the crowds press in because they hunger for his instruction and wait in anticipation of seeing the works of his hands. I have seen it with my own eyes. Hundreds can validate his stories! He is more than a teacher, he..." Chanoch stopped himself, carefully weighing his next words. Finally, he spoke with great hesitation. "Perhaps he is more."

Mary wished she could see the expressions on the faces of the other men. She was not well educated when it came to things such as this, but she knew if he insinuated that someone was a prophet, it would not go over well. Israel had seen no new prophets since Malachi.

Yokim sounded frazzled. "What are you saying, Chanoch?" He seemed to know what was being insinuated but wanted to hear the words come out of Chanoch's mouth.

"I'm saying that John the baptizer has been telling us that he was paving the way for someone greater, and we didn't pay attention. Many say Jesus of Nazareth is the one John spoke of, because things that have happened surrounding him line up with ancient prophecy. Perhaps it is being fulfilled right before our eyes. And now we are seeing Jesus perform mighty miracles. Maybe John was not so crazy after all."

Mary's heart melted at the sound of Jesus' name. His family had been dear friends of theirs since she was a small child. It was strange to think of him as anything more, but she did not doubt the stories of the wondrous things people had claimed he had done. At first, it was hard to believe any story of a miracle. Those things happened in the time of Moses and Abraham, not to them. Not now. Nevertheless, the stories kept spreading like wildfire, and if a miracle was going to happen, Mary knew it would be at the hand of Jesus. Now the conversation had her attention for reasons other than keeping an eye on her brother.

Yokim's words dripped with sarcasm. "Oh, yes, Chanoch! Let's take the word of a man who eats bugs in the desert! Do you hear the words coming out of your own mouth? You believe a man who stands in the river all day over the words of the Pharisees? All he does is yell about someone coming to bring fiery judgment. You are a fool if you think Jesus is going to do that. Such a claim borders on blasphemy, Chanoch! Only the Most High God can do that. I will not believe Jesus is any more than a carpenter until the temple declares him as something more."

Another voice that Mary did not recognize chimed in. "Yes, he has won over some crowds with fancy storytelling, but the so-called miracles could be nothing more than the foolery of a common magician. There is nothing miraculous about that."

As Chanoch began again, Mary could hear the growing impatience in his voice. "Yokim, were you there the day Jesus came down to the river, and a dove descended on him? I was! A voice came from the sky. How do you explain that? Was that also a magician, casting his voice from above? It was also then that John told us the dove was a sign and we are to call Jesus the Lamb of God."

Yokim avoided the question about the voice as he replied, "A bird in the sky over a river is a sign? That happens every day! It was mere coincidence that it was flying over Jesus. A dove is a wild bird and John is a wild man! He dresses in clothes made of camel's hair, like Elijah, as if that alone will convince people that he himself is a prophet. Yet, he does not even make the proper offerings at the temple. He does not even wash himself! He is physically and spiritually unclean. What would he know of prophets?"

Chanoch challenged, "Many believe John the baptizer is a prophet himself, and we should listen to him. He has baptized hundreds, maybe even thousands, and brought them to repentance. Even Rome has taken notice. We have waited for prophecy to be fulfilled our entire lives. If he is pointing to Jesus, I think we should pay attention."

Other men were talking now, and their voices jumbled together. It was difficult for Mary to tell who was saying what, but their input seemed to quiet Yokim and Chanoch for the moment.

"The only reason Rome noticed John or Jesus is because the sizable crowds were getting in the way. It had nothing to do with their message. It just caused an inconvenience. Rome knows from experience that a gathering that size could quickly become a riot that they will have to disperse," said Yokim.

"Perhaps," replied Chanoch. "But word has spread that John has been taken for questioning. By whom, we are unsure. It's not unlawful to stand in a river and baptize, so someone in Rome must feel there is a greater threat. The question is, are they threatened by him or by his warnings about Jesus?"

Another voice said, "Rome doesn't concern themselves with spiritual interests. They are just afraid of an uprising if John's followers continue to grow."

Chanoch continued. "People are reporting miracles. It seems every traveler through Bethany has another story of what Jesus has done. Maybe Rome is not afraid of what they know of John, but perhaps they are afraid of what they don't know about Jesus. John said Jesus is greater than he, and John has many followers. The only greatness Rome is comfortable with comes from Rome. Anything else is a threat."

Yokim's voice could be heard again, but it had a distinct ring to it. His words were now slow and steady, as if it caused actual pain to allow them to escape his throat. "Are you buying into this hogwash that Jesus is actually performing miracles? And if so, by what power? Or are you saying that he is ... what? Another prophet? You just said John may be a prophet. You think we've gone since the time of Malachi with none, and now we have two in one town? Nonsense."

It was then that Mary recognized her brother's voice, loud and clear, and it was void of the hesitation shown by Chanoch. Lazarus spoke boldly and plainly in front of his elders. "It means that Jesus is not a prophet. He is the Messiah."

And with that, every voice fell silent.

# Chapter 2

## Trista's Journal Entry

### Never?

March 6, 2005

"You are never going to have your own child."

Why do I still feel so silly sitting down to journal? No matter how many times I try it as an adult, it feels like I am in sixth grade again, sitting on my double bed in my peach and brown bedroom, writing about the sleepover I had with my friends who lived up the street, or how unfair it was that my mom and dad didn't let me go to the sleepover and how it was going to ruin my life forever. As ridiculous and self-absorbed as it feels, I'm going to try it again. I remember the constant encouragement of my former counselor about journaling on a regular basis. It can help reduce depressive symptoms.... It can help shift your perspective about stressful situations.... It can help to build connections between events and feelings and possible solutions.... I guess if there was ever a time to start, the time is now. I just feel so defeated.

Well, last week Andy and I had our first interview with our foster care intake worker, Betsy Davidson. I am still in shock about how it went. I cannot believe she said those things to me in my own living room. This was the first time meeting her in person. We've taken the required thirty-two hours of classes from "C.P.R./Basic First Aid" to "Emotional

Effects of Abuse and Neglect" to "Empathy and Compassion for the Biological Parent," to name a few. They have approved our fire inspection. We've passed our physicals and gotten the appropriate paperwork completed. Our medicines and cleaning supplies have been locked up. We've filled out all the pages and pages of forms. This was supposed to be our meeting where we set up our individual interviews with her and started nearing the finish line of becoming certified for foster care and adoption. It was not supposed to go this way. I thought it was going to be more of a formality than anything else.

After introductions and a brief tour of the house, we returned to the living room, where Betsy sat down in our secondhand brown leather chair and Andy and I sat down on the newly Febreezed couch across from her. She took out her paperwork and confirmed some basic information about each of us, including our dates of birth, how long we have been married, and the date we completed the required courses. She then focused her attention on me. I was expecting her to thank us for our application and ask a few "getting to know you" questions, but shockingly she zeroed in on me similar to the way a predator focuses on its prey. Her remarks were pointed. "Mrs. Trista Haskins, you are never going to have your own child. Your husband (pointing to Andy) has no trouble procreating. In fact, he already has a child of his own. And you are never going to give birth to your own perfect child. You are never going to have that perfect child that you dreamed about all these years," she spouted.

Wait. Was she serious? My face started to burn. My stomach instantly became queasy. Before I could interject with anything, she continued with her monologue, stating, "Our children in foster care are not like that perfect child in your mind. They have often been abused or neglected, and some have severe issues."

Did she really just say these things to me?! Honestly,

I half expected to look over my shoulder and see a camera crew and realize we were on one of those shows where they would tape your reaction to horribly awkward situations. The things she said were just too over-the-top to be happening in real life! I still can't believe it as I am writing her words down on paper! I looked over at Andy, and his mouth was hanging open. He had a dumbfounded look on his face that mirrored the look I was trying to hide myself. It looked like he wanted to say something to defend me, but he remained silent, unsure if having my back would help me or just make an already awkward conversation with Betsy even worse.

I hoped in that moment that she could not tell that my face and ears were on fire with madness. They had to be scorching red by now. I prayed she couldn't tell my stomach was flipping with the uncertainty of how this conversation may affect the rest of my life. Stay calm, Trista!

How do you even respond to that? I managed to reply, "Well, I have never imagined that I would have a perfect child. No family, no matter how they are created, has a perfect child. In fact, one reason we feel confident that we can be successful foster/adoptive parents is our extensive experience with children who have severe behavioral and emotional issues."

The nerve of this woman! I tried hard to keep calm and appear unrattled by her accusations and shaming session. I wanted to say something in defense, but I didn't trust myself not to say something that would get me into trouble. If she only knew our hearts and the journey we had been through to be sitting in this interview, she would understand.

I have never been able to become pregnant. When Andy and I fell in love and were considering marriage, I already knew that I struggled with infertility. I had been married and divorced already (which is a story for another day) and had not become pregnant during years of trying. Andy knew about this and my strong desire to become a mommy. He shared that he was on board if we had to try different routes to become parents together, even though he had already been blessed with a wonderful daughter from his previous marriage. Soon after we married, so began the dreaded ovulation kits, Chlomed, prayers, shots in the butt, tearfully attending other people's baby showers, more tears, artificial inseminations, planning baby showers for family members, more tears, more prayers.... It was a continuous cycle of getting our hopes up and then having them crushed, along with daily reminders of what I didn't have.

Infertility has been a long and painful roller coaster. First of all, when you are actively trying to get pregnant, you notice way more pregnant women and babies than you have ever noticed in your normal life. It seems that everywhere you turn, every call you take, and every email you receive brings the news of yet another person blessed with a baby. And everyone and their cousin has a "helpful" piece of advice for you. They all have a friend of a friend who stopped trying and then immediately became pregnant, and they share this with you as if it is encouraging. In reality, all this does is insinuate that your worrying is preventing you from getting pregnant, like it is your own fault. It is not my fault. It is not my fault!

Then there is the guilt factor. Yes, I want to be happy for my loved ones who easily became pregnant on the exact time schedule of their choosing. No, I don't want to be a jealous person, wishing it was me instead. Yes, I want to "ooh" and "ahhh" with the rest of the women at the latest baby shower about how cute a frilly pink dress will look on my co-worker's baby. And I would be rich if I had a nickel for every time my dad said, "I just don't understand it.... All I had to do was look at your mom and she would get pregnant." But the longing for motherhood is so strong, and the more time that goes by, the more it seems it will never happen for me. The possibility of never having the privilege of being someone's mommy is a dark cloud that follows me wherever I go, whatever I am doing. It is always there.

Many disappointments and a couple infertility specialists later, we started having serious talks about our options. Would it be weird to have one of my sisters carry a baby for me? How would that go? What would the cost even be for that process? Then, how much does it cost to do the adoption? After many long talks and assessing our financial standing, we realized that surrogacy and the "traditional" route to adoption were not going to work for us. We decided our route to parenthood was going to be fostering, with the intention to adopt if the situation presented itself. I dug out the yellow pages and found our county's fostering agency and made the call. We began the weekly training sessions and filled out the extensive applications and prepared our home for little ones. We acquired cribs and car seats and looked forward to getting on with the interviews. I was so excited about the first meeting with our social worker that I spent a stupid amount of time in the grocery aisle trying to decide which assortment of cheeses and crackers to buy. Then, Andy told me that the social workers won't be eating anything when they come to the house because it would be considered unprofessional. It's probably more likely that they take the teacher approach like we did at school.... Always assume any food brought in has been sneezed on at least once, smile politely, thank them profusely, and then don't eat it under any circumstances. Okay, fine. But I held on to them just in case!

Then the day of the first meeting finally arrived! I was afraid to think about it, but this may actually happen! We are getting closer and closer to being able to share our lives with a little one who needs a safe and loving home. And then, Betsy Davidson sat down.... It didn't take long to realize that I was being verbally and emotionally abused in my own home. Here she was, sitting on our furniture in our space, somehow trying to use my husband's blessing of fatherhood against me. She seemed to enjoy the fact that she has the power to decide if I become a mom or not. Andy and I were both so shocked. I managed to reply to her calmly, explaining that I was not trying to substitute this fictional perfect child that I had supposedly been dreaming about with the county's neglected and abused children. I explained that we are excited about serving these children in our home and are hoping to be lucky enough to adopt a child if the need arises. Who did she think she was, telling me what I was never going to have? Only God knows that! I am furious! And, furthermore, who actually uses the word "procreate" anymore??!! That is just gross!!

I DESPISE BETSY DAVIDSON!
I DESPISE BETSY DAVIDSON!
I DESPISE BETSY DAVIDSON!
I DESPISE BETSY DAVIDSON!

Okay. Maybe my counselor isn't as silly as I thought. It really does feel good to get that out on paper! Contrary to what Betsy thinks, we are not going into this next phase of our lives naively. Andy and I actually met at a special school for kids who have severe emotional and behavioral disorders. I was the teacher, and he was the therapist in one of the classrooms. This school serves as the "last chance" for kids to have some success at school and turn it around before they are put into group homes. Andy has moved on, but I have worked there for 8 years and counting. All this to say we both have experience working with children who have mental illnesses and educational delays, which are both likely to happen with children in care. Neither of us have had any trouble creating bonds with these kids, whose behavior would turn many off, because we love them! I mean, we have had oranges, chairs, and desks thrown at us, been yelled at, cussed at, spit at, kicked, and had to restrain children in order to prevent them from hurting themselves or others. Even so, I love these kids so much that I have spent more years of my teaching career here than at any other school, and for a lot less pay!

So, to answer your question, Betsy Davidson, I have not been "dreaming of that perfect child!" I have been too busy teaching and encouraging and bonding with my students who are very far from perfect. The funny thing is, God has shown us both that we can love and bond with children who the world may see as "imperfect." Maybe they aren't perfect for other people, but they may just be perfect for us ... if we could just get through this next phase.

Andy and I have gone over what happened many times since that upsetting meeting last week. Dissecting, analyzing, venting ... discussing what we should have said, and what we wish we could have said, and what it all means. We figure it comes down to this; I told the whole truth in my application, stating that I had been to a therapist to help me with my sadness about infertility years ago. Not only was this true, but I thought it to be a positive attribute that I sought out help for a problem I had. I did not realize this before, but I found out the subject of infertility is a hot topic in the land of fostering/adopting. There were even a couple pages about it in the fostering handbook that I must have missed. Evidently, there is a concern that people who struggle with infertility may try to replace the child they could not have with a child in care, and this would lead to problems. So, the interrogation is starting to make a little more sense at this point. Still inappropriate! Still totally out of line! And I still despise Betsy Davidson!

Before she left, the bossy and belittling Betsy requested that I get a statement from my former therapist saying I have accepted my infertility and have no remaining issues with it. She gave me the address to pass on the statement.

Seriously? Accept the fact that I cannot have a child? With no remaining issues with this loss?! How is a woman who dreams of having a child supposed to ever be totally over the fact that her body will not do what it was created to do? What seemingly every other woman's body is able to do? Who is ever totally over a loss like that? I still feel a twinge of pain whenever I drive by a hospital, knowing that I will probably never be that mom the nurse hands the precious newborn baby to. But, if that's what it takes, I will play the game. I have tracked down the therapist and emailed her my request but have not heard back yet. I saw her nine times because my employer offered ten free visits through the E.A.P. (Employee Assistance Program). You would think it would be a positive step to take for my mental health during all the disappointments infertility brings. Will she write such a ridiculous statement to placate the powers that be? I have no idea!

I see one last chance at being a mom, and I have a strong suspicion that the person who is supposed to decide this doesn't like me. And now I have to rely on a counselor who I saw years ago to sign her name to a statement that she knows is not true.

*Lord, I am so tired! Tired of jumping through never-ending hoops. Tired of not being able to have what comes so easily to those around me. Please know I am so grateful to you for all the ways you have blessed me. Thank you for giving second chances. Thank you for my sweet husband. Thank you for the wonderful children you have already put in my life. You know my heart, though, Lord. You know how much I hurt at the thought of never being called Mommy. Please, God, let me be a mommy some way, somehow, whether it's through this crazy process we have started or through another path. In Jesus' name, Amen.*

# Chapter 3

## Tradition

31 A.D.

All eyes turned to Lazarus. Did he just say that Jesus was the Messiah? His youthful tongue lacked wisdom. Surely, he didn't understand that such bold and unfounded claims would be considered blasphemy. Not knowing what to say, the men looked to the elders in silence, waiting for their reaction.

Chanoch stood with his mouth open, like a fish gasping in air. He could not believe that young Lazarus had spoken the words he, himself, had considered in his own heart, but had been too fearful to voice in front of the others. In a selfish way, he was thankful that Lazarus said it out loud so he wouldn't have to, but now he feared the fallout of such words from his young friend. He considered it bravery on the part of Lazarus to speak at all in front of the elders, especially about something as heavy as this. Yet, he knew Yokim and a few others would not react well. Chanoch had to quickly consider whether or not he would speak up in the defense of Lazarus or be silent and let him take the fall.

Their people had been waiting for a Messiah to deliver them from despair for hundreds of years. Generations had been looking for signs that would fulfill the prophecy. Although everyone had faith that it would happen one day, few dared to expect it would happen in their lifetime. Such a claim would change the world as they knew it. Everything would have to be weighed and tested against the ancient prophecies. Only the true Messiah could fulfill them all. Few dared to imagine that prophecy could actually be playing out right in front of them. Even fewer would say it out loud.

Chanoch had his suspicions about Jesus ever since his cousin had returned from a wedding in Cana where Jesus was said to be in attendance. There were whispers that he had made water become wine. A miracle, they said. Chanoch wanted to believe, but his mind was that of a scholar. He needed proof. Validation. He hoped it would come from the other elders but never thought it would come from Lazarus. He wondered what grounds Lazarus had for such a claim. Did he have any idea what he was talking about? Or was he just saying something to try and fit in with the other men? Yes, he was younger than the others but still old enough to be held accountable. Whatever it was, it better be good.

Yokim broke the silence first. He turned, standing aghast at the words he just heard from Lazarus. He seemed to take a breath between each word. "What did you say?"

Lazarus spoke with the voice of a man and the faith of a child. "I said Jesus is the Messiah. Everything Chanoch said is true, and, given the circumstances, my father would have told you the same."

Yokim shot back, "How can you say such things about your own father when he is no longer here to defend himself? Do not bring shame to his good name!"

"Respectfully, Yokim," continued Lazarus, "he would not defend himself to you, and he would not be ashamed of my words. He would defend Jesus."

Chanoch was amazed at Lazarus' cool composure. He seemed pretty sure of himself.

Like Mary, Lazarus often thought of their parents and wished he had more time to learn at the feet of his father.

Their *abba* had been very handsome and wise, and although he was monetarily better off than most, he didn't show it. Instead of using his wealth for power, he gave it away to those less fortunate. He was strong and firm, yet kind and approachable. He was known for his sharp mind, strong faith, and fair dealings. His humble demeanor demanded respect from others, and Lazarus hoped the men standing before him now saw the same attributes in himself.

As Lazarus looked around at the other men, he saw they were all making eye contact and waiting for a further explanation. Yokim had covered his own face with one hand as if to deflect the words from reaching him. Yet now, even he stood silent, waiting for Lazarus to address the group. Yokim probably figured his pointed words would not be necessary because Lazarus was digging his own grave.

Having their full attention, Lazarus stood tall as he continued. "As you know, my family has been acquainted with the family of Jesus for many years. My father, who you all knew and held with high esteem, told us before every visit that we were to listen carefully to Jesus and commit every story to memory. He would repeat these stories to us at bedtime, or on long journeys so that none of us would forget." Lazarus looked around at the face of each man. Still having their full attention, he continued. "*Abba* said he knew Jesus was doing the work of God ever since he heard him teaching in the temple when Jesus was just a twelve-year-old boy. Even the Pharisees were astonished at his wisdom. *Abba* said the words came straight from God because no boy of his age would know such things."

"An intelligent twelve year old with a knack for holding a crowd's attention does not make a Messiah," challenged Yokim, smugly.

"Perhaps not," answered Lazarus, "but it became more apparent as the years went by. After hosting the family of Jesus in our home multiple times, we had the privilege of hearing dinner conversations turn into teachings beyond anything my *abba* or Joseph, the father of Jesus, had ever known or understood in all their years of study. Jesus was different. Anointed, just like John the baptizer has been preaching. And now, Jesus is performing miracles! How can you witness that and deny that Jesus was given the power from God alone? Jesus is more than an ordinary man. He is the one who will fulfill the prophecy. If he could, I know that my *abba* would tell you himself that Jesus is the Messiah."

Another man, whose voice Mary didn't recognize, spoke up. "Yes, we have seen the family of Jesus enter your house, but we did not have the benefit of hearing his stories. Forgive me for saying so, but throughout all those years, we saw nothing remarkable about Jesus. As far as we know, they ate, drank, and struggled to pay taxes just like the rest of us. If he were the Messiah, would we not have known? Would there not be some sign from heaven? Would he not be a great military man, organizing armies to overthrow the Roman occupation?" The man's words were not accusatory; rather, they were searching.

There was a pause while those words were considered, then Lazarus continued. "My sisters, Mary and Martha, heard the mother of Jesus tell my *aima* that even the conception of Jesus and everything surrounding his birth was a miracle. Do you remember the killing of the innocents, when every baby under two years of age was struck down by Herod? That was because Herod saw a threat. He wanted to kill the one people were calling the newborn king, did he not? Guess who was born there at that very time? Jesus. They fled to Egypt for his safety. Does it not make sense that it would be him? That John the baptizer pointed to him? That the dove and the voice came from the sky? That he would be performing mighty miracles now?"

Still listening from behind the wall, Mary was frightened for her brother, yet proud of his confidence. She wished she were more like him. It wasn't a matter of whether or not her faith was strong enough to stand up for what she believed. She had plenty of stubborn, strong will. She just hated confrontation and tried to avoid it at all costs. She knew that their *abba*, their father, had been piecing together the signs, and that he suspected Jesus would one day reveal himself as the Messiah, yet the consideration of it never went outside the walls of their own home. Their father told them God would unveil this in His own time, and that they would somehow know. Mary wondered if that time had come? Apparently, Lazarus thought so. She would have never thought her little brother would be so bold but knew their father would be proud of him for doing so.

Just as Lazarus said, their mother had met Mary of Nazareth, the mother of Jesus, when they were all in Jerusalem for Passover many years before. Lazarus was not yet born but had heard the story many times. Mary remembered it well. They had stayed a couple of extra days to visit friends while her father attended meetings at the temple. Mary and Martha spent most of their time strolling the markets with their *aima*. While they were perusing over fresh fruit, Mary the Nazarene rushed frantically past them, asking if anyone had seen her son, Jesus, and quickly described what he looked like. The girls' mother sprang into action, helping to search for him, but first gathered Mary and Martha in her arms, looking intently into their eyes so they understood. She said, "See how easily it can happen for you to get lost in this crowd? Stay close!" She instructed Mary and Martha to hold on to her *tunic* as she rushed quickly, from one merchant to the next, describing the boy the way his mother did. She would motion with her hand and say, "He's about this tall. He's wearing a green *tunic*, and he's twelve years old. Have you seen him?"

Each of the merchants would shake their heads and go about their business, letting the women know they had more important things to do than look for a lost boy. Her own mother could see the desperation building in the eyes of the mother of Jesus as one person after another dismissed them.

Finally, they saw the woman run and embrace her son in the street. His father was with him. Taking in the scene before them, young Mary looked up to their own mother's eyes, and the relief was visible. Her mother always had such great compassion for others, even if they were strangers. She knelt down and took one girl in each arm and held them, as if they were the ones who had been lost. Mary was too young to understand how scary that must have been for Jesus' mother at the time, but it became clear to her after talking with Adinah this morning. She was grieving the loss of her parents, and Adinah was grieving a barren womb. The circumstances were different, but the pain was the same. Grief is grief. She supposed it must be the same with mothers. Fear is fear. Love is love. It's not held within the boundaries of one family or one situation or circumstance. Mothers must have a way of understanding one another's pain when it comes to how they love their children.

Mary the Nazarene had walked over to their mother and introduced her husband, Joseph, and her son, Jesus, and thanked her profusely for helping to search for him. While they were talking, young Mary could see their own father making his way through the crowd, and he joined them as they spoke in the street.

After they made introductions, her father motioned to Jesus. "Ahh, so this is the young man I could not walk away from at the temple!" He looked at Joseph. "He speaks with such wisdom for such a young man! You must be a great teacher, Joseph. I am pleased to make your acquaintance."

Joseph seemed pleased with his son, yet somehow uncomfortable with the compliment. He replied only with a smile, then explained how they had been halfway home after Passover when they realized Jesus was not in their caravan.

Mary and Joseph had to turn around and rush all the way back to Jerusalem. In all, it was a three-day ordeal, and they were both physically and emotionally exhausted.

Mary's father did not hesitate. He invited Joseph and his family to accompany them to Bethany and stay at their home for as long as they needed. Bethany was not far outside the city of Jerusalem, and they were on their way back home themselves. Joseph and his family were more than happy to take them up on the offer. After that, it had become a yearly tradition. Their family always looked forward to visits from the family of Jesus after Passover.

Mary had been lost in her own memories so deeply that she missed part of the conversation between the men. Judging by the tone of the conversation, she regretted doing so. The graveled voice of Yokim cut through Mary's thoughts, and she could tell that he was struggling to maintain self-control. "We have much to discuss, and words like this should not be spoken on the street. Let us go inside."

With that, together the men turned to enter the house of Yokim. Mary stepped out from around the wall just as the men were walking through the doorway. Instinctually, Lazarus looked over his shoulder and caught his sister's eye. They both knew that things were about to change.

Once home, Mary saw Martha dumping the water she had gathered from the well into clay jars. The day had just begun, and her sister already looked tired. They still had to bathe, fix their hair, tidy the house, gather flowers for the table, and make all of the preparations for the next two days. It just occurred to Mary that Martha didn't yet know that she had invited guests. Before Mary was able to speak, Martha started in with the inevitable reprimand.

"Mary, I could have used your help at the well. You know you were only supposed to gather dates for a short time and meet me there. I had to make two trips myself! It's just like you to wander about with your head in the clouds and push your responsibilities onto me."

The preparations for *Shabbat* always required an extra trip to the well, so they would have enough water for both days. After sunset, they could not make another trip until the Sabbath was over the following evening. It had been the same every week of their lives, so Mary knew what was expected. It would have been hot, but she still would have gone for her share of water when she got back. She didn't know why her older sister had to make such a fuss. If she didn't want to do it, she could have waited. Yet, she had given her sister her word and did not keep it, and she did feel badly about that.

"I'm sorry, Martha. I intended to help, but I saw Adinah along the path on the way home. I'll tell you in a minute, but first, I have to tell you what Lazarus just did! You won't believe…."

Martha cut her off. "Don't change the subject, Mary! What's your reason this time?"

Mary continued. "I was on my way back and stumbled upon Adinah. She is once again stricken with grief, and you know I could not leave her like that. It was as though she couldn't gather a thought outside of her heart's mourning." Mary paused, unsure of how the next part would be received. Hesitantly, she said, "I invited her and Levik to join us for *Shabbat* dinner."

At first, Martha was angry for even more work put upon her without it being discussed, but she knew exactly what Mary meant and immediately softened. She understood her delay and wouldn't have left Adinah's side either. "That poor girl's heart is broken into so many pieces. I suppose it will always carry an infant-shaped hole that only God can heal."

A few seconds of silence hung between them as they both pondered the thought, then the two young women busied themselves with pulling out table coverings, bowls, utensils, and spices as they spoke softly about the blessing of *Shabbat*. They had done this together so many times that each knew their own unspoken duties to be carried out. Preparing for *Shabbat* was no small task, yet it was done with reverence. Instilled in them by their parents and friends, it was a joy to honor God through the fruits of their hard work and then have a day to rest in His creation.

Instinctually going back to the task she had as a child, plucking out stray leaves that had fallen into a bowl of olives, Mary suddenly realized she had left the basket of dates sitting on the ground where she had been talking to Adinah. She hoped Martha wouldn't notice. It was one thing not to help with the water, but if she left Martha to continue the work while she walked all the way back for her missing dates, she would hear about it the rest of the day. How could she not have anything to show for the entire morning? It would mean listening to her sister go on and on about how she needed to be more responsible instead of being such a dreamer.

Then, as usual, Mary would remind her older sister that she needs to enjoy life more and not take everything so seriously. Martha would defensively respond that she enjoys life just fine, so Mary would feel compelled to make her prove it. She had to get more creative in how she went about that last part. She learned the hard way that tossing flour into her sister's hair and telling her to stop acting like a gray-haired old woman didn't seem as funny to Martha as it did when Mary played it out in her mind.

They were two very different creatures, and Mary often wondered how they came from the same parents. But no matter how much they teased and tormented one another, she loved her sister profoundly. She was both a sister and a friend. When Mary was being truthful, she knew Martha carried a heavy burden, and she needed to be more careful in how much she allowed her sister to endure alone. They weren't children any longer. They were too old to be considered orphans, yet in many ways they still needed their parents. Mary wasn't sure exactly where they fit in, but she knew her place was right here, in their family home, with the siblings that she loved.

When Martha walked over to inspect what she was doing, she quickly moved the bowl and started up the conversation again. "All of this must weigh heavily on Levik as well. Lazarus said there are times he will just stare in silence, as if he is unable to hear the words being spoken right in front of him." Mary wondered to herself if he was actually in grief, or was he thinking of how to cover up his tracks from whatever rendezvous he had been on. She didn't want to tell her sister about Adinah's suspicions, as she was hoping they would be proven wrong. No need for Martha to think poorly of Levik for undue reason.

Martha added, "Yes, I suppose a man's heart is no different from a woman's in the way it aches for a child. You did well to invite them to dinner."

Mary paused for a moment and turned toward her sister. "Martha, what words would you have offered her?"

Martha didn't return the gesture, but stood in silence, thinking seriously about what she might say. Then she simply walked over to the shelf on the wall and took the five candlesticks from their familiar place. They were handed down from their mother, and Mary knew they would be used later that evening. Martha set three of them on the table but held the other two with great care. With one in each hand, she paused for a long moment, as if feeling their weight for the first time. As she spoke, her voice was gentle and serene.

"I guess I would start by saying I understand how *Shabbat* preparations could be a reminder of what Adinah doesn't have."

Mary's forehead wrinkled. "What do you mean?"

Martha weighed her words carefully. "Well, although celebrating the Sabbath is a holy reminder of what God has blessed us with, our customs surrounding the day itself can unintentionally be a continuous reminder of the family He has not yet given us." Her voice trailed as she turned away. "Or family that is no longer with us."

Mary's head cocked slightly to the side, as if trying to look deeper into Martha's thoughts, but she still wasn't following. They celebrated God's day of rest together as a family every week, and to Mary, it brought a sense of comfort and closeness. Perhaps the void left in their home without their parents weighed on Martha more heavily than Mary realized?

Her sister held up the two candlesticks. "Take these for instance. Most every family lights two candles for observance and remembrance. Did you ever wonder why *Aima* had three more?"

Mary hadn't. That's just what her mother had always done, so that's what they continued to do. She knew there was a reason behind everything they did for *Shabbat*. Why had she not questioned more from her mother when she had the chance? She supposed she just always thought there would be more time to learn such things as they got older, so she never thought to inquire about it. Martha must have.

Mary's silence prompted Martha to continue. "Every home lights at least these two. But in a home with children, the woman of the house may light not only these, but an additional candle for each child. Our home did not always have five. *Aima* added an additional candlestick for you and me and Lazarus when we were brought into the world."

Martha walked over to the window and looked out into the sunlight. She continued talking, but it didn't feel as if she was talking to Mary anymore. It was more as if she were talking to herself. "When we were leaving the well this morning, Basharel was so proud to tell us that her oldest daughter has learned to make candles. They light seven each *Shabbat*. These two, and then five additional for each of her children. I was glad Adinah wasn't there to hear it. I understand the grief she must feel when she is never given a reason to add an extra candlestick."

Now it made sense. Mary spoke, but more to confirm her own thoughts than to reply to her sister. "Oh, yes. I guess you're right."

It hadn't even occurred to Mary that this simple ritual could bring anguish to a barren woman. That must be what Adinah meant when she asked how many *Shabbats* would pass with the constant reminder that she has not given an heir to Levik.

Martha set the remaining candlesticks on the table with quiet contemplation. For the first time, Mary thought she saw an ache in her sister's eyes. Martha never spoke of it, but it would make perfect sense that she longed for a husband and children of her own. When their parents died, Martha didn't even question what would happen. She just took over all the household responsibilities and inadvertently put her life on hold to provide for their little family. Maybe taking care of her and Lazarus wasn't enough anymore.

As if wanting to change the subject, Martha turned and asked, "Now, what were you saying about Lazarus?"

Just then, Lazarus came through the door in such a rush that he nearly tipped over the water jar on the floor. Catching his breath, he said, "You'll never believe what just happened!"

Lazarus bent over, hands on his knees, trying to catch his breath before he could speak. Mary knew he had only come from Yokim's house, and it wasn't far enough to cause a person to lose breath like that. She also knew he didn't run as quickly as he used to, as the injury on his foot from the Roman soldier was still causing him pain. Such tormentors! That wretched man probably forgot about wounding her brother the second he walked away. In fact, he probably delighted in it. But for Lazarus, every step was a painful reminder of what tyrants Rome had become, and every day made him more eager to find relief from the oppression in which they lived.

So, what was causing this reaction now? Excitement or fear? What did the men in the village do to her brother? Were they chasing him? The girls came to his side, eager to hear what he had to say.

Martha spoke first, with anxious anticipation. Whatever Mary had told her earlier must have been more important than she realized. Why had she let her carry on about *Shabbat* candles? She was sure something horrible had happened, and she was checking over her brother's body as she spoke to make sure there were no obvious injuries. "Lazarus, is someone hurt? Are you in trouble? What happened?" She looked over her shoulder through the window and quickly went to close the door. She pulled the latch tightly, just in case.

Mary put her hand on her brother's back because he was still bent over. She said, "I was afraid something like this would happen. I knew I should not have left you, but Martha was waiting for my help. Lazarus, please, tell us!"

Martha was still confused. "You were afraid what would happen? Someone please tell me what is going on!" Mary started to answer but signaled to Martha to wait for Lazarus to tell the story himself.

He hadn't moved after a few moments, still trying to slow his heartbeat to a steady rhythm. Finally, Lazarus carefully raised his shoulders until he stood towering above both of them. He took after their father, who was tall, broad and strong. The girls were petite like their mother.

When he finally spoke, his words came quickly, his mind racing. One sentence wasn't yet complete before he started the next, and his sisters had to listen closely to keep up. Mary held her breath as Lazarus recapped the part she had overheard as she stood behind the wall. She wasn't sure if she was ready to hear what happened next. Had they accused her brother of blasphemy? Would there be repercussions?

She listened intently as Lazarus continued, "… then as Yokim asked question after question, it amazed me that I actually had answers! I was so scared, Martha! But the words just came to me."

Martha held his hand in hers. "Oh, Lazarus. I'm not sure how these men are going to react, but I have a feeling that our *abba* would be proud!"

He continued, "As I spoke to Yokim, the men standing behind me started whispering to one another. I thought the whispers were about me, and I was praying they weren't discussing whether to make a formal accusation. My heart was racing, and I was trying to keep my voice calm. Yokim must have thought the same, because he turned and asked them if they wanted to address the group. It was not out of politeness; I can assure you. As a friend of Father's, he probably just didn't want to make an accusation himself, so he was going to let them talk first, sure they would do the dirty work for him."

The sisters moved toward one another and grabbed hands, bracing for terrible news. They just lost their parents. They couldn't lose Lazarus, too! The penalty for a formal accusation of blasphemy was death by stoning.

Lazarus went on. "They addressed the group, one by one. First Aharon, then Kozel, then others."

Mary's eyes immediately swelled with tears. "Oh, Lazarus! Were you accused? Did you have to flee?" Her mind was racing with where they could hide their brother from merciless stones.

"No, that's what was so astonishing! Not one of them came forward to speak about me at all. Each had personal accounts about Jesus! They told of him healing a paralytic and a woman who had been unclean with blood for many years. How Jesus reached out and touched a leper, and the lesions dried up right before their eyes! He even made a blind man see!"

Eyes wide, both sisters looked at one another as they listened in awe. Mary let out an audible sigh of relief, and it was Martha's turn to feel her eyes grow moist with tears. She felt such a sea of emotions. A wave of relief was followed by a wave of worry, but to her surprise, most of what she felt was nothing short of astonishment. Their father had taught them prophecy that pointed to the Messiah, and it all came rushing back. The Messiah would come from the tribe of Judah. He would be a descendant of Isaac and Jacob. He would be in the line of Abraham and David. A virgin would give birth to him in Bethlehem, and they would end up in Egypt.

Jesus fulfilled it all.

Lazarus continued. "Then Gershom, who has not yet lived in Bethany a full season, told of a miracle that his family saw with their own eyes! In their travels, they came upon a large crowd that had gathered near Bethsaida. Gershom had wanted to see what was going on, so he questioned a man standing there to see what all the fuss was about. It turns out that all of those people had come to hear Jesus speak. His best estimate was over 5,000 men, not even including the women and children with them. He said even though he could not hear all the words being spoken, he still clearly understood the little he heard, which has never happened to him before. He was near the back of the crowd, and as evening approached, the disciples of Jesus asked all the people to break into groups. They did as they were told, and before long there were baskets of food passed around to all of them. He watched in astonishment as Jesus fed all of those people with only five loaves and two fish! The loaves and fish multiplied right before them. He watched as the men continued to pull food out of baskets that should have long since been emptied. It was as if the baskets had no bottom! They each ate until they were full and then had food left over!"

The girls were overflowing with excitement. Martha smiled and nodded her head as she spoke. "Father told us that Jesus would one day do great things! How lucky for Gershom to witness such an event!"

Lazarus went on. "Chanoch started sharing that his cousin was at a wedding in Cana, where Jesus, his mother Mary, and some of his disciples were in attendance. It was only the first of several days for the wedding celebration, and the parents of the groom were embarrassed to find that the wine had already run out. Unfortunately, there was no money left for more, which would leave them standing in embarrassment and shame. One servant told Chanoch's cousin that he was instructed to fill six stone jars with water. Big ones, for ceremonial washing. Each jar holds about twenty to thirty gallons. Jesus asked them to leave the room, and when they returned, the water in all of those jars had turned to wine!"

The sisters stood, mouths agape. They were amazed at what they were hearing, yet they truly believed. One person could make up such a story, but there were so many accounts. So many witnesses.

Mary was soaking in his words like a cool rain on a hot day. "If these men have witnessed miracles of Jesus, surely, they will know there is truth in what Lazarus told them."

Martha added, "So, do you think the ones who shared stories suspected that Jesus was the Messiah all along, and no one was brave enough to speak up until then?"

"Yes, I suppose that is true! And there is more! Just when Yokim was ready to toss us from his house, there was a knock at the door. I heard the voice on the other side ask for me, which is strange because why would anyone ever look for me at Yokim's house? How would anyone know I was there?" Lazarus shrugged his shoulders and his young forehead wrinkled in confusion as he spoke.

Martha's concern grew. "A man asked for you at Yokim's home? Who was it, Lazarus?"

"A follower of Jesus! It was as if he knew what our conversation was about and walked in on cue!"

Martha's mind was still not at ease. "What business did

he have with you?"

Lazarus shook his head, "He just had a message for me." He paused for effect and motioned to his sisters. "Well, he had a message for the three of us."

Mary still wasn't following. "Why would a follower of Jesus ask for you? In Yokim's house of all places? And what does that have to do with us?"

Lazarus raised his eyebrows as if in complete surprise, as he laughed. "He just said Jesus sent him ahead to tell us that he requests to stay at our house!"

The girls were overjoyed! Mary clasped her hands together in delight. "What a gift to spend time with him between Passovers!"

Still not convinced her brother was in the clear with the other men, she asked, "What of Yokim?"

"The disciple asked to speak to Yokim alone, and Yokim dismissed all of us from his home. The others were patting me on the back when we were clear of sight from Yokim's window. I think they are as excited to see Jesus as we are!"

Martha hugged each of her siblings in celebration. "When will he arrive?"

His voice went higher as his excitement grew, "He will be here the day after *Shabbat*!"

Martha's face dropped. "So soon?"

Mary knew her sister worried enough for all of them, but how could she create worry in such a joyous moment? She teased her sister. "When is it ever too soon to be in the company of Jesus?"

Martha quickly scanned the room, taking an inventory of supplies in her head. "But we aren't prepared! We only have a few more hours in this day to prepare the *Shabbat* dinner, and even more so since Levik and Adinah plan to join us. In addition, we must prepare the meals for the Sabbath tomorrow. When will we find the time to prepare for Jesus?"

Lazarus spoke. "Didn't *Abba* tell us to always be

prepared for Jesus? Perhaps this is what he meant."

Mary put an arm around her sister. "Martha, you worry for nothing. I'll help. How much trouble can it be to prepare for one extra man?"

Martha just shook her head at her siblings, knowing that neither one of them had any idea how much work it was to be a suitable host, especially to such an honored guest. Their mother had always planned so carefully and taught her well, but to be honest, Martha didn't always pay very close attention. When their mother was in charge, the girls acted as assistants because their *aima* was a natural at making people feel at home. The girls were learning, but it took them all day to do what their mother could pull together at a moment's notice. Now that it was their turn to be in charge, Martha felt pressure to get it absolutely perfect. She was secretly happy Jesus didn't say he was coming for *Shabbat*. If that were so, she was sure her nerves wouldn't be able to take it.

She was confident that even her mother would not be entirely sure how to properly host the Messiah.

# Chapter 4

## Trista's Journal Entry
## Ten Foot Pole

June 19, 2005

"I am going to be frank. I wouldn't license you with a ten-foot-pole."

She did NOT just say these words to us!! Sitting at our newly disinfected kitchen table, she spread out official paperwork detailing our entire lives in several neatly arranged piles. This is not happening!! This CAN NOT be my life now... but it is. Responding to problems the county has with our pasts, our paperwork, and our "fitness" to be foster/adoptive parents is becoming a part-time job. Our assigned home study assessor, Todd Combs, dressed in khakis and a slightly wrinkled button-down shirt, sat across from me. Nina Williams, his boss, wearing a black suit with pumps and clutching a matching briefcase, sat across from Andy. The topic we were going to be discussing was so uncomfortable, and the news being delivered was so bad, Todd brought out his boss to help him navigate the discussion. What is this about? What now?!

It seems like it took forever to jump over the hurdle of obtaining the statement from my former therapist. I've been dealing with that request since March! She was as taken aback about the odd request as I was, but she gladly wrote up a letter and promptly sent it to Betsy. I hope she's happy. The county now has their official piece of paper stating that I, Trista Haskins, have resolved all the issues I had related to not being able to have my own baby. AS IF I am no longer going to have tears running down my face during church when the baby in the next pew plays peek-a-boo with me. AS IF I am not going to imagine the nurse handing my baby to me, with Andy lovingly looking on, every time I pass by a hospital. AS IF I will be able to walk by the adorable baby skunk costume at the store without being filled with intense heartache, fearing I may never take my baby out for that first trick-or-treating experience. There are so many painful reminders about what I don't have in the course of a regular week. How dare she even ask for that!!!! I am still so mad about this request, and I really wanted to tell her what she can do with that piece of paper, but I must keep my end goal in mind. I want to be a mommy. My pride, my dignity, my privacy…they don't matter, they can't matter more than the great privilege of becoming a mommy.

And here we are, at the next stage, only to be told this! How many things from our pasts are going to come back to haunt us? Now that decisions from my past have been judged and dissected and "resolved," it looks like it is Andy's turn. Admittedly, his first marriage was not a healthy one for many reasons, but they were blessed with an amazing daughter named Lilly. By the end, he and Clare separated, she filed for divorce, and she hired a cut-throat lawyer. Unbeknownst to Andy, she intended to restrict his access to his daughter.

It was a sad situation, as divorce always is. Andy has always expressed regret that he was not the husband he should have been to her. They married very young, and he was immature and self-centered, as many young men are. He made many mistakes; one being eventually turning to porn to satisfy his sexual needs. At the time, this option seemed easier than putting in the effort it would take to improve his marriage. I guess one day in a heart-to-heart with her, he shared details about this very personal topic, hoping it would all be out in the open and could finally be dealt with in their marriage. Instead, she took notes on his admissions and his part of the conversation ended up in letters to family, friends, and fellow church members. She shared that she was worried about him and was reaching out for help for him, to almost everyone in his life! This wasn't the end of their marriage. More confrontations, therapy appointments, marriage books, and sleeping arrangements would be tried and fail before it would end.

I am still mortified at the thought of all these people opening that letter!! What their faces must have looked like! He told me about all of this before we got married, and I appreciated his honesty about this struggle. I know many people struggle with this, especially in marriages that are no longer intimate. It's unfortunate but true. We are both on the same page that God's plan for marriage includes regular intimacy, so we were not worried that this struggle for him would continue into our marriage.

Cue the long and drawn-out, harrowing custody battle. Andy mistakenly thought this was going to be an amicable divorce and hired a family lawyer, who did not have the skill set necessary to fight the enormous feud ahead. He was depressed, exhausted, broke, and desperate for a resolution to occur so that a new "normal" could be established with his daughter and her time with him. By the end, I don't think there was a paper he wouldn't have signed, as long as it meant he had consistent time with his daughter.

Fast forward to our situation now. The paperwork that Nina, the boss, was looking at in my kitchen contained all the demands Andy had agreed to in his grim state, including a promise to attend sessions with a psychologist to create a safety plan. Now, coming up with a safety plan to put passwords on computers so that children cannot access inappropriate things sounds good. It is actually a responsible step most parents should consider. However, the psychologist that Andy agreed to work with just happened to be well-known in the area, specializing in sex addiction. He also happened to be interviewed in the local news fairly often about sex crimes.

Needless to say, this did not look good. A potential foster parent handing over his child custody arrangement with this well-known psychologist's name all over it did not make for a glowing application packet. Even though Andy was never accused of doing anything to harm Lilly, and she was in no way exposed to anything inappropriate at any time, being associated with Dr. Albert Simmons was enough to put a shadowy cloud over the entire application process. What was Andy thinking???!!! Albert Simmons! No sane person would have agreed to this, but it is what it is at this point. :(

The horribly awkward conversation in the kitchen continued.... After Nina dropped the bombshell about the ten-foot-pole, I looked over at my husband. His face became instantly bright red. I could tell he was clenching his jaw, and he was silent, trying to think of his reply. I jumped in first. "Well, I'm not ready to give up. I know it looks bad on paper, but Andy was in a no-win situation and agreed to this crazy contingency for the best interests of Lilly. The custody arrangement needed to be finalized so that his daughter could start feeling some stability," I managed to explain.

The mortifying topic was already broached. Could it get any worse? And I am known to keep talking in uneasy situations, long after I should just shut my mouth. True to form, as I heard more words coming out of my own mouth, my mind kept telling me to shut the heck up already. But I didn't. I hate this about me! Ugh!! I went on. "I recently read an article that stated 64% of men in the United States watch some pornographic material on a regular basis. Sadly, it almost seems to be an epidemic, even among Christians.

I do not intend to stick up for this behavior, only to ask if you quiz all the applicants about this topic. If so, does it mean they cannot become foster/adoptive parents if they admit to it? My guess is some of those 64% of men are fostering and adopting through your county right now."

Nina sat up straight and fumbled with the papers in front of her as she responded. "No, we do not question all applicants about this topic. It is personal and private and able to be kept so in most situations, except in your case, where it is written about in an official court document. Because it is in our paperwork, it has to be addressed now."

Todd, the assessor, seemed a little embarrassed that he brought his boss with him to handle this delicate situation. He cleared his throat. "There is one option we may possibly want to look at. I am not guaranteeing anything, but a full psychological evaluation from a psychologist would be necessary to even consider keeping this case on the books," he stated.

Andy, with his eyes still scanning the papers outlining all the embarrassing secrets and mistakes of his life laid out for all to see, declared, "Okay, I'll do it."

Neither of them, the boss or the home study assessor, looked convinced that a flawless full psychological evaluation would help, but they at least pretended that it may.

I have to keep hoping that it will work, because I cannot get away from the reminders. Walking by the nursery at church with the cries of babies spilling into the atrium, the adorable onesies at our local shop, even the diaper aisle at the grocery store.... Driving by the hospital wondering which floor is the baby floor, passing the lake crowded with neighborhood kids having a blast.... I just got back from running a few errands in town and saw three billboards begging people to be foster parents! Three!!!

"The best gift you can give a child is a home."

"You don't have to be perfect to be a perfect parent."

"We need good homes for great kids in tough situations."

I am continuously being mocked at this point and can't seem to get away from it. I feel as though my childlessness is a humiliating, disgraceful stain that I wear wherever I go. And I can't get the stain out, no matter what I do.

*God, I feel so empty! Oh, Heavenly Father, where are you in all of this? Why did you create me with such a yearning to be a mommy if you weren't going to let me be one?! It hurts so much! Father, I promise we will make you proud if you allow us to be parents. I will not let a day pass without taking time to teach about you, praise you, pray to you always and forever. I know Andy regrets his sins of the past and has asked you for forgiveness for these. Please do not let his past prevent us from expanding our family together. I beg you, please! This is so messy! Lord, do you see me? Do you hear me? You turned water into wine and fed over 5,000 people with five loaves and two fish. You can do anything! We need you and your help more than ever before. In Jesus' name, Amen.*

# Chapter 5

## The Plan

31 AD

Mary, Martha, and Lazarus had renewed joy in their hearts. Over the next several days, they were to enjoy the presence of good friends, both near and far, and that brought with it excitement that had been absent from their home for a quite a while. Mary kept looking at the colorful, yet slowly-darkening sky, thinking their friends better hurry if they were to get there in time. She was beginning to wonder if being in the company of friends proved to be too much for Adinah and Levik after all. Maybe they had changed their minds, but there was not enough time to let them know before the sun set. At last, she spotted their friends making their way down the dusty street. As they entered the doorway and stood talking with Martha, the words on the wall above them captured Mary's attention. They had been there for as long as Mary could remember, so they usually just blended in, unnoticed. The words had been written in their mother's hand, and they read *Adonai el Roi*. 'The God who sees me.' It seemed terribly ironic that Adinah would stand beneath them now, when just hours earlier she had told Mary how unseen she felt, by both God and her husband. Mary had never given it much thought before, but now she wondered why her mother had chosen those words. Had she felt unseen as well? Or, had she wanted to speak that truth into the lives of her family so they knew God was always watching out for them? Maybe she simply knew how important those words would be for all who entered. As her sister welcomed them into their home, Mary silently prayed that God would make His presence known, even now, in the middle of Adinah's pain.

As they walked toward the table, Levik wasted no time starting a conversation. "Lazarus, everyone is talking about the discussion among the men in town today. From what I heard, Yokim was pretty fired up. I can't tell if that man is genuinely trying to stay true to the scriptures, looking for drama, or trying to get on the good side of the higher-ups by siding with them against Jesus. I would love to hear your side of the story to find out what actually happened." Martha, true to form, told them it would have to wait until the meal had begun and invited everyone to gather around.

Mary's heart was happy to have friends join them for *Shabbat* once again. It had been a regular custom when their parents were still with them, but the girls and Lazarus didn't host very often. She could tell Adinah was still masking pain with a smile, but hoped it wouldn't be long before the joy in her friend's heart wasn't buried so far beneath the surface.

The friends made their way to the beautifully decorated table. Martha had thought of every detail. The group grew quiet as they stood in reverence. Martha lit only two candles, waved her hands over the flames, and covered her eyes with her hands. She said, "Blessed are You, Lord our God, King of the universe, Who has sanctified us with His commandments, and commanded us to kindle the light of the holy *Shabbat*." She whispered a prayer that only she and the Lord could hear, then uncovered her eyes and looked up at her sister.

As soon as Mary's eyes caught her stare, she recalled their conversation about the candles earlier in the day, and she knew what Martha must be thinking. At this point of the Friday evening meal, their father would usually say a blessing over his wife and the children after the additional three candles had been lit. Mary felt a tug in her heart. She closed her eyes in case the memory became a tear and drew more attention to the fact that there was only a need for two candles in each of their circumstances. How awful that would be for Adinah! They had never discussed it, but after Mary had explained the custom more thoroughly, she was sure Adinah felt the same emptiness at that part of the celebration.

Next was the *kiddush*, which had also been recited by their father, but was now delivered by Lazarus. He lifted a cup of wine and went on. "And there was evening and there was morning, a sixth day. The heavens and the earth were finished, the whole host of them. And on the seventh day, God ended His work which He made, and He rested on the seventh day...."

When the prayers were complete, they each washed their hands. As their hands were dried, they said, "Blessed are You, Lord, our God, King of the Universe, Who sanctifies us with His commandments, and commands us concerning the washing of hands."

When everyone finished, they stood around the table as Lazarus led the group in song and prayer. Afterward, he uncovered the two loaves of bread that served as a reminder of a double portion of manna in the desert. He held them up and said, "Blessed are You, Lord, our God, King of the Universe, Who brings forth bread from the earth. Amen." With that, he ripped off a piece for everyone, and they were seated at the table. Their meal could begin.

Lazarus had everyone's full attention as he regaled their friends with the events from earlier that day. He was still unsure how it would all play out, but he was proud of himself for speaking out on behalf of Jesus, even with the risk that came with it.

"I can't believe I missed that!" exclaimed Levik. He liked to think he would have jumped in to back Lazarus, but in all honesty, he wasn't sure. It was more likely that he would have waited to see the response from the other men before he spoke up. He had to hand it to Lazarus; that was brave. It could have gone either way. When there was a silent lull at the table, Levik changed the subject. "So, tell us, what was it like to grow up knowing Jesus?"

Adinah perked up at the suggestion. They were enjoying the carefully prepared meal, but the stories from friends around the table were a welcome distraction from her reality. She looked at each of their friends with wide eyes. "Yes! Was he different from the other children? Could you tell he would be a miracle-worker, even back then?"

Martha, Mary, and Lazarus exchanged knowing smiles with one another. It brought an exceptional closeness between them to share something so special. What a relief it was to now be able to talk about it openly!

Lazarus, being the youngest, had always looked up to Jesus like a brother he never had. Joseph, Mary, and young Jesus had quickly gone from being sporadic guests to most trusted friends. Since their families had met before Lazarus was born, many of the stories were fun for him to hear as well. Their father was such a superb storyteller, and Lazarus had heard them so many times that he felt as if he had been there for all of it himself. It had become an undeclared custom for their family to regale one another with their favorite memories with the family of Jesus as they walked into Jerusalem for Passover each year. The fond remembrances made each of them look forward to what new memories might be created after they met up again.

Mary was first to share. "Well, he wasn't any different from other boys his age on the outside, but he was much more intelligent than any boy I have ever known in Bethany."

Lazarus jumped in, pretending to be insulted. "Hey

now! We aren't so bad." The friends all laughed.

Martha's eyes sparkled as the thoughts of those easier times came flooding back. "Remember when *Abba* kept trying to stump us with his riddles, and Jesus would get the answer every time?"

Mary giggled and said, "His mother asked him to let others answer first so we would have a turn, but it was always the same. We could never come up with the correct answer. *Abba* would let us guess until he knew it was utterly hopeless that we would ever get it right, then he would signal to Jesus that it was okay to reveal the answer. Jesus would give such a thorough reply that one would think he had written the riddle himself."

Lazarus recalled, "Remember when I talked him into tossing the ball with me in the street? I threw it too high, and when he reached up to catch it, the leather burst open and dried corn spilled all over his head!" He told the story with such enthusiasm that each of them could picture the scene in their mind, and the delight in their eyes was evident. Knowing what they did about Jesus now, it was strange to think he had been a clumsy boy just like any other.

Martha laughed. "He was always a good sport. He would never turn down a foot race with you either, Lazarus. Even though he was much taller and could easily win, he would let you pass him right before you reached the finish line."

Lazarus looked genuinely surprised. "What? He didn't let me win. I did that all on my own!"

Levik winked in the direction of Lazarus and whispered, "I'm sure you did, my friend." Everyone had a good laugh, and it brought Mary delight to see everyone with light hearts.

Then Mary's voice grew quieter. "I think my favorite part was when we would gather around in the evenings and listen to the men talk. When any other guests were here, the men would go off by themselves, and the women would tend to the children. We weren't allowed to be part of their conversations. But it was different with them. We were all invited to sit at their feet and listen, and it always made me feel so grown up and special."

"Joseph and *Abba* would begin," added Martha, "then Jesus would start talking about Moses and Elijah, and before we knew it, an hour's time had passed, and Jesus was still talking. It was his second nature to take the role of the teacher with the rest of us soaking it all in like eager students. Even at that age, he had such a way about him that everyone wanted to listen. He had wisdom and confidence beyond his years."

"Joseph must be quite a scholar," said Levik. "I can't wait to meet him as well."

The siblings' eyes met one another, trying to decide who would speak first. Lazarus spoke up. "Jesus and Mary now come alone. Joseph has died."

"Oh, I'm sorry to hear that. Forgive me," said Levik.

The room felt solemn for a moment, and Martha was deep in thought. She had been rolling bits of information around in her mind, trying to connect pieces of the Torah with conversations she had been a part of when she was younger but didn't understand until now. When she spoke, she weighed her words carefully. "Joseph taught Jesus well, it's true. He was a great and noble man. However, as more is revealed about Jesus, I've been carefully considering in my heart what Jesus' mother Mary had told our *aima* about the conception of Jesus." She hesitated, unsure of how the next part would be received. "Joseph is not his true father."

Everyone sat in silence, looking at her with questioning eyes. She went on. "Mary said that an angel told her that the Holy Spirit would come upon her, and she would conceive a son in her virgin womb. The baby would be holy and would be called the Son of God. She and Joseph were already betrothed, so the angel also came to Joseph. His message was that Mary was telling the truth, and that he was to name the child Jesus."

"That would be difficult for a man to accept and understand," said Levik. "Even though I have never met Joseph, I can tell that he was a man of faith and honor."

"Very much so," added Mary.

Martha continued. "Of course, there were few that the mother of Jesus trusted with this information, but she was very close to our aima. I clearly remember overhearing their conversation and thinking that it was probably something I should not have heard. I did not understand what it meant then, but now it's all coming together."

"Yes!" exclaimed Lazarus. "We know Jesus was born in Bethlehem, when Joseph had to register under the house of David for the census. And we know they fled to Egypt to avoid the killing of the innocents."

Levik's eyes grew wide. "So, if that's true, the conception and birth of Jesus has fulfilled the prophecies of Isaiah, Micah and Hosea."

"It does," replied Martha. "And I would assume *Aima* shared the story with *Abba* and he saw the prophecy coming together as well. That would explain why he always told us to pay close attention and commit the words of Jesus to memory. He knew even then that Jesus would be the Messiah."

Mary added, "And with all the signs and wonders Jesus is doing now, some must believe the Messiah has come, even if it is creating a divide among the Jews and religious leaders. There are still those like Yokim who believe what Jesus says is blasphemy."

"They see him as a threat," added Adinah.

"I fear that things could get worse before they get better," said Levik. "The people who are likely to be against Jesus are very powerful. They will want him gone at all costs, even if it is by taking his life."

"That is possible," added Adinah, "but let's not darken the mood with such thoughts. We will worry about that when it's time. But for now, let's enjoy more of the fun stories.

"The only encounter I had with young Jesus was when I was in the garden one afternoon with Kunya and Asher. We were trying our best to lure a wood pigeon nearby with berries and ground corn. It would come within an arm's length, but just as we would reach to touch it, it would fly away. Jesus was walking by and saw this and smiled as if he was thoroughly amused by our attempts. He asked if he could try, so of course we stepped aside to see if he could lure it in. He squatted down, reached out his empty hand, and the pigeon walked right up and perched on his palm! We teased that he must be like Noah himself, and we even called him Noah a few times after that. Asher was looking around for a second wood pigeon to come along behind it!" Again, the sound of laughter filled the room.

The stories continued one after another as they passed food around the table. The later it got, the more anxious Martha became. Mary noticed.

"Martha, what's wrong? Are you already fretting over his arrival after Sabbath?"

"You know I am. I want everything to be just right. This is the first time I have ever wished I could get some work done on our day of rest."

"No need for that!" said Adinah. "You know that if you honor God's day of rest that He will reward you. Besides, your house is already in perfect order for *Shabbat*! What more do you need to do? He's only one man, Martha. There can't be much more to prepare, and you have plenty of room."

"I suppose you are right," Martha said reluctantly.

They enjoyed a moment of comfortable silence, as close friends can do, and finished their wine in the candlelight. Levik leaned over and whispered in Adinah's ear. Her eyes lowered, and she nodded in agreement with whatever he was saying. She took his hand, and they looked up to search the eyes of their friends. Levik wasn't sure if this was the right time to bring this up, but he supposed now was as good a time as any.

He cleared his throat. "Adinah and I have something to discuss with the three of you, as our dearest and most trusted friends. We are not sure how it will be received in Bethany. Many might view it as unclean, but we have decided to take the risk of public ridicule and do it anyway. We would like to bring it to you, because we know you will give us good counsel. As we lay out this idea, please be honest with us. You will not hurt our feelings if you tell us to go a different direction, because we know you will only steer us in a direction that honors God."

The three put down their glasses and gave their friends their full attention. "What is it, Levik?" Martha asked, but she looked at Adinah as she spoke.

Their collective concern was growing. What could their friends be associated with that would be considered unclean? It wasn't like them to even talk of things that were outside of the law. Mary wondered if it had something to do with Adinah's suspicions.

In Adinah's silence, Levik continued. "As we are well aware, the Roman Empire carries with it some hideous practices. I apologize in advance to the women at the table, as it is not even easy for me to talk about." He took a sip of watered-down wine to moisten his throat that had already grown dry from nervous expectancy of what he was about to say. He began again. "It is a common Roman practice to dispose of unwanted babies. If they are close to the sea, they leave their own crying infants out on the rocks to be swept away by the waves. Others are piled in the garbage, or even thrown on top of dung heaps while they are still alive."

Mary gasped and brought her hand to cover her mouth. She had heard rumors of this but did not know it was by such disgraceful means. How could a person do such a thing? She felt her stomach curling as if she could vomit right there at the table.

Lazarus voiced what they were all thinking. "God will surely punish such people."

"They don't see it that way," explained Levik. "They believe in many gods, and many times this is done as a sacrifice to one of them. It is also in the table of Roman law that a deformed child must be quickly killed. They are murdered, right there in front of the mother that brought them into the world."

Martha's eyebrows came together as she questioned Levik. She felt silly asking such a question, but it wouldn't leave her mind. "Do the Romans have that many deformed children?"

"The law says the deformed must be immediately killed, which is an act of mercy compared to what they do to perfectly healthy babies that are not wanted. Those are exposed. That is, they leave live babies out in the elements to suffer whatever fate may bring them to their death. For whatever reason, we do not know. Maybe it was a female, and they wanted a male. Maybe they already have as many children as they desire. Maybe they want to use it as a sacrifice to whatever god they serve. Or maybe a baby would simply cause an inconvenience."

Adinah explained further. "We have heard of this happening in Rome, but we have only recently heard it reported outside the gates of Jerusalem."

Mary couldn't believe what she was hearing. "Our holy city? It cannot be so!"

"We believe it is so," continued Adinah. "A widow I was caring for at the infirmary said she saw it firsthand. The wives of Roman soldiers stationed in Jerusalem are taking their unwanted children to the woods on the south side of Mount Zion, opposite the Valley of Hinnom. They are just laying them right there on the ground, left to be carried away by wild animals."

Martha didn't want to believe it was true. "Are you sure

the widow wasn't sick with fever and talking out of her mind? How can she be sure the babies suffered such a fate? Surely they didn't just pass by and leave them there?"

Levik finished Adinah's story. "She said at the time they passed, there were Romans still standing around and ordered them to move along. She was told by other travelers that if the babies are still alive at first light, the Romans have put a sword right through their heart. Maybe the crying is too much even for them."

Mary felt as if a sword was just put through her own heart. She had never heard of anything more horrific.

It was Lazarus' turn to speak. "What does this have to do with you and Adinah, Levik?" Mary and Martha could guess, as they knew how much Adinah grieved not having a child of her own, but they had discussed no details with Lazarus.

The couple paused and looked at one another. Levik could see Adinah's eyes filling with tears. He cleared his throat again. "Well, as you know, we have been unable to bring a child of our own into this world. I will confess to all of you now that it has put a great strain on our marriage and has led me into temptations that I am too ashamed to say out loud."

Adinah's eyes widened as they met Mary's. Her husband had never spoken those words to her, let alone to others. Her heart was mixed with emotions. She was partially thankful that he had acknowledged his sin before his friends and before God but partially sick with the truth. What did he mean when he said he was led into temptation? Was he unfaithful in act, or in thought? She knew they would have to discuss this further, but now was not the time. She let Levik continue with what he was saying.

"Adinah and I want to locate the woods where these infants are thrown and take one into our home. Although we know it will be from a Roman bloodline, and perhaps even meant to be a sacrifice to a pagan god, we don't care. We want to raise it as our own."

Mary, Martha, and Lazarus looked around the table from one set of eyes to the next. Mary had so many questions and thoughts swirling that she wasn't sure how to even voice them.

There was a long silence as each one of them processed the information they had just heard. Lazarus spoke first, decidedly. "I'll go with you."

Levik's eyes filled with tears. In that one sentence, he knew that his friend not only understood their heartache but also forgave him for any unspoken transgression. He knew that Lazarus loved them enough to risk his own life to help them. He had never felt so covered in grace.

Martha, always protecting him more than he wished, grabbed her brother's arm. "Lazarus! I know you want to help our friends, but what of the Romans? You have yet to recover from the last wound they inflicted."

"Martha, Levik and I will be careful. We can go just before nightfall and watch from afar. If we see them discarding a baby, we will wait for them to leave and sneak in carefully so they don't see us."

"But the baby is surely going to be crying out. What if they follow the cries as you carry it away? They will hunt you down!" Martha added.

"We have thought of all those things," said Levik. "It is true. That is a risk we will be facing. We are unsure how often these babies are laid out, or even the exact location. It will likely require many trips before we are successful. I want to be clear up front that it will be a risk. It is one I am willing to take myself, but I did not intend to have Lazarus take that risk with me. We simply wanted to know that we would still have your friendship if we brought a child into our home that has been disposed of by a pagan Roman."

Mary looked across the table to both of her siblings, trying to sway Martha into giving Lazarus her approval.

"What other choice do we have but to help? Every child is made in the image of God, regardless of whether their parents believe in Him. Aside from helping Adinah and Levik, I think we have a responsibility. Now that we know these babies are in such danger, we cannot leave them there!"

"I agree." Lazarus was firm in his speech. Knowing Mary was in agreement, he looked to his oldest sister, searching her face. "Martha?"

She was quiet with her thoughts for a moment. They had already lost their parents. She couldn't even allow the idea of losing Lazarus to enter her mind. She pushed the thought away and tried to focus on the plight of their friends.

The room was silent. Lazarus was hoping she would see it the way they did. He was old enough to go without her permission, but he didn't want to do anything that would cause his sister grief. She had always taken such good care of him, and he respected her as much as his own *aima*.

Martha gave a decided nod as she spoke. "Let it be so."

Adinah let out her breath, unaware that she had even been holding it. A tear of relief streamed down her cheek, and it was nice to know it was not from a place of grief this time. It was out of love for her dear friends. The hope of having a child in their home might actually be within reach! And if it helped save the life of an outcast child, it was even better. She turned to the three as she spoke carefully. "You understand that there will be many in our village that will not agree. We may even be shunned. Even though the child is not in your home, if you support us, you may still be considered guilty of the same sin in their eyes. If I am being truthful, it scares me for you. There are already people up in arms because of what Lazarus said to the men earlier today. This will only add to their anger."

Martha leaned over the table and took Adinah's hands in her own. "We are willing to take that chance," she said.

It was settled. They said a prayer together that God would bless their travels and lead them to the baby that He wanted them to find.

# Chapter 6

## Trista's Journal Entry
## Broken

December 22, 2008

"You gotta find a place to pull over. You're going to get us in a wreck trying to drive in this condition!"

I blurted this out to Andy through my sobbing and wailing as Andy slowly and grudgingly drove down the street. "Mommy, you and Dadda okay?" asked our sweet little Bella from her car seat in the back. She looked so confused, her blue and yellow ducky pacifier halfway dangling out of her mouth. Andy found a place we could safely pull over to let the first of many waves of anguish wash over us.

This was hands down the worst day of mine and Andy's lives. I don't know how we will ever get through this.

Looks like it's been a while since I've picked up my journal. Since we got our foster care and adoption licenses, I haven't really had the need! Excitement about the possibility of becoming a mommy had me on cloud nine, and we were blessed with Brandon, the first child placed with us, soon after. Bella came to us six months later, and life was wonderful. Stressful and chaotic and full of unknowns, but wonderful! Until November 21st came.

The call came in the middle of lunchtime. Brandon and Bella were in their IKEA highchairs, eating black beans and carefully cut up grapes, and sipping on apple juice from their sippy cups. We were all laughing as we were listening to the muffin man song for the gazillionth time and watching the dog and two cats wait under their chairs for anything they may drop. Brandon's case worker called and reported the information like it was just another appointment reminder. "Since Brandon's father is out of the picture now, and the weekly visits have been going well, the judge has decided reunification will begin as soon as possible. Are you available to drop Brandon off at Rachel's place around 2:00 P.M. tomorrow? Along with all of his belongings, of course," she added.

Brandon's biological father was recently found guilty of child abuse and sent to prison. Since he is no longer a danger to Brandon because he is no longer at the home, reunification will be able to happen. Rachel is Brandon's biological mother, who has been having weekly supervised visits with him for the past fourteen months, the amount of time he's been with us.

What was I going to say? When you are a foster parent, the county is like your boss, and not an especially nice or empathetic one. They say "jump," you say, "how high?" This is just how it is. They don't want your opinions. They don't want your suggestions. And they definitely don't want to see you, God forbid, cry about this emotional rollercoaster you willingly got on. They wanted Brandon to be safe and in a home where he was loved, but they don't really have the time or inclination to hear about that love. I've been doing this for over a year now. The rules are not unknown to me. I got it. Act like a robot, but at the same time love them like they are yours, because they just may be someday. Make the appointment that will tear your heart in two and don't show any emotion about it. Got it.

"Sure," I replied in a daze before pressing the red X on the phone's screen. Sure, I will pack up this child, who means everything to me, who I love more than I could ever imagine loving. The one who taught me to be a mama, the first little person to ever call me "Mommy." Sure, I'll drop him off at Rachel's apartment. Tomorrow. Rachel, who has questionable judgment at best (choosing her abusive husband over Brandon for the past fourteen months), and who I fear may worship Satan because of some of her public posts online. Sure, I'll do that.

After the long and messy home study process, we were finally approved. We had three cribs and were certified for three children ages 0-5. We were so excited to serve God by taking care of His children who desperately needed a safe home. And, of course, we welcome the idea of adopting if the court deems that is in the best interest of the child. It looks as if Bella's case may head toward adoption eventually, and Brandon's case was ending with reunification. It is challenging to even explain how hard it is to foster. I find it so difficult to even pray about these situations because, of course, you want the child's mother to get her act together and become the mom God wants her to be. And yet, if you pray that way, you are literally praying to lose a child you have come to love, most likely to never see them again. I try to just pray for God's will to be done, but it is a continuous battle between your heart and your mind. At least it is for me.

Of course, we knew that the purpose of fostering was not to adopt. The purpose of fostering was to give the parents time to gain the skills needed so the children may be reunified with them. We knew this day may come and had been preparing for it since our first fostering class years before. But knowing these facts does not take away the love we have for him. These facts do not take away the pain we feel as we consider life without him. These facts also did not protect us from the pain we felt as the biological grandmother had to peel Brandon's hands off me as he was hugging me goodbye for the last time, not really realizing it was the last time.

The most agonizing thing either Andy or I have ever done in our lives was walking out of that door as we heard the baby we had raised for the last fourteen months crying and calling out for us, knowing we may never see his sweet face again. Before this day, I'm not sure what I would have said my hardest moment of all was. It doesn't even matter because I know it didn't compare to this moment. This was definitely the hardest moment of all my life. I don't even know how I got my legs to take the steps necessary to walk to the car, hand in hand with Bella. All the while Brandon's dejected cries were flooding our ears.

The reality is sadly setting in. Rachel is probably not going to let us be any part in Brandon's life. She has not responded to one call or text. I have sunk into a deep, dark, all-consuming depression. How do I describe the love I have for Brandon? I had always seen mommies doing things like put a pacifier in their child's mouth to clean it before giving it to their baby, wondering if I would ever love a baby that much. It seemed kind of gross to me, honestly! And what about a baby who wasn't even biologically related to me? Would I be able to love like that? Brandon gave me that answer. It was a definitive YES!!!

We were so nervous when the social worker brought him to the house that Thursday afternoon and handed him to me to hold. We briefly chatted about upcoming appointments and signed the papers about his new official residence, and she drove down the driveway, leaving us standing on the front porch with a sweet, chubby-cheeked, blue-eyed, smiling boy looking up at us. He was a fun and wonderful addition to our family. And Andy's daughter (who we call Silly Lilly) was turning out to be the best big sister ever. And yes, just to get a laugh from that sweet baby, I would put his binky in my mouth and suck on it. He thought it was hilarious, and I did not think it was one bit gross! Yes, we knew there was the possibility that he would be reunified, but that did not limit that love we shared with him, hence the pain we feel losing him. We were able to adjust to fostering and babyhood with Brandon for six months, and then Bella (a girl close to his age) joined us. We now had two fun-loving toddlers, one doting older sister, the sweetest dog, and two cuddly cats. As hard as foster care is, we were loving every minute of our sweet family time.

Brandon…the boy who made me a mommy. That kid loves Barney and Elmo and dancing and suckers. He loves suckers so much that I caught him on more than one occasion putting two in his mouth at the same time! He had a smile on his face almost all the time until the times I dropped him off at daycare to go to work. I could hear him crying even after walking down two long hallways and out the door to the reception area! One of his absolute favorite things to do was walk down the road to visit our neighbors' goats. Some days, the first thing he would do after waking up is walk to the front door and point to it, saying "goat-goat," and we all knew what that meant. We had special brushes for Brandon and Bella to use on the goats, and he would go find both of them, repeating "goat-goat" as he gave Bella her's. The love I had for him grew every single day, despite knowing how it may end.

The demands of working full time as a teacher of kids with special needs, and having two one-year-olds, were many. When I added in the regular meetings with social workers, visits with biological parents, and various therapy appointments for both children, I wasn't getting to spend too much time with them. As soon as we thought we could afford it, I left my teaching job and became a stay-at-home mom. Brandon and Bella and I were a little trio: we had so much fun together! If we weren't hunting for animal tracks or picking berries on our land out back, you could find us swimming at Long Lake's beach up the road. It was official. DNA did not matter. The love I have for these precious children could not be stronger. So, the pain of losing Brandon is not lessened one iota by the facts I already knew.

The depression is terrible and can be inescapable. It's not like I am feeling suicidal, because I know Bella needs me. I love her way too much to do that. However, I am having thoughts that are embarrassing to admit but are very real. I have never experienced sadness or loss like this. I will sit here late at night, Andy at work, Bella safely tucked in bed, and I will hear a noise. The typical me would get up and look out the window, freaked out about a possible intruder, or more likely a bear making his way up to our porch looking for leftovers. The depressed me actually sits on the couch and hopes it is an intruder, and that he will hurt me or take me out of my misery. Every minute without sweet Brandon is full of pain and heartache. Every single minute is almost unbearable.

Some of my former students were into cutting. The psychiatrist at work would try to explain this behavior in our staff meetings. The thought was that they were experiencing so much pain, the only way they could think about something else was to put a razor to their arm. Their attention would be drawn immediately to that pain, hence giving them relief from the emotional pain they were feeling. I don't know if I ever really bought into this reasoning. I know many times I thought the students did it for attention. But now, it makes so much sense to me. A pain so immense, the only way to experience relief from it had to be another, more acute pain. I finally understand the behavior. I have not begun cutting, but I daydream of walking downtown late at night and letting brutal things happen to me. It seems that would be the only way to escape thinking of life without the sweet Brandon we have come to love.

I want to seek help for this depression, but I have already been judged for seeking therapy for my sadness around infertility. If my therapist hadn't written that statement that I was totally over it, we probably wouldn't have gotten our licenses. As foster parents, our lives are literally open books for the county to read and judge. If I sign up for therapy to help me through this loss, they will find out. Will that make me look bad to them? Will they question my abilities to care for Bella? When I admitted my innermost, disturbing thoughts to Andy last week, he agreed with me that therapy is not an option. Even if we risk the county finding out I am in therapy again, I wouldn't be able to share the extent of my sadness with my therapist, anyway. What would be the point? An anti-depression medicine? I fear I would be judged for this as well. After many talks with Andy, crying sessions into my pillow so Bella can't hear me, hours of staring into space, wondering how I am going to get help, I have concluded that I have to go it alone. No therapist. No meds. I cannot bear losing Bella, too!

To make matters even worse, I am finding this is not a loss that many understand. I'm not friends with any other foster parents. There are no foster parent support groups I can find out about on my own, and I am afraid to admit I need one to anyone who may possibly know, like the case workers. Friends and family try, but they do not understand. I "signed up for this." I knew this loss was likely to come. So, I should not be hurting this much. I should be getting over it by now. The judgments and expectations of others who have no experience with this pain are heavy burdens I carry with me wherever I go.

I'm so desperate to find some help with this unbearable pain, but I have to be careful that it is help that the county will not use against us. There doesn't seem to be a book for grieving foster parents anywhere. I've even gone into bookstores and personally asked about the topic. In my search on the web, I finally came across one website that another foster parent started, and a handful of foster parents in pain shared their stories. One total stranger named Kathy shared a poem she wrote about the loss she and her husband felt when they said goodbye to their foster daughter. I have read that poem a hundred times in the past week. Somebody else knows our pain. Why is it so important that I know that somebody understands our loss? It has been refreshing for both Andy and me to read this poem and know that another couple, somewhere in this world, knows our same pain. But more importantly, in the last lines of the poem, the poet is reminded that Someone else also knows the agonizing pain of handing over a child to people who may not love them like you do.

Wow! This hit me like a ton of bricks.... I've been a little frustrated about my mom and the church and my friends not understanding or recognizing the depth of the pain our family is suffering. We gave our whole hearts to a child who we will probably never see again. The last time we saw him, he was crying out for us and clutching me in a hug and had to be physically removed from me. And we walked away as he screamed, never to return again. We have no idea how he is being cared for and no way to find out. No, I don't want to go on with life as if Brandon never existed or was part of our family. No, I am not capable of having a conversation about a t.v. show or vacation or someone's new car when I am worried that Brandon is not being kept safe. All the thoughts.... Does he think we don't love him anymore because we never came back? We tried to explain what was happening with picture books we made, but did he understand? Does he still look out the window for us thinking we will come back? My heart shatters while reflecting on these. But then I remember the One who has been through worse.

*Heavenly Father, here I have been searching for someone else in this world to tell me they know my pain, and yet I realize the Creator of the universe knows my pain better than anyone! You know what it's like to love a child so much, and then turn that child over to a potentially harmful situation, because you did that with Jesus, and you did it for me! Father, you know my pain. You see my tears. What now, Lord? I so desperately wanted to be a mommy for so many years. You know all that I went through. And then you finally brought me this wonderful, sweet baby I fell in love with.... He made me a mommy.... And I am never to see him again? How can this be? Please, God, let me be in his life in some way!! As a babysitter, as an auntie, as anything!! And Father, heal me. I am a broken mess, and I need to be whole for Bella. Hear my prayers and see my tears and heal me as you healed the leper. Please, Lord!*

# Chapter 7

## The Preparation

31 A.D.

The morning after the Sabbath dawned fresh and new. Despite the fact that Martha had tossed and turned all night, she awakened with the rise of the sun, with only one thing on her mind. Jesus was coming today! She rose and dressed, then quickly awakened Mary and Lazarus. Although they had been very careful to leave the house in good order, there was still much to be done. The messenger Jesus sent ahead said that he was coming, but he didn't say for how long. Was he coming only for dinner and a rest? To stay for the night? For a week? Was he coming alone, or with a traveling companion? These were all things she would have asked if the messenger had come to her, but it never even occurred to her brother to ask such things. Lazarus rarely involved himself with those preparations, so he gave no thought to the details that she was now listing in her mind. She tried to remember Jesus' favorite foods as best she could and had the meal planned in her mind since she heard he was coming. She seemed to remember him saying he grew tired of gruel, as they ate it so often when he was growing up. It was a staple meal in many homes in Israel because it was inexpensive and there was usually an abundance. But he never grew tired of her mother's bread dipped in oil and vinegar. That was first on the list! She would also make fresh fish with sesame, legumes, sliced peaches, and pistachio nuts. For dessert, they would have small cakes covered in carob syrup.

Lazarus walked into the kitchen next, stretching with a yawn. His hair was a mess, and Martha told him as much. She guessed he probably already knew and didn't really care. He stood in the middle of the room, trying to wake from sleep, just like he had done as a small boy. It had always been difficult to get him moving in the morning. He grabbed a few dates and a piece of bread off of the table. "Lazarus, when you have eaten, please go out for more wine. I didn't realize we had gone through most of it when we hosted Levik and Adinah for *Shabbat*."

He bent at the waist and held out one hand, as if addressing royalty. "Anything for you, Martha."

"I'm glad to hear that, because when you return, I will need you to gather wood for the fire and take care of the animals, and...."

While she was still talking, he walked over and gave her a big squeeze, lifting her feet off the floor. "Is that all? Is there more? Would you like to tell me now, or do I have to shake it out of you?" he joked.

Martha smacked at his hands, pretending to be angry. "Stop that! Put me down! Just because you're bigger and stronger doesn't mean you can pick me up on a whim!"

Lazarus gently lowered her to the ground and patted the top of her head as if she were a toddler. "I'll be on my way now."

"Not with your hair looking like a madman!" Martha reached up to flatten the cowlick, but Lazarus ran to the door before she could reach him.

"What people must think!" she said to herself, as she smoothed out the wrinkles in her skirt.

"Who are you speaking to?" asked Mary. She was still pulling her hair back as she entered the room.

"Oh, to nobody, it seems. Mary, please go to the well to fetch water with the other women." She sounded a little smug when she added, "You may have to make two trips. I'll be staying here. There are many preparations to take care of."

The look Mary shot her sister let her know that she understood what that comment was really about. They usually only got extra water before *Shabbat*. Martha was intent on teaching her sister a lesson for making her fetch all the water on her own a couple of days earlier, when Mary was consoling Adinah. Mary's voice was thinly veiled with guilt as she replied with a tease, "Yes, *Aima*…I mean, Martha." She smirked over her shoulder as she made her way through the door. The fresh air was quickly becoming hot. She was hoping her early start would mean the line at the well would be shorter.

When she stepped out onto the dirt road, she could see Adinah headed her way. "*Shalom*, Mary!"

"*Shalom*!" Mary said in return. She noticed that Adinah was carrying an extra water jug. "I suppose you didn't get to the well in time before *Shabbat*?"

"No, silly! The extra is for you! I told you that I would help." It was true that Adinah was more than happy to lend a hand, but she was secretly hoping her help would mean an invitation for herself and Levik to visit with Jesus as well.

Mary laughed to herself, thinking how Martha would be a tad bit agitated when she found out that Adinah's help meant that Mary didn't need to make two trips to the well after all. The lesson would have to be learned another day.

"Today is the big day! I bet Martha is beside herself," said Adinah.

"You know my sister too well." Mary smiled as she said it, knowing Martha's list of chores for them was surely getting longer by the minute. There was no telling what would await her when she returned home.

"Mary, do you think he will remember me?" Adinah

asked. "It was so long ago when we last spoke."

"It is very possible," replied Mary. "Jesus remembers everything. After our families had met that first time, I was still very young. He remembered how fond I was of watching the ducks, and he carved one for Martha and me. He surprised us with them when they returned at the next Passover. They still sit in our kitchen."

Adinah's eyes widened. "Yes, I was admiring those wooden ducks when we were there just the other day! Ah, what a special gift!"

"Indeed, it was," continued Mary. "Yet, the bigger gift is Jesus himself. He makes each person feel as if he is there just for them. Like, if nobody but you lived in Bethany, he would still make the journey just to talk to you."

As they neared the well, they could see that a line had already formed. That wasn't unusual for the day after Sabbath. However, it was unusual that the women were all standing with their water jugs on the ground. None of them were actually drawing water, but they were looking in the direction of Mary and Adinah as they approached. Mary turned to see who or what was behind them. What were they looking at? She scanned their surroundings but saw nothing out of the ordinary. She looked at Adinah for an answer, but she just shrugged her shoulders. The closer they got to the well, they realized the women were waiting for them.

"*Shalom*," said Mary, in a voice that was more confident than she felt. Why were they staring at her?

She stood waiting for a return greeting, but none came. Instead, they began to speak all at once, with questions coming at her from every direction. She didn't know which to answer first.

"Is it true, what Lazarus said?"

"Has the Messiah actually come?"

"Have you and Martha seen any miracles?"

"Do you think the elders will make a formal accusation?"

"Is Jesus to stay at your home as the messenger said?"

"Tell us what he's like!"

Mary wasn't used to such attention, and she didn't much care for the pressure of everyone waiting to hear how she would respond. If she misspoke, the ripple effect could put the lives and reputations of many on the line. Their questions all floated and swirled in the air. Their voices blended, but then dissipated like the fading image of a mirage when she heard one of the women say, "He could be here any time. Someone said he was only coming from Jericho. He was staying just on the other side of the Mount of Olives for the Sabbath."

For a split second, Mary was overjoyed with excitement. He is near! It won't be long now. Then her thoughts went to Martha, and how she would react to the news. "Wait," said Mary, trying to process all of the information that was just thrown at her. "Did you say he could be here any time? We weren't expecting him until supper!"

"Well, it's just a guess, but that's only a short distance from here. It surely won't take long once he starts heading this way."

Suddenly, Mary felt an urgency to get the water back to Martha. She was sure her sister's heart would beat right out of her chest when she heard how close Jesus was. The other women graciously stepped aside and allowed Mary and Adinah to fill their water jugs and be on their way. They understood the responsibilities of hosting guests.

When the girls returned to the house and told Martha what they had heard, they watched Martha begin to pace around the room, talking to herself more than anyone else. She would walk to the table and pick something up, only to set it back down and walk to the other side to begin something else, undecided on where to even begin. If he was coming early, the fish she had in mind would not do for a morning meal. If she made it for lunch, there would be nothing left for dinner. How had their *aima* made this look so easy?

She knew Jesus wouldn't mind if everything wasn't perfect, but she wanted only the best for him. With the promised help from Mary and Adinah, she supposed it wouldn't be too difficult to make enough food for just a couple more people.

# Chapter 8

## Trista's Journal Entry
## Wildflowers and Poop

June 24, 2010

Today was a glorious, freeing, momentous day! I told the kids that not all the wildflower seeds we planted this summer will bloom this year. I explained that we will get to see the rest of them bloom next year, and I meant it. They didn't know how much I really meant it!

Why is this seemingly mundane statement momentous, you ask??? I will tell you.... This summer day started off normal enough. Booker and Bella woke up first and headed into the living room for their Barney fix. I made oatmeal and juice and brought it out to them on their miniature red and blue plastic picnic table, which was placed in between the couch and the television. This set-up started out as temporary but has morphed into something a little more permanent since the kids wake up at different times and it just makes life easier in the mornings. Booker's diaper looked full, so I scooped him up and changed it before putting him back on his side of the bench, just as Baby Bop began singing about shapes. Daddy walked in the front door from working his night shift, and the kids started gleefully yelling for him, then remembered to quiet down, as we all know Amelia is very grumpy when she gets woken up before she is ready. Daddy came over to their table and gave them big hugs and gave me a kiss, went to the kitchen to make my coffee, and headed to bed to get some much-needed sleep.

In stomped Amelia with a concerned look on her face. "Did I hear Daddy go to bed without giving me a hug good morning? I've told him I don't like that. I'm going to go tell him he hurt my feelings."

"Good morning, sweetie, how was your…" She was already stomping down the hallway on a mission, her pink satin nightgown tucked halfway into her underwear and half her hair twists sticking straight up into the air. Guess her hair wrap fell off again in the night. Mental note to get a new one.

After we got Amelia squared away with her hug and breakfast, and I grabbed my coffee, we sat down for some stories. *Wheels on the Bus* is a favorite for all of them, and Booker always insists on the one that you can press the buttons to hear the different dinosaur roars. We finished story time with our *Beginner's Bible* about David and Goliath.

Next activity on the agenda was our morning walk down the road; past the goats, past the bison, and back down to the trails on our property to check out all the new blooms coming up in the yard. During the spring, Andy had tilled up part of a meadow, and we planted wildflowers. Part of the mix was annuals and part perennials, and the seedlings were really taking off. Bella was especially excited about the new blooms we hadn't noticed the day before. "Mommy, look at all the pretty colors of flowers God created … pink, yellow, white! We're so lucky! Thank you, God!" Bella and God are pretty tight, even at this young age of four.

As we all took notice of the new blooms in the meadow, I leaned down and explained to them, "If you think this is pretty, just wait until next year. Some seeds we planted won't come up until then, so we'll get to see even more flowers next summer." As we all held hands, admiring the flowers and looking forward to what was to come, it hit me. I just talked about something in the future with my children. I didn't have to avoid the conversation or be wishy-washy or say a bunch of disclaimers about it because I didn't know if they would still be in our family. Next summer, we will all get to see the new flowers bloom together. Tears of joy streamed down my face. These are my children. I am their mommy. I get to talk about and plan for the future with them. Is there a word that means happier than happy? If so, that is how I feel on this day. From the corner of my eye, I saw Andy walking in our direction with his mid-day coffee in hand. As he came over to us, Booker quickly climbed up to his spot on Daddy's shoulders as I held the coffee. Bella and Amelia started recounting the names of the new blooms and about how there will be more next year. They were talking at the same time, getting louder and louder to compete with each other, but he heard enough to get the gist. He looked over knowingly at me with a content smile all over his face. He understood immediately why I was wiping tears from my cheeks.

What an experience this fostering thing has been.... A while after we said goodbye to Brandon, we fostered two sisters for a short time before they were placed with an aunt. In the following year, we got calls about both Amelia and Booker when they were born because they were both related to Bella. Since they were related, all their cases ended up getting tied together. Soon after the case went to court, and the judge ruled in favor of placing all three in adoptive custody, the judge was convicted of a felony. All decisions made by him were thrown out and a new court case had to begin again. So, this meant a prolonged time of uncertainty for all involved. Finally, the adoption worker called with a date. The future will no longer be unsettled. We will be a forever family.

The adoption day was wonderful, a dream come true, with a few unexpected laughs if I'm being honest. Bella, Amelia, and Lilly (who was excited to be their forever sister) were wearing matching yellow princess dresses and Booker looked handsome in his suit with a coordinating yellow tie. Andy and I and our families wore yellow also to support the special day. The magistrate was up on her large, elaborate podium, which felt a mile away and at least twenty feet tall. She was a large woman with a stern face and wore a long black robe. I was a little intimidated by her, and it all felt so formal and official. Our adoption worker sat with the three littles and us at the attorney's table, which happened to have a long microphone we could talk into when we were asked questions. This long microphone also just happened to be the right length to reach Booker's mouth if he sat on my lap.

The magistrate began with explaining why we were all there and facilitated the process for going under oath. After we did this and we all introduced ourselves, she explained in no uncertain terms that adoption is a permanent and lifelong commitment to ... *poop* ... and both Andy and I must be equally committed to … *poop*!

I was so nervous that I didn't realize the poop interruptions were being made by Booker. He was sitting on my lap to get himself tall enough to reach the microphone and cracking himself up with his funny word of the day. As much as I tried to prevent him from reaching the mike, I didn't want to break the microphone or cause a big scene, so we just kind of went on with the hearing with some funny interruptions along the way. As stern as the magistrate looked, I could see a brief glint of humor in her eye by the end. She then signed the decree of adoption for all three children and let them each come up and bang the gavel. What a beautiful sound that was!

*Dear God, how awesome are You that You can take my infertility, which brought me years of agony, and turn it into a blessing for me in the end! I am in awe every time I see You work Your Romans 8:28 magic! Speaking of the way the wildflower meadow will look next summer seems like such a small thing, but it means a future for this family. I also want to take this time to pray for their beautiful biological mother, Serenity. I don't know much about her life, but I do know that she chose to have these dear little ones instead of aborting them, and I am so grateful to her for this brave choice. She's been through so much and experienced loss after loss. Please wrap your loving arms around her and comfort her during her pain. Protect her from harm and give her wisdom and courage to make healthy choices for herself. Give her hope and a future filled with Your grace and blessings. Help Andy and me to raise these sweet children in a way that brings honor to her and You all the days of our lives. In Jesus' name, Amen.*

****

June 24, 2011

Not today, Satan!
You will not rob me of my peace!
You will not steal my joy!
You will not destroy my love and
overwhelming sense of gratitude!
Not today, Satan! Not ever!

Life is absolutely wonderful! The winters here can be long and cold, but the snow has melted, and school is out for the summer, and I thank God every day for these amazing children.

Scrolling on Facebook memories today, I ran into our big adoption day post.... It had pictures of the special day: the courtroom, the magistrate, everyone dressed to the nines, big smiles, extended family and all. I had written, "Andy, Lilly, Booker, Amelia, Bella, and I are official according to the state of Wisconsin and the powers that be! Hooray!" The kids were engrossed in yet another episode of Wild Kratts, so I killed some time and read through the messages from the original post. It was so nice to read the many heartfelt congratulations from people we have shared our lives with. We are so blessed to have so many supportive people in our village. Yet, one recurring theme kept showing up in the messages…I can't believe the number of people who wrote something along the lines of, "Watch, now you'll get pregnant and have one of your own."

What do you mean? Can't you celebrate our family the way it is, or does there have to be a biological connection before it is authentic enough for you? Can't you just say congrats or put a smiley face emoji and call it a day? Why must you insinuate that our family is not real enough to be celebrated until we have a biological child? I know this may not be what these Facebook friends were consciously thinking, but this is how it feels to me.

Hence the poem I just wrote…. Not today Satan!! I am right where I am supposed to be. Loving the children that I am supposed to love. Pouring myself into the family God gave me, and I am grateful, oh so grateful!

And as imperfect as the journey was that led me here, I would do it all over again with no hesitation. Of course, I wouldn't change a thing about the obvious blessings of the adoptions of Booker, Amelia, and Bella! Even the difficult cases that ended in reunification were blessings in disguise from the foster care system, as broken and messy as it may be. Even Brandon's case. It was one of the greatest privileges of my life to share our love and create a family for Brandon during a time when his whole world was being decided (unbeknownst to him) by parenting plans and social workers and judges.

But more importantly, I hope he was blessed by our decision to become foster parents. He did not deserve to be hurt by his father. He did not deserve to go through the pain of being separated from his mother. No child ever deserves to become a member of the dreaded foster kid club. However, he did deserve to be loved on and doted on and prayed for every single day. The foster care system allowed that to happen, too. The never-ending paperwork, the loss of privacy, the constant social worker visits, experiencing the greatest heartbreak in all my life when it was time for him to go. All worth it.

*Dear Father in Heaven, As I sit here reflecting on our fostering journey, my thoughts are drawn to the foster parents still at it, signing up for that emotional roller coaster time and time again, child after child. Give a never-ending supply of strength to these parents who choose to love kids who are not their own, kids who may very well show up at the door at 1:00 A.M. with only the bug-ridden clothes on their back. Lovingly mend the broken hearts of these parents who choose to spend their days mending the broken hearts of children. Give them the words to say when the children in their care ask why they have to be separated from their mommy, why their mommy didn't show up to their visit, why they can't go home and live with their mommy now. There are so many others as well, stepping up to the plate for children in desperate need of love and stability; aunts, uncles, grandparents, stepparents... Pour your blessings on each of them, God. Give them the strength they need to get through that last tantrum or unappreciated meal or battle of the day. Give them the peace and joy that can only come from You. Find a way to whisper into their souls that they are right where they are supposed to be, loving exactly who needs their love at this exact moment. In Jesus's name, Amen*

# Chapter 9

## The Visit

(31 A.D.)

It was but a few hours later when Lazarus popped his head in through the kitchen window. "Jesus is here!"

Mary ran out into the street to see many people already gathered around him, talking as they walked together toward their house. She was surprised. She didn't think that many people in Bethany welcomed his teaching. Perhaps they had heard what Lazarus and Chanoch had said and discussed it with their families over the Sabbath. Did they have a change of heart? But as they neared, she realized most of them weren't from Bethany at all. They must have followed Jesus from the last village. Oh, my! Were they all coming to her house? Martha would surely faint when she saw.

After tidying up the flowers on the table, Martha hurried out to Mary's side. She took in the scene for a moment and whispered to her sister, "Are they all with him?"

"It seems so," Mary hesitantly replied, and she felt Martha grab her hand.

Lazarus had already joined Jesus, and they were exchanging light-hearted pleasantries as they approached. As Mary and Martha walked up, Jesus smiled and held his arms open wide to receive them in a hug. Mary couldn't help but think of how much it felt like the warm embraces they had once gotten from their father.

As the eldest of the household, Martha stepped back and formally invited him to stay with them. "Jesus, it is so nice to see you again! Please, come stay with us in our home as long as you wish."

"Thank you, Martha! I'm glad the messenger I sent ahead of me got word to you in time. I hope he also let you know I would be bringing guests?"

He hadn't. Martha felt a wave of panic. Were they really all staying?

Jesus could read her face. "I see that part did not get relayed properly. No need to worry, Martha. We don't require much."

Mary could see her sister looking over the shoulder of Jesus to count how many she didn't plan for. She didn't want Jesus to feel as if he were inconveniencing them, so she extended her hand toward their house and said, "Make yourselves at home! All are welcome."

With that, the friendly chatter continued as Mary, Martha, and Lazarus watched everyone pile into their family home. Yes, it was bigger than most others in their village, but it was not nearly large enough to fit them all comfortably. Luckily, most were accustomed to taking a seat along the walls, both inside the house and outside the window. Martha was so glad she had given the floor some extra attention!

Jesus made introductions all around and warned his disciples that his 'little brother' Lazarus might challenge them to a footrace before they left. It was true. That's the first thing young Lazarus would say when they were children, because Jesus would never turn him down. Everyone had a good laugh, and Mary soaked in the way Jesus and Lazarus seemed to pick up right where they left off. Conversation came so easily between them, and she knew Jesus always had a special fondness for her brother. Adinah helped the girls make sure their guests had a drink of water. It was a good thing she had gone along with Mary to the well to draw extra jugs! She felt honored to have helped serve Jesus, even in such a small way. Now they could save the wine for dinner.

The room grew silent for such a large number of people, because they didn't want to miss a word that was said. Lazarus noticed that Yokim was among those standing at the window, listening intently, but probably not wanting to be seen by Lazarus. He wasn't sure if that was to be taken as a good sign or not. Was he there to listen and learn, like the rest of them? Or was he going to confront Jesus the way he had confronted him and Chanoch? Lazarus hoped Yokim's intentions were not to challenge their guest. But even if he did, he knew Jesus would handle it with grace, mercy, and wisdom from above.

Aharon and Kozel were just inside the doorway. They wanted him to tell the stories they had heard about healing a blind man, a leper, a sick woman, and a paralytic. One after another, the people of Bethany would ask questions and tell of the stories they had heard. Jesus verified that all they heard was true. However, he did not retell the stories simply for their amusement. That would bring attention to himself. He always pointed back to his Heavenly Father, and how every miracle he performed was in God's name and for His glory. He only wanted people to see and believe. Then Jesus turned the conversation away from things he did and turned his attention back to those in the room. He spoke about loving God, loving others, and believing in their hearts that what he told them was true. If they did these things, they could inherit eternal life.

The crowd was clinging to every word he spoke, and the room was filled with pleasant camaraderie. That is, until Yokim's voice came from the window. "Teacher, you have spoken nothing of the law, so I am confused by what you are telling us. Tell us again. What exactly must we do to inherit eternal life?" Those in the room probably thought he was taking the role of a student, trying to learn from a superior scholar. But after their conversations a few days ago, Lazarus was afraid he was trying to frame Jesus with his words.

Jesus said to him, "What is written in the law, Yokim? How do you interpret it?"

Yokim answered assuredly. "You shall love the Lord, your God, with all your heart, all your being, all your strength, and all your mind. And you shall love your neighbor as yourself."

Jesus looked directly at him as he replied, "You have answered correctly. Do this and you will live."

Yokim wasn't sure what to think. He wasn't expecting Jesus to agree with him. And how did he know his name? Had the messenger he sent before Sabbath gone back to tell Jesus what they had discussed? For some reason, he felt the need to justify himself. He spoke again. "And who exactly is my neighbor, Jesus?" he asked.

Jesus replied with a parable, but this time he addressed the answer to all who were gathered. "A man was going down from Jericho, and he fell among robbers. The men stripped him and beat him and then departed, leaving him half dead. By chance, a priest was going down that same road. When he saw the man who had been beaten, he passed by on the other side. Shortly after him came a Levite. When he came to the place where the beaten man lay, he also passed by on the other side. But a Samaritan, their sworn enemy, came along behind them. As he came to where the man was, he went over to him and was full of compassion. He went to him and bound up his wounds, pouring on oil and wine. Then he set him on his own animal and brought him to an inn and took care of him. The next day he took out two denarii and gave them to the innkeeper. He asked the innkeeper to spend whatever was needed to take care of him. He promised to repay him when he came back, and he did."

Jesus turned once again to look at Yokim. "Which of

these three, do you think, proved to be a neighbor to the man who fell among the robbers?"

Yokim replied, "The Samaritan, who showed him mercy."

Jesus said to him, "You go, and do likewise."

Although Yokim agreed with his teaching, he felt insulted. He didn't appreciate being told to go and show mercy, as if he wasn't a merciful person already. The tension could be felt in the room.

Martha hoped some people from the village, especially Yokim, would go on their way. She wanted Jesus all to themselves like they had when their parents would visit, yet she had a feeling those days had passed. His following was much too big to allow that to happen. She wanted to be a good hostess, yet she had no idea how to accommodate this many people. She had to prepare something for them to eat. As the day was growing short, she didn't have enough supplies to give Jesus the special meal she had planned. As the minutes passed, she grew more frustrated because all she had in a large enough quantity to feed them all was gruel. Of course! That was the only thing she could remember Jesus saying he grew tired of as a child, and gruel was the one thing she was trying to avoid!

Her words broke the tightness of Yokim's reaction. "Jesus, you and your friends must be hungry! I will prepare you something to eat."

He replied with a smile. "Ah, what a kind gesture, Martha. Thank you!" With that, he went on answering questions about how to pray.

Martha looked over at Mary, who was still sitting at Jesus' feet, in the spot she had always taken as a child. She motioned to her sister to get up and help. Mary shook her head 'no' and pointed to Jesus, then turned her attention back to him, completely ignoring Martha's plea.

Ugh! Martha was astounded at her sister's

inconsideration, especially knowing the task ahead of them! Her temper got the better of her, and she walked over to where Mary was sitting. "Jesus, don't you care that my sister has left me to do the work by myself? Tell her to help me!"

For a moment, Mary's eyes grew wide with anger. How could her sister call her out like that, in front of everyone? She would be so embarrassed if she were reprimanded by their most special guest. Instead, Jesus came to her defense.

He looked at her sister tenderly. "Martha, Martha. You are worried and upset about many things, but you should only be worried about one. Mary has chosen what is better, and it will not be taken away from her."

Mary was surprised that her emotions immediately softened towards her sister, as she knew her fear of being reprimanded in front of the crowd had just become Martha's reality. Instead of resenting her for her actions, she patted the floor next to where she was sitting and asked her sister to join her.

Although it wasn't the response she was looking for, Martha felt a weight taken off her shoulders and accepted the empty spot on the floor. Mary grabbed her hand. As Jesus began to teach, Martha leaned over to whisper in Mary's ear. "You have chosen better. But when he is finished, you will still help me make gruel and fresh bread."

Mary smiled as Martha's gaze fell upon the face of Jesus.

# Chapter 10

## Trista's Journal Entry
## Room 10

July 25, 2011

"Is he going to live? I know you keep saying we have to wait and see, but we have four children counting on their dad coming home. What should I be telling them at this point?"

Dr. Grave (which is not his real name—we just nicknamed him that because he almost always delivers the bad news) surely knew what my question would be before he asked if I had any questions. What else am I going to ask him? What else matters?! It is the same question I ask each morning from my new permanent spot by Andy's hospital bed. Usually, at about 7:30 A.M., there is a knock on the door, and the many doctors, doctors in training, and nurses quietly come in and form a semi-circle in the room. The head doctor for the day stands in the middle near the nurse pushing a cart with a laptop on it, which they look at from time to time when sharing specific numbers with me. This was just part of our new daily routine. Andy's medical team rounded and gave me the morning update in Room 10 of the S.I.C.U. (Surgery Intensive Care Unit). This was the eleventh day of the coma. On most days, the answer went something like "I can't answer that yet" or "We have to give the medicines time to work." But today, the answer was different.

"I would prepare your older child that her dad may not make it through this and have her come say her goodbyes. I'm not sure what to advise about telling the younger ones," the doctor answered. My guess is there were around twelve medical professionals circled behind him as he delivered the news, as this is a teaching hospital. It was like a sea of doctors in blue, turquoise, and green scrubs. They all seemed to blur together, and it was so quiet you could hear a pin drop. All I could think about was how I have to start researching how to tell your children, ages 3, 4, 5, and 12 that their dad is dying. How in the heck do you tell a child this news?

This can't be real. The team is losing hope. How did my life change so drastically in such a short amount of time?! Life was somewhat predictable just two weeks ago. At least as predictable as it gets around here. Our three littles are now ages 3, 4, and 5. I am a stay-at-home mom who rarely stays at home. On a typical summer day, we get in the golf cart and ride up to the beach, where I give the kids daily swimming lessons in our community's lake. We then walk across the street to the bait shop to say "hi" to Missy and pick out some treats. Booker's favorite is a Cow Tail. Amelia usually picks a Drumstick ice cream cone, which always starts melting before she gets to the end, and Bella gets Skittles every single time. When we aren't at the lake, you can usually find us playing "duck, duck, moose" in the yard or on a day trip to the zoo with the help of my new triple-stroller. Lilly is with us on Wednesdays and every other weekend, and we love to go cheer her on at her ice hockey games. Andy still works night shifts at the hospital, so he joins us on our outings when he doesn't have to sleep.

Exactly two weeks ago, we went to church as usual. We headed home for some freshly picked raspberries and playtime before napping. Out of nowhere, Andy developed a fever and decided to go to Urgent Care. They said it may be an ear infection and prescribed some antibiotics for him. A couple of days later, he started having trouble sleeping because of some back pain. This time, he went to the emergency room to see what was going on. It was a Thursday evening when he decided the pain was too much. I was trying to get the littles settled for dinner at that time, and this is no simple task, so we just had him slip out of the house without saying goodbye. And now the doctor is telling me he may not make it. I didn't allow the children to give kisses and say bye-bye to their daddy that night. That may have been the last time they could ever do that. I cannot even deal with this possibility right now. Although there was no way I could have known, the guilt and shame will eat me alive.

They admitted him that night into the S.I.C.U. for a possible gallbladder removal the next day. Friday morning came, and we found that he may be sicker than we realized. Plans were changing. He had a high fever at that point, so they didn't think he could handle surgery. Instead, they began preparing for a smaller procedure that would be less dangerous. Thankfully, I had arranged for someone to come over and watch the kids so that I could be there with him. This was the last time I saw him conscious. When they wheeled him back into the room, he was intubated and sedated. I guess it is called a medically induced coma. Wires and tubes were everywhere. My husband is in a coma. Does this really even happen? I seriously thought this only happened in the movies, like in "While You Were Sleeping," but not to real people like us.

While he was having the procedure, I was texting my sister Abigail. She is the family nurse we all go to for advice about medical problems. I could hear doctors outside the room, talking in hushed and concerned voices. There seemed to be a lot of them. I could not make out most of the words they were saying, but I thought I heard the c-word that everyone dreads. When I texted that to Abigail, she left her work and came to the hospital to be with me. She knew what we would be facing if it was, indeed, cancer.

His fever would not subside, and the team of doctors was trying to figure out what was making him so sick. Their best guess (and yes, they admitted it was a guess!) was still the gallbladder, but it was not safe to take it out when he had a fever. I watched as the doctors tested and rounded and consulted and waited. I put cold, wet rags on his forehead and prayed for his fever to go down. The chaplain brought me a Bible to read, and my mom brought my computer so that I could get on Facebook and ask for prayers. Someone got me some tape so I could display pictures of our family, and I showed each of the doctors on his team the four children who were counting on him to make it out of this. At the advice of the nurses in our family, I am allowing no residents to perform procedures on him, only attendings. Basically, I am THAT wife.

I have decided I am staying by his side, only leaving to use the restroom or get food, or when the nurses kick me out for his daily 5:30 A.M. x-ray. Thank the Lord, my family and friends are working together to make this possible! Clouds almost always have silver linings if you look close enough, and the support system I have to take care of my children so that I can take care of Andy is definitely one of them! They are literally stopping their lives, canceling their vacations, and even taking off days at work so that I can be here to hold Andy's hand.

After a couple more days of high fever, Dr. Grave came in to deliver more bad news, hence his nickname. He explained that Andy was getting sicker, and they wanted to remove the gallbladder, even with the fever. I would need to give consent for them to do an emergency surgery, which has a 30% mortality rate. It sounded scary until I realized that they thought he would die for sure if they did nothing. It seemed so surreal. We just thought he had an ear infection not too long ago! Yet, here we were. Eleven days into this coma and he still had a fever of 105 degrees, and the doctors had only a guess about what was making him sick. They told me it was time. I signed the papers.

After I signed the consent, they kind of went into what I refer to as 'Grey's Anatomy panic mode' to get him ready for surgery. It seemed like people in scrubs appeared out of nowhere in a rush to get his many machines packed up, unhooking wires and tubes and all his different medicines so he could be wheeled away to the dangerous surgery, which may or may not help his condition.

As all this was going on around me, I was standing at the side of his bed, thinking this may be the last time I saw him alive. We like to think he can hear us talking to him, but really, we have no idea. I could just reach his ear if I stood on my toes, so I whispered to him how much I love him. Hopefully, he heard me tell him that he is strong and that I know he will get through this surgery. I continued whispering into his ear that this will all be a distant memory when we get our cabin at the lake with a dock, which is one of our dreams for our family. We will be laughing in the sun as we swim and jump off the dock with the kids all day. Then, after we put the kids to bed, we will sneak back down there and enjoy the moonlight on the lake, talking about all the fun memories we are making as a family. And they wheeled him away.

By this time, more of our family members had arrived, and they gave us "the room" to wait in. It was this night that I led my first group prayer. I had asked for the chaplain to come up to lead it, but he wasn't able to be there that minute, and the time was now! If this wasn't out of my comfort zone, I don't know what was! Never did I even imagine I would lead a group prayer, in front of actual people, many people, some of whom are not church-goers or even Christians. This was for the wiser Christians who knew what they were doing, who knew more about the Bible than I did, like my Bible study buddies. But I did it. I asked everybody to hold hands in a circle and prayed for God to help Andy live through the surgery and to give the doctors wisdom to find out what was wrong. And our prayer was answered!

We were all so relieved and hopeful for what seemed like a minute and a half. We quickly realized that the guess the doctors had made about what was making him sick was not the right one. He made it through the emergency surgery, and the gallbladder was out, but things are not improving. The fact is that Andy's body is dying. The updates are just as hopeless now as they were before surgery. They guessed wrong. All of his organs are failing. The reports are consistently along the lines of "He is sicker now than he was three hours ago, and we don't know why." It seems like I am living out an episode of E.R., with teams of doctors coming in regularly to update, getting consent for this or that, and sending in a variety of specialists. I have met with the kidney guy, the liver guys, and the infectious disease guys. Andy is on dialysis, has a machine breathing for him, a feeding tube, and is hooked up to eight different I.V. medicines at this point. There is now only one part of his face that I can get to if I stand on my tippy toes that isn't covered by a tube, and that is where I kiss him. I am so grateful to have that two-inch by two-inch square to kiss him and touch him. How quickly and drastically one's perspective can change.

This morning is when I had the conversation with Dr. Grave about preparing the kids that Andy may not make it. I just got off the phone with Silly Lilly. She is coming tomorrow to see her dad, knowing it may be for the last time. She may be fatherless soon. I may be a widow soon. And what am I going to tell the littles? They have already lost one set of parents when they were placed in the foster care system. Bella has already lost two sets of parents, as she had foster parents before us who could not continue because of their medical issues. Please, God… tell me you wouldn't take a third father away from this sweet child in less than five years!

This thought alone haunts me continuously throughout my days. She cannot go through more loss. Her daddy has to live. For so many reasons, but especially this one.

*Dear Father in Heaven, I know that You give and You take away. I understand this. I also understand that we are to expect problems in this life because it is not heaven. Why should a sinner like me expect my life to be problem-free when Jesus, who was perfect, faced horrible trials? But I am not coming to you on my behalf tonight, Lord! I come to You on behalf of the four innocent children who need their daddy. Lord God, you know the importance of a father's love and guidance. These children love and depend on Andy. They've been through so much loss already! Please let them keep their daddy. I am coming to You on their behalf, asking for a miracle. We have all heard what the doctors have to say. They gave us their report today. That pales in comparison to what You say. What DO You say, Father? You are the Healer of healers, Lord. Send us some help. Please save their daddy. In Jesus' name, Amen.*

# Chapter 11

## The Journey

31 A.D.

Much too soon, it was time for Jesus to depart from Bethany. His visits were never long enough, yet they knew he had important work to do in other regions. The siblings were helping him gather his things to leave, but not before Lazarus challenged him to a foot race. Martha bulked when her brother suggested that he take part in something so childish, but Jesus was happy to have a physical challenge instead of an intellectual one. Besides, they had to keep up their goofy tradition.

Joy and laughter were palpable as Jesus and Lazarus took their starting positions in their usual spot on the street outside their home. Everyone lined up on both sides to watch. Jesus sent two of his disciples to stand a distance away and instructed them to stand with their hands out to their sides. He and Lazarus were to circle around them, then race back to the finish line that he had marked in the dirt with his heel.

The two stood ready, waiting for Mary to bang a spoon against a pot, which was their signal to start. The crowd grew silent while they waited for the sound to start the race.

*Bang!* They bolted off as the bystanders cheered them on. Oh, what fun!

Always before, Lazarus had come out the winner,

but this time, Jesus beat him by several lengths. Of course, Lazarus blamed it on his injured foot, but he knew that even his best effort would not have beaten Jesus this time. Perhaps Jesus really had let him win when he was younger, after all?

As the laughter faded, they knew it was time for Jesus to go, although nobody wanted to see him leave. Well, almost nobody. If they asked Yokim, he would probably see it differently, but no one was asking him. Mary selfishly wanted Jesus to stay there forever, teaching and telling stories how only he could. She had been lucky enough to have parents who would teach the word of God to their son and daughters alike, but she knew others weren't so lucky. Many women had never been formally taught and were hearing much of it now for the first time. Even the elders in their town admitted that hearing Jesus teach was like learning it anew.

Mary, Martha, and Lazarus knew what a blessing it was to have such a close connection with Jesus and were honored to be able to host him and his friends. They got to see firsthand how hearts, minds, and souls were changed. Although Jesus had not come straight out and said he was the Son of God, he didn't deny it when asked directly by Yokim, even at the chance of being accused of blasphemy. So, it was true! Lazarus took cautious delight in this. It was a relief to know that the Messiah they had been waiting for was in their midst, and he was privileged enough to spend time with him and call him a friend. Yet, he knew Yokim was trying to frame Jesus. For what extent or purpose, he was still unsure.

Surely, Jesus was here to fulfill all the prophecies their parents had taught them. If only they were still alive to behold such things unfolding, right there in their home! Their *abba* always expected as much and said Jesus would change the world as they knew it. Mary didn't know about the rest of the world, but one thing was sure; the people of Bethany would never be the same.

# *But*, Even Now

****

It was the day after the Sabbath of the following week, and Mary and Martha were helping Levik, Adinah, and Lazarus pack what they thought they might need for their journey. They were about to embark on a trip to the forest they were told about somewhere on the outside of the walls of Jerusalem, where newborn babies were thrown as sacrifices to pagan gods. How does one pack for a trip like that?

They had debated whether Adinah would accompany them or stay back. Levik preferred her to stay home, only because he didn't want to put her in any danger, but she insisted on going along. No offense, but what did the men know of caring for an infant? If they were lucky enough to get to one before death found it, what would they do with a sick or crying baby all the way back to Bethany? Besides, if this was the path God was preparing for her to become a new mother, she wanted to be among the first to lay eyes on her baby.

Mary's heart was heavy. Where exactly was this journey taking the people she loved most in this world? What danger could they encounter? What gruesome sights might meet their eyes but never leave their minds? How long before she would see them again? Would they even be successful, or would they come back with hearts more broken than they were now? Time would tell.

As she and Martha stood side by side watching them walk away, she felt her sister's arm come around her waist. Martha squeezed a little tighter as she prayed out loud for the safety of their brother and their friends. The sisters had a newfound faith, and Mary felt a strange sense of peace come over her as she joined Martha in prayer. Even though the odds were against them, she just knew in her heart that Lazarus would accompany their friends back safely.

Although the journey wasn't long compared to most, it took two full days for them to locate the woods in question.

Too afraid to inquire anyone about it, they followed the directions the widow had given Adinah. As close as they could guess, the location had to be near. The first day, they walked to the general vicinity and hid among the trees to observe the comings and goings of passersby. Most were just travelers like themselves, but they hoped to be close enough to overhear a conversation that could be helpful.

They slept near a small stream, under the cover of the trees. Lazarus was awakened by a loud raucous. When he first opened his eyes to the branches hanging over his head, he was sure it was a dream. It took hearing Levik's gruff voice asking, "What is that?" before he remembered where they were. The three sat up and looked around, scanning the horizon for the source of the sound and any danger that may await them. Levik stood and peered around a tree, only to discover vultures in the distance, carrying on and fighting over food. "Stupid things!" he said, spraying a bit of spittle as he spoke. He was tired and had been sleeping surprisingly well. It was incredibly annoying to be awoken so early, in such an abrasive manner.

Speaking of food, his grumbling tummy reprimanded him for not having eaten since early the day before. Knowing they would be more conspicuous if they brought a donkey, they had left it behind, and each of them carried only the things they thought were completely necessary. They were trying to stretch out their meals in order to make their supplies last. There was no telling what to expect or how long this journey might last. Lazarus walked over to the stream, cleaned his teeth and freshened up, then he joined the other two on the ground to pray over the unleavened bread that was to be their breakfast.

They saw nothing out of the ordinary in the spot they had chosen the first night. The three wondered if they were in the wrong place altogether, or if they were exactly where they needed to be. Perhaps this morbid process didn't happen as often as they thought it might. After much debate, they decided to move in a little further. They opted to walk the traveler's path in order to blend in and then veer back off to hide in the woods when they were close enough to detect what the Roman soldiers were saying. Maybe that would at least give them some clue as to how this was to play out. They knew they were taking a tremendous risk, but hopefully they would be able to hear the conversations of the Romans without being detected themselves.

The path took them in the direction of the vultures. They could see the ugly birds still greedily chasing one another away from the feast they had discovered. The closer they got, the more they could smell the carcass the birds were fighting over. Lazarus' curiosity got the better of him. He covered his nose and mouth with his sleeve to mask the atrocious smell as he snuck up behind the pugnacious birds. It wasn't often they saw a flock like that, and he wanted to see what all the commotion was about. The vultures scattered as he made his way closer, and he was horrified to see what lay before him. There in the dirt lay the bones of tiny human remains. He immediately bent at the waist as the bread he had just shared with his friends came lurching back up. The putrid smell would not leave his nostrils, and although the contents of his stomach had been emptied, he continued to heave.

Levik started to come toward him to see if he could help, but Lazarus held up his hand to signal his friend to stop. It was too late. Levik was close enough to make out a human skull. It had been crushed. This child must have been deemed deformed in some way and killed immediately after birth before it was carelessly tossed out like garbage. He did not walk any closer but prayed out loud for the soul of this unnamed and precious child.

Adinah couldn't make out what it was but heard her husband's words and understood what Lazarus must have seen. They had come too late to save this one, and she cried for the infant whose life was snuffed out before it began. If they had only left a few days sooner! She was appalled to find that what she had heard from the widow at the infirmary was true, but at the same time, she was relieved to know they were finally in the right place. She prayed in silence. Levik and Lazarus covered the remains of the infant with dirt, sticks, rocks, and leaves as best they could after they had to chase off stray dogs that tried to carry it away. The thin layer of debris over the remains was as close as they could get to a burial without being deemed unclean.

The three slept under the cover of the woods for several more days, with nothing to report. It made them wonder if they actually were close to where this hideous act took place, or if animals had carried the infant to that spot from somewhere else. *Shabbat* was once again upon them, and they decided to go into Jerusalem for food and lodging. They needed to replenish their supplies and honor God properly for the Sabbath. When the day of rest was over, they would again return to keep watch from their hiding place in the trees.

Two more nights passed, and Adinah wondered if they had made a mistake. Her heart balanced on the precipice between exhilaration and pain. With every passing day, it seemed her hope of becoming someone's *aima* was slipping further and further from her grasp. She and Levik had long since acknowledged the fact that their own bloodline would end with them, which was difficult to accept in their culture. Her emotions were all over the place as she sat in silence, waiting day after day with great anticipation, only to be let down again. One moment she would feel great determination because their mission was not only going to complete their family, but it would also save the life of an innocent child. Then, the next moment, she would feel utterly hopeless. She always prayed through times like this, but in this situation, she wasn't even sure how to pray. To ask God to give her a child in this manner would mean it had been abandoned, sick, or abused by its parents. How could she possibly utter those words? She felt selfish for even entertaining the thought. She gave it much consideration and finally decided that she would not ask for a child to be brought out, but if it did, she promised God to love him or her like her own. Not a day would go by without teaching them to honor Him in all ways. If given the chance, she knew she and Levik could give a child a home full of love and security.

Those thoughts were scrambling around in her mind like a prayer not yet formed when they heard a stick snap not far off. The reflexes of all three made them startle to attention. Was it just an animal, or was someone else in the woods? Her heart was racing. Had someone seen them and suspected their motives? Had they sent a Roman to arrest them?

The three lay flat on their stomachs behind a fallen tree, afraid to peek their heads up to see who or what was in their company. Adinah's heart was beating so rapidly that the rush of blood pounded in her ears. Her breathing was quick, but she was trying to keep it shallow so they would not be discovered.

At last, from the shadows, they saw the source of the footsteps. It was indeed a Roman, but to their relief, it was not a soldier. Not far from where they were hiding, a young girl slowed her walk until she came to a stop. Adinah guessed her age to be around 14. She appeared to come from a family of wealth. The girl was wrapped in a white *palus*, a robe made of very fine linen, and it was fastened over one shoulder with a golden hummingbird. One didn't see such fine clothing in Bethany. She had a crown of flowers around her head, and her long hair flowed down her back. She was beautiful.

In her arms was a baby, wrapped in a beautiful silk blanket, but it wasn't crying like they all expected to see. The infant appeared to have been taken care of. The girl had tears streaming down her face as she gently kissed her baby on the head and laid it on the ground. She caressed the baby's hair as she removed the swaddle until bare skin was exposed. She softly sang a lullaby, and they could see the baby's arms and legs reaching up to what they assumed was its mother. As she stood, she began to weep. The girl gasped through her hands as she covered her mouth, likely in disbelief at what she was about to do. Her shoulders raised and lowered in rhythm with silent sobs. Then, just as quickly as she had appeared, she turned and ran in the direction in which she came. It seemed she was trying to put as much space between herself and her baby as possible before she changed her mind.

Adinah didn't understand! This was no pagan offering. This girl obviously loved her child. If her dress was any indication, it seemed their family could afford another mouth to feed. Adinah's mind was whirring with different scenarios that could possibly lead the girl to abandon her baby like that. Was it pressure from Roman culture? The Jewish culture pressured women to have a baby. Did the Romans pressure them not to? Or perhaps the girl was a young bride and abandoned by the baby's father? Did her affluent family lose their money? It was rumored that depending on the circumstances of what caused that to happen, the family was often forced into suicide. Adinah had heard of that horrid Roman custom. Could the life of that beautiful young mother also be in jeopardy? The answers would forever be out of her reach. Adinah felt sorry for her. Even from such a brief encounter, something about the young woman made Adinah feel a strange kinship with her. Under different circumstances, it's possible they would even be friends.

Adinah's thoughts shifted from mother to baby when they heard it begin to cry. She wanted to run to it, but Levik's hand on her back told her to stay still. There were more voices. Men this time. As the voices got louder, they could see that it was two Roman soldiers. They walked toward the infant that was just left by the girl, and Adinah gasped and hid her eyes, certain one of them would put a sword through the baby's heart. The widow had told them that happens if the soldiers didn't want to hear it, and so far, she had been right about everything else. They didn't draw their swords, but instead, one handed a bag to the other and he tossed it onto the ground next to the crying baby. Without concern, they turned and walked away.

Their actions were so nonchalant. How could they behave as if this was normal? Had they no souls?

The three waited for what seemed like an eternity. The baby was now wailing so loudly that its cries were broken and quivering and sounded more like a baby lamb. Adinah could stand it no longer. She started to get up, looking around, but the tears in her eyes were so heavy that she couldn't see through them. Levik and Lazarus stood but did not speak. They signaled for Adinah to remain quiet as they carefully scoped the area to make sure they were alone. Not seeing anyone, the three carefully snuck toward the infant.

Lazarus got there first, but stood and looked toward Adinah, not sure what to do. When Adinah reached his side, she dropped to her knees and scooped the babe up to her chest. She quickly wrapped it in her *tunic*, both to comfort and quiet it. The poor thing was shaking from both fear and cold. She was so intoxicated with the thrill of finally holding a child that could be her own, she instinctively wanted to run away to shelter this tiny little treasure. Funny how she had just laid eyes on it but already knew she would protect it with her own life if it came to that. Turning to escape back to the spot they had been camping, as was the plan, Levik grabbed her arm and pointed to the bundle that still lay on the ground. She was so caught up in the moment that she almost forgot. Giving her husband a nod, he carefully picked it up. It felt empty. Why would they have made a trip to that spot to discard an empty bag? Did it have something to do with the baby? As Levik held the bag open, Lazarus gently slid aside a dirty blanket that had been stuffed inside. He peered in with both caution and curiosity. It could be anything. Squinting through the layers, he was astonished to discover a baby so tiny that it almost didn't even look real.

In whispered excitement, he said, "Levik, it's another baby! I've never seen anything so tiny."

Levik peered in, and his face fell. "I'm afraid this one didn't make it. It must have come too early."

Lazarus spoke to his friends but couldn't take his eyes off of the lifeless newborn. "What shall we do with it? We can't leave it here."

"I supposed we can cover it with rocks like we did for the other. At least it will keep the animals away," offered Levik. He looked around to make sure they were not being watched, then he nodded toward their hideout. "Let's go."

They turned to leave, but Adinah turned back. "Wait! Lazarus, please grab the swaddling blankets from the ground. That's the only thing this child will have as a remembrance of the mother who loved it first. I will use it to wrap the baby in salt to guard against any illnesses. It's not much, but surely it will help a little." Lazarus did so, then led the way back to where their few belongings were lying. They would bury the little one and make their way back to Bethany before anyone discovered what had been done. They didn't know how close the Romans kept guard over something like this. If it wasn't a sacrificial offering, would they even care? Or, if they did care and realized the baby was no longer crying, would they assume an animal found it quickly? Or would they become suspicious of thieves and come looking for all of them? Had this happened before, or were they the first to do this?

Adinah had finally gotten the baby to settle down. Warm once again, it had cried itself into exhaustion and slept in her arms. She couldn't take her eyes off the sweet face in front of her. It seemed ironic that something so innocent could be surrounded by a world so malicious. She wondered if the baby knew what had just happened. For the child's sake, she hoped not.

The men laid the bag that held the other infant under the biggest tree they could find. It looked like a proper place to be buried. Though it was nearly dark, Lazarus could tell there were flowers sprinkled about. They went looking for rocks and met back under the sprawling branches, where they prayed over the child. Lazarus bent down to fold the blanket over the little one and jumped back.

"What is it?" asked Levik, a bit alarmed.

"The blanket moved! I think." He bent down to move the blanket back and stared at the little one, watching for signs of life. He thought he saw the tiny chest rising and falling, barely. "Yes, it…the baby is alive!" exclaimed Lazarus, unable to believe his eyes.

Adinah looked up, in complete shock. "Are you sure, Lazarus?"

He leaned over again to make sure his eyes weren't deceiving him in the shadows that were growing darker by the minute. He could see the baby taking shallow breaths. "Yes! It's breathing!"

"Bring the baby over here, Levik," said Adinah softly. She was trying not to wake the babe in her arms, but she knew they had to move with haste. "Dip your little finger into the goat's milk and see if the baby will suckle it off of the end of your finger. I'm sure it has been given no nourishment."

Levik did as Adinah instructed, and sure enough, the baby's lips slowly moved enough to allow the milk to dribble in. He was ecstatic. "It's taking it! Adinah, look! It's taking it!"

The three celebrated with quiet laughter through tears, as they watched the tiny infant seem to come back to life. Levik looked up, and his eyes met his wife's. This moment was so surreal. They were both standing with an infant in their arms. He was so moved with emotion that he could barely speak, and the tears that were filling his eyes were those of joy. "Adinah, can..." He had to pause and collect himself before he could continue. "Can you believe this? We came in hopes of maybe rescuing one infant. Did you ever think we would be going home with two?"

"No!" she cried through her laughter. "Not at all. But I knew God would make a way. If His will is for us to have two children, let it be so!"

They watched the tiny baby take in the milk, one drop at a time, until it fell asleep. Lazarus wished Mary and Martha could be here to see the tenderness that would forever be a part of their friend's family history. It dawned on him that either he or Levik would have to care for an infant all the way back to Bethany. Being the youngest of their family, he had always been coddled. His heart was in the right place, but he did not know how to take care of something so small. If he was being honest, he was fearful that the smallest one might not even make it back, but he wouldn't dare voice that out loud.

He hated to interrupt such a gentle moment, but knew they needed to get moving. In any other circumstance, they would never travel at night, but they knew they would have to take the chance this time. They were uncertain what the penalty would be for taking a deserted Roman baby, but they could guess. If this child was meant to be an offering to some pagan god, they were sure it was an unpardonable offense. Nobody takes from a Roman. If they were found and arrested, these babies would be killed on the spot. They had to get them back to Bethany and possibly even get care for the smallest one at the infirmary. Adinah and Levik each held a babe in their arms, and Lazarus gathered up their belongings. They walked in silence. Even after they were out of earshot of those who might be keeping watch over the discarded babies, they remembered the parable Jesus told about the man being robbed on the road near Jericho. They had to keep watch and alert to robbers and thieves.

After a couple hours of walking, the baby Adinah held woke and began to cry. She supposed it must be hungry as well. They stopped alongside the road and Lazarus found more goat's milk as she got out the shredded rags she had brought along to change the ones it had soiled. She laughed aloud.

"What's so funny?" asked Levik, happy to see his wife so happy.

"It's a girl!" she said. The friends all chuckled and celebrated the news. They had been in such a hurry that they hadn't even thought to look!

"Levik, what about the other one? Girl or boy?" she asked. He shrugged his shoulders and gently moved back the blanket covering the precious gift that lay in his arms. Levik's face beamed. "It's a boy!"

# Chapter 12

## Trista's Journal Entry
## Four Times

July 28, 2011

"It's going to be okay. It's going to be alright."

I still can't believe He talked to me. Out of all the people in all the world and all the many problems others are going through, He took time to speak to me! I feel so special. I am so unworthy, yet so grateful. As He said it a second time, a third time, and then a fourth, I realized it was Him. God was giving me a message.

"It's going to be okay. It's going to be alright… It's going to be okay. It's going to be alright… It's going to be okay. It's going to be alright," He repeated.

The first time He said it, I looked around, thinking my favorite male nurse, Eric, had come in the door without me realizing it. But, to my surprise, no one had come into the room. Not one single person was in that room besides me. I even got up to check the adjoining bathroom, just to be sure. The voice was so loud and clear, as if someone right next to me was speaking. As the calm male voice repeated Himself, I began to realize what was happening. By the fourth time, I could actually feel the weight of the heavy burden I was carrying lighten a little. It was the middle of the night, so dark and calm and quiet. The only sound was that of the steady beeping from Andy's dialysis machine, interrupted by the comforting words from my Heavenly Father. I am in awe!

Let me back up and explain this a little more. So, so much has happened in three days! Lilly came to see her dad. I picked her up so that she could reach the uncovered spot on his face, and she was able to kiss him. I held one of his hands, and she held the other, and we prayed for her daddy to get better. One by one, Andy's organs were failing. The team's tone when they came into the room seemed to get more and more grim. I began telling family and our closest friends that it was time to come say their goodbyes. The littles were not allowed in the S.I.C.U., but they came to visit me in the lobby, and we went to the hospital's chapel to pray together. To see their heads bowed and peanut butter and jelly covered hands clasped.... To hear their sweet voices pleading with their heavenly Father to help their earthly father live.... To witness two tears streaming down each of Booker's cheeks as we told God how much Andy meant to us all...it was almost too much for me to bear.

During all this chaos, one of Andy's old friends from high school, Lori, had read on Facebook how sick he was and was texting about if she could come up to help with anything. She is a doctor. Honestly, Abigail (my sister who had been by my side since I got worried) and I were kind of ignoring her because I was busy with the constant doctor updates, and she was busy arranging who was going to watch the littles and be with me at the hospital. Well, Lori ended up just showing up on Sunday morning, and I gave her permission to round with the doctors.

People were coming in all day to say goodbye, bringing food, cards, plants, and even wine. We officially took over the waiting room, and the consultations began. Lori and another of Andy's doctor friends were speaking and researching via phone. I told them that at the beginning of this, the doctor had questioned me about any traveling or anything out of the ordinary he should know about. I shared all about the trip our family took to a lake in Missouri three weeks prior and explained how we found tons of tiny ticks all over us when we got home. They were so tiny that they looked like little freckles. We had to use flashlights to find them on our bodies. In the middle of the night, we were all standing in the kitchen in our underwear with flashlights doing tick checks on each other. It was crazy, and I didn't realize ticks came this small. Dr. McSteamy kind of blew this information off, saying that common things are common, and showed no further interest in the story. (He was Andy's admitting doctor, whose nickname came from one of our favorite television shows. Why we chose it should be self-explanatory.) I told every doctor I spoke with about this tick story, thinking it may be important, but none of them seemed to agree.

The steamy doctor might have ignored it, but Andy's doctor friends focused on this piece of information and wanted to know what kind of tick it was. I remembered that Andy had saved one of them on a piece of tape and put it in a baggy because he was kind of concerned at the time. I also recalled that the next day we found a tick on his belly that we had missed the previous night, meaning it had been on him for 24 hours. My dad and youngest sister, Anna, were sent to my house to hunt for this little baggy so that we could identify the type of tick. The normal me would have been mortified about them going to the house and rooting through our many junk drawers, but the highly overwhelmed me just had to let it go.

A couple hours later, they returned with the tick and confirmed what the doctor friends were suspecting already, the lone star tick.... Dr. McDreamy (another doctor on the case who we nicknamed after our favorite television show for obvious reasons) was willing to join a meeting with the infectious disease guy, Lori, and myself. Lori convinced them during this conversation that the lone star tick could be the cause of ehrlichiosis and suggested the recommended treatment. Andy was put on this new treatment within thirty minutes and tested for the tick disease, although it takes weeks to get that result back.

I have reason for a little hope because of the added treatment, but we have no idea if this is the cause of his sickness or not. Andy has still gotten sicker and sicker throughout the day. Facebook friends are probably tired of hearing requests for prayers. As I sat by Andy's bed in my halfway reclined, vinyl, turquoise-blue chair in the wee hours of last night, I held his hand. I began to envision the future without my husband. What am I going to do? Do I have it in me to raise these children alone? I can't imagine. And without Andy's visitation schedule, I will lose Lilly. How am I going to do this? What will the finances be like? I will have to go back to work, but won't all my earnings just go to daycare? How am I going to be a good mom when I am suffering the loss of my love? ... And then God spoke to me.

His words changed my perspective immediately. There was no uncertainty for me about who that was or what He meant. The doctors' updates were a little different for me this morning. In fact, they were poles apart from my expected reaction to them. Yes, he still has a fever. Yadda yadda yadda. Yes, he reached his eppy limit—which I know is a bad, bad thing because I have watched a lot of Grey's Anatomy! Yes, he is very sick. Yadda yadda yadda. Yes, his organs are shot. Yadda yadda yadda. Yes, he needs a C.T. scan right away....

BUT GOD just told me that it's going to be OKAY.

It's going to be ALRIGHT.

Who am I going to believe?

He is on day 14 of his coma. There are no signs of turning around. Not one single medical professional, friend, or family member thinks he's leaving this room alive. Yadda yadda yadda. I choose to believe God today!

*Dear Heavenly Father, You are my rock, my refuge, my comforter! I can't believe it! You amaze me! During our last Bible Study, we learned that "but God" appears about 45 times in the Bible. Situations may look one way from down here, no matter how many perspectives you use, BUT GOD often makes a path that we could never even imagine. I believe in my heart You are about to bless my family with one of Your famous "but God" moments. I wholeheartedly believe it was the Holy Spirit who talked to me last night. I believe it is going to be okay. It is going to be alright, just like You said! I sit here weeping in awe of you! A roomful of physicians have agreed that Andy is dying, but You are the one and only Great Physician! I choose to believe You. Thank You for the comfort You have provided me in my hour of need. I will cherish those words You spoke to me forever. I thank You in advance for saving my husband's life, however You choose to do so. I thank You not only on my behalf, but on all four of his children's behalf. I love You, Lord. I have never felt closer to You. In Jesus' name, Amen.*

Now, time to go tell the family I think he's going to live because God talked to me.... I'm sure this will go over well! NOT! I know they're going to think I'm crazy or I hallucinated. I don't really care because I know the truth.

****

August 7, 2011

Well, I am sitting in Room 207 in a regular hospital room (not the I.C.U.), and Andy is sleeping next to me, just snoring and farting away. Not in a coma, just sleeping! And he is getting a little better every day! God realized that the doctors weren't going to figure it out in time, so He sent in reinforcements. It ended up that Andy's two doctor friends were right about the sickness coming from the tick and the recommended treatment! God already knew he was on the right treatment plan and going to get better before He comforted me that night. He knew it was going to turn out okay all along.

A couple of days later, Andy was showing signs of improvement, so the docs woke him up and pulled out his breathing tube. The question on all of our minds was would he be able to breathe on his own…. Yes!! He looked up at me and I could tell he was trying to figure it all out... who I was, where we were, why we were there…. He pointed to his severely chapped lips and made a scratchy sound in his throat, and I immediately knew he wanted some ice chips. I asked the nurse if we could get some and looked straight up to where I imagined heaven was. I raised my hands and said, "Thank You, Lord, for keeping Your promise!"

Before I turn the lights out and try to get some sleep in this awkward, bumpy, puke-green chair, I'm gonna try to write down some memories from this crazy time before I forget them....

I got in trouble with the lady at the desk for not wearing shoes in the lobby. By day three, it felt like I lived there, so I stopped taking my gym shoes off and on and just wore hospital socks. I didn't get caught for a week!

I will never forget the time my dad got frustrated with all the confusing medical updates and which organs were going into failure, and declared loudly, "Why don't they just pick a ******* organ!"

It had been a week since I saw the kids and I was so excited that my sister-in-law was bringing them to the hospital so that I could visit with them. I got busy with doctor updates and was not able to go to the gift shop for some goodies like I had planned. Five minutes before I was supposed to meet them, I pressed the down button on the elevator and within three seconds, some friends came out of the same elevator with a basketful of snacks and gifts for me and the kids. God even cares about the little things, and I was so grateful! The peanut butter snacks and teddy bears made our visit extra special!

The pastor of our church came to talk with me and pray for Andy. I gave him a big hug and thanked him before he left. I then realized I had major body odor and promptly asked one of the nurse aides if I could snag some hospital deodorant! Ugh!

Janie, one of my sisters-in-law, brought some wine to the hospital for me when she visited, thinking a glass may help me sleep at night. I had a glass while talking with my brother one evening in the waiting area and forgot to eat dinner that night. He left, and I went to use the restroom in the lobby before heading back to my chair. I will never know how long I was passed out on that toilet with my pants down, but when I woke up, the toilet paper was still folded neatly in my hand! Passing out on the toilet was definitely a first for me!

Since Andy works at that hospital and is beloved by all, many visitors came in to see him. Many of them came during the middle of the night because he worked the night shift. The reason I would know they stopped by is I often found money and get-well-notes right by my chair when I woke up. Knowing I can go to the cafeteria to eat without worrying about my bank card being declined is such a blessing right now!

On weekdays, the Starbucks downstairs is open. The lack of sleep and constant decision-making must be affecting my social skills because the barista knows all the details of Andy's coma and medicines and the doctor's plans for the coming days. I am THAT customer!

# Chapter 13

## The Gift

31 A. D.

Adinah and Levik knew their world was about to be turned completely upside down, but in a way that was unimaginably rewarding. They discussed what to name their children on the long walk home, and the decision came rather quickly. Their daughter would be called Drozah, *my dear little one*. It seemed fitting to Adinah, who couldn't get the picture out of her mind of the young mother stroking her dear child's face. Their son would be Hess, meaning *strengthened by the Lord*. They all knew little Hess would need all the strength the Lord could give him if he were to survive. Nobody dared say it out loud, but anyone who laid eyes on his tiny little body knew it would be a touch-and-go situation until he got some real nourishment and gained some weight.

As Levik held him in his arms, he marveled at how beautifully and wonderfully made Hess was. How much care the Creator put into forming every facet of his little body! Even the minuscule fingernails were amazing to contemplate. They were so small they could scarcely be seen! Yet God cared about even that minor detail. He wondered if their hours with Hess were limited. Were the few drops of goat's milk enough to keep him alive? Would the milk itself make him sick? He did not know, but that's all they had to give. Did he have any other medical issues they were unaware of? He prayed that the Lord would give their son the strength of a lion in order to withstand any obstacle he might come against. It was shocking that little Hess didn't suffer a blow to the head like the first infant they had found. It made him nauseous to think about it. He guessed Hess's saving grace was that he was probably already assumed dead. With each step he took, Levik thanked God over and over and over. Even if their son didn't make it and it caused them unbearable pain, he would be thankful for every minute God allowed him to be theirs. Every second that passed, every breath Hess took, was a gift. The Almighty had given them a son!

Levik knew he and his wife could give their children a life full of immeasurable love and laughter. They knew Drozah came from Roman blood, but they knew nothing of Hess. They presumed that he was also Roman, but there was no way to know. He could be Greek. It didn't matter at all to Levik. These were now their children. Yet, he couldn't keep from thinking about Moses being raised in Pharaoh's house and then leaving the family that raised him in order to rescue his people. Would Drozah and Hess be content to be raised as Jews? Or would their bloodlines one day sway them to choose loyalties? Would he and Adinah even tell them the story of how they came to be a family, or would they keep it a secret? If it were to be kept a secret, they would have to make a home in another town because the people of Bethany would talk. There were so many questions that could only be answered in time. Levik prayed for discernment the rest of the walk home.

Adinah was entertaining many of the same thoughts. Praise be to God! He had, indeed, provided a way! It was strange to already feel like a mother to children who were strangers just a few hours before. She wondered about the mothers who brought them into the world. What were their stories? Did the mother of Hess love him the same way Drozah's mother seemed to love her? Was it their decision to abandon their babies, or was it forced upon them by someone else? She prayed they would heal, both physically and emotionally, and that each of them would someday know the God that created and loved them. Adinah would probably never uncover their stories, but knew that every time they went to Jerusalem, she would look into the face of every woman she passed on the street, looking for similarities between their features. One of them might be Hess or Drozah's birth mothers. What emotions would be stirred within her then? Would her heart be thankful, jealous, or burning with judgment toward them for doing something so atrocious? One would likely not know how they would react until the moment it happened. Even though those women had brought Drozah and Hess into the world, God had brought them to her and Levik. Perhaps his plan all along was for each of them to be an instrument in the lives of these little ones. God's ways were so far above their ways! It was difficult to even imagine how all the pieces of their lives fit together for His glory, but she was glad she was a part of it.

Adinah had other concerns as well. For many years, she had prepared for a newborn, but she was concerned about how to care for little Hess. Never had she seen a baby so small! Not knowing how the people of their village would accept these children and what she and Levik had just done, her mind was scrambling to come up with a plan for their care. Hess would need more than she could give. Drozah was a good size and probably already nearly a month old, by her best assessment. But Hess would likely need the help of a physician. Would he be denied care? She decided that, even though it was taking a risk, she would approach Basharel, who was still nursing her youngest child, and ask if she would be a nursemaid to their babies. Hess, especially, needed a mother's milk.

Lazarus was lost in his own world. He was exhausted but elated for his friends. It felt so good to have just saved the lives of two babies, and he wished Jesus was there to share the story with. Life was good, other than the bug bites itching his ankles. Although they all had reason to celebrate the success of their mission, he couldn't get out of his mind the sight of the picked-over bones of a deserted newborn. How many more babies would suffer the same fate? And now that their eyes had been opened to this practice, how could they sit idle and allow it to keep happening? There was no stopping Rome. No one dared oppose them, and those who did found prison or death. He knew in his heart and conscience that he could not face his Creator and confess to only saving the babies that were convenient for them. He would feel the same guilt as if he had laid the infants out to die himself.

Even as they walked, he wondered if another baby was crying in the night, and it haunted him. He knew he was being called to save as many as he could, and his mind raced with possibilities. If he were to do this again, he couldn't do it alone. He would have to find others willing to help. Maybe they could take turns going on rescue trips and intercept any new infants that were exposed. But what then? What would they do with them?

It's possible they could get care at the infirmary in their village, but it was usually full of abandoned widows, or those who were sick and cast from Jerusalem. Or perhaps they could start a new infirmary, just for infants? They weren't all sickly. It's likely that many, like Drozah, were just unwanted. If they rescued the babies before they got sick or injured, they wouldn't even need a physician as much as they would need caretakers. Surely some women of Bethany would overlook where they came from and see the heart of an innocent child. It's possible that some would even bring a child into their home, like Levik and Adinah were doing, but it was a stretch. Adoption wasn't very common where so much importance is placed on bloodlines.

A thought came to his mind out of nowhere, but it wasn't his thought. It was as if a voice were speaking to him.

*There are many others. Establish a home for the innocents.*

It was as clear as if it were an audible voice spoken to him by God himself. When he heard it a second time, he knew it was more than just a thought. It was so audible that he glanced over at Levik to see if he had said something. He hadn't. Levik was watching Hess sleep as they walked, as if they were the only two people in the world. Adinah was softly humming a lullaby, so it wasn't her, either. Lazarus had heard nothing so clearly without actually hearing it. Not only had Levik and Adinah not said it, but they had not even heard it. If there was a voice that only he could hear, he knew it must be God convicting his heart. He most certainly had never entertained this thought on his own. He tried to shake the idea from his mind and looked up at the sky for some kind of reassurance. Surely, if God was speaking to him, there would be some sign. An angel? A cloud? A burning bush? He saw nothing but the stars that were slowly fading into the first light of morning.

He was unsure of a lot of things in life, but he was suddenly very sure about this. God was very clearly calling him to start an orphanage.

The idea had barely entered his mind before the doubts started rolling in. What if the people of their village reported them to Rome instead of supporting their endeavor? What if they brought disease into their village? What if they got caught trying to rescue the babies? Would they be killed? Tortured? Jailed? He didn't know the penalty but knew it would be harsh.

What if they weren't able to find enough people to care for these babies after they rescued them? It would be a lot to ask the people of Bethany. Some were barely surviving as it was. For most, it was difficult to provide enough food and tax money for the families they already had. He almost voiced this to Levik, but he held it in his heart for now. At this moment, nobody knew but him and God, and strangely, his heart was happy that God had entrusted him with it.

He replaced the doubts with something Jesus had told them during his last visit. He had reminded his listeners that the birds were unable to provide for themselves, but God takes care of them. And the flowers are here one day and gone the next, but God dressed them beautifully. If God takes care of even these, why do we waste any time worrying? It will not add a minute to our lives. How much more would God care for these innocent children? Lazarus decided right then to stop the worrying. He would remain faithful and obey. If this was God's will for him, God would provide a way for it to happen, just like he provided a family for Levik and Adinah.

As they neared their village, all they wanted was sleep, but the babies were beginning to stir. They were never so happy to see their village, and they could finally see the home of Levik and Adinah just up ahead. Nearing their front door, Adinah caught the eye of her husband. "Can you believe this? We are entering our home for the first time as a family of four!"

Levik managed an exhausted smile, but his eyes still sparkled. "My love, these are the most fortunate children in all of Judea to have you as their mother."

Adinah's eyes grew moist with tears of emotion. "And they are blessed to have you as their father."

The five of them entered the front door and Lazarus helped his friends get the babies settled and unpack their belongings. Not knowing what to do next, the men stood looking at Adinah for guidance. She gently asked them to hand her this or please hold that. She was a natural. To watch her, one would think she had been a mother for years.

Drozah got fussy, and Adinah knew it was past time

for her to eat, yet it was too early to knock on Basharel's door with such surprising, and perhaps controversial, news. She pacified them with what goat's milk they had left until they began to hear movement out on the street. What must people think who walked past their home and heard the cry of infants? People in town knew she was barren.

Lazarus didn't know how to make himself useful, so he bid his friends goodbye and walked home to give his sisters the good news. They were ecstatic to see him and embraced him for an unusual amount of time. Lazarus filled them in on the most important parts, and the girls were thrilled to hear their mission had been successful. However, the rest of the story would have to wait until after Lazarus had time to sleep. He had never been so tired, and it seemed the mental exhaustion was almost worse than the physical. Giving each of them one more hug, he collapsed in his bed and drifted off almost instantly.

When they saw that Lazarus was asleep, the girls hurried out the door to the home of Adinah and Levik. They wanted to meet the babies and see how they could be of assistance. After doting over the little ones for a bit, the ladies came up with a plan. Levik would go to the market, Martha would stay there to help Adinah, and Mary would make a couple of trips to the well. Martha knew she would get those extra trips out of Mary at some point! Mary was instructed to find Basharel and request that she follow her back to Adinah's house. The three of them would present the situation to their friend together.

As they parted ways to carry out their assigned duties, Mary prayed for God's guidance with every step. She didn't see Basharel on the first trip but was pleasantly surprised to see that she was just filling up her water jars as Mary approached the well the second time. She was alone, which was unusual. Basharel usually had at least one child following along with her. Mary saw this as a good sign and took the opportunity to talk with her on the walk back. She invited Basharel to stop with her at the house of Adinah and Levik and visit for a little while so she could drop off a water jug. Basharel said she would gladly welcome the adult conversation. She let out a sigh of exhaustion as she laughed that she needed the company of other women before the children drove her out of her mind. Mary smiled. One more piece of God's plan was fitting into place.

Mary was wondering how to explain the situation but soon realized that she didn't have to. Their conversation quieted as they drew near Adinah's house, and they heard the cry of an infant with very healthy lungs. Basharel looked at Mary, puzzled. Mary squinted and shielded the sun from her eyes with her hand, trying to gauge Basharel's reaction.

"It's the reason I asked you to come," explained Mary in a careful voice. She wasn't sure what to expect but knew full well that Basharel may just keep on walking to her own home.

She didn't.

There was no hesitation as Basharel walked into Adinah's house without even knocking. She scanned the room to find Adinah holding a crying infant, and her eyes filled with tears of happiness for her friends. She didn't know how they acquired the baby and didn't even seem to care. It was clear that the cries were because the baby was hungry and Adinah had no milk. She walked over to where Adinah was standing, swaying Drozah back and forth. How long had she been trying to calm her, to no avail? Basharel could recognize that frazzled look of a tired mama from a hundred paces.

She looked into Adinah's tired and almost panicked eyes. As a seasoned mother, she knew that feeling all too well. She smiled and held out her arms. "May I?"

Adinah could not hold her sentiments back any longer. The tears came flowing as she handed little Drozah to her friend. She was relieved to have the help and was enormously grateful to have someone who understood their needs without even asking. It was a pleasant change from having to dictate every move to Levik and Lazarus. They meant well, but sometimes it felt like one more thing on her very full platter. Yet, it was cute to watch them move so carefully, as if the babies might break if they held them the wrong way.

Standing there now, a part of Adinah was overwhelmingly sad that she was unable to nurse her own child. She felt selfish entertaining that thought even for a moment. God had just made a way for her to be a mother! She had no right to be anything but joyful. But when Basharel sat in the chair and pulled Drozah to her breast, a lump grew in Adinah's throat. She looked away as the baby began suckling fiercely and couldn't help feeling a bit jealous. However, she knew this was exactly what Drozah needed, so she would swallow her feelings until it choked her, if that's what needed to be done. She supposed this was the first of many times she would feel this way as a mother.

The four friends sat in silence and soaked in the emotions that saturated the room. Just then, little Hess began to fuss in a voice so faint it was barely audible. Mary and Martha caught each other's eye and realized Basharel didn't even know about him yet. They wondered if their friend would still be so willing when she saw him and learned their stories. To satisfy Basharel's questioning look, Martha walked Hess over to show her that the noise was coming from the sweet little bundle in her arms. It was suddenly making some sense to Basharel, but there were still many questions.

She looked from one face to the next, wondering who would speak up first. "Now," she said, "let's start from the beginning." The four women laughed and cried together as Adinah recounted the story that would forever change their lives. Basharel not only understood why they did what they did, but she volunteered to be a nursemaid to both babies as long as they needed her. At last, Drozah's fervor slowed and Basharel looked up from the nursing infant, who was beginning to fall asleep, with a dribble of milk running down her cheek. She scanned the room, pleased with herself that she was able to help Adinah.

Little Hess even drank his fill, to their great surprise, as the women dribbled the breast milk into his mouth from a spoon. Adinah felt an immense weight lifted and knew in her heart that their prayers were answered. Hess would be okay. Perhaps she was feeling what everyone called a mother's instinct.

As they were talking, Levik returned from the market, looking as tired as Adinah felt. It was a good feeling to walk into his home, knowing it was filled with all the people he loved most in this world. He had a package in his hand and another in a sack around his shoulder. He put one on the table and held the other one out for his wife. "For you," he said tenderly. Adinah was frankly a bit taken aback. This was not usual for him. She had felt so depressed over the suspicions of another woman that she had grown accustomed to feeling overlooked by her husband. She loved him deeply, but her emotions had grown guarded. As he stood in front of her, she felt her heart soften toward him.

He knelt down on the floor in front of her and watched excitedly as she carefully unfolded the linen wrapping. When she saw the gift that lay before her, she brought her hand to her mouth and let out a noise that was half gasp and half sob. She leaned over and embraced her husband, unable to believe he had been so thoughtful. She sat up and looked him in the eye, so in love with the man she married. "Thank you, my love. I can't believe you remembered."

"I want this *Shabbat* to be the best and most memorable we've ever had," he replied as he took her face in his hands.

Adinah finally had her four candlesticks.

# Chapter 14

## Trista's Journal Entry
## Babe

October 7, 2017

"I just tried to call u hun... My other phone is out of minutes... Why won't u say anything babe?"

Who in the heck is this texting my husband? I feel like I am living an after-school-special where the husband is leading a double life, and the wife is too clueless to see the signs right in front of her. I can see the people sitting on their couches yelling at the screen, "Look at the phone bill! Check his phone! Why do you think he ALWAYS has his phone in his pocket, even when he's sleeping?! Open your eyes, lady!"

Where do I even start? It's been so long since writing in my journal, I almost forgot where it was. At the beginning of this year, the doctor noticed something unusual about some routine labs with Andy. Long story short, he has a rare and weird disease which is harming his immune system. When we almost lost him because of the tick bite, we initially thought it was because it was a rare tick. Come to find out, he just couldn't fight off what other people could because of this disease. As soon as he was diagnosed, I began researching and found that there is one doctor in the world who knows about the rare L.G.L. Leukemia and has experience treating it. I made an appointment for Andy immediately and we flew to Virginia so that we could get him on Dr. H's patient list and get the diagnosis confirmed. Now, he has a local oncologist here in Wisconsin who consults with the specialist in Virginia. I've made it my part-time job to research the disease, keep up with communications from both of his doctors, and accompany him to his appointments to take notes and advocate for the best treatments for him.

So, this chilly fall day was set up to be a pretty typical day for me. The day's plan consisted of the following:

- Get kids to school
- Put something in crock pot
- Meet Andy at monthly oncologist appointment
- Head to kids' school for my volunteer shift in the Explorers' Club
- Drive kids home for snack/homework time
- Take our usual walk through the national forest trails across the street.
- Chill with kids until Daddy gets home and have dinner together.

Well, the day did not end up being a typical day after all. In fact, it is hard to remember back to who I was before I knew the information I found out on this day. I am an empty shell of that person now. I function because I have to for the kids, but the person who walked into that appointment with Andy is surely gone.

Since he got his diagnosis, Andy has switched jobs and now works day shift. He was using his lunch break from work for the appointment, so we met in the lobby and sat in the waiting room before being called. It was not a typical lobby as they had someone playing soft music on a grand piano at the entrance, which spilled out throughout the open waiting rooms. I noticed that he had a coffee spot on his shirt and went to the drinking fountain to get some water on a tissue to try to get it off for him. He looked at me with his arm around my shoulders and said, "What would I do without you, sweetheart?" and kissed me. I looked up at him and kissed him back and told him I had no idea, gently squeezing his knee just as we heard his name being called to go back. Just like any other doctor's appointment, the time was broken up between the nurse and docs coming in to gather information, taking vitals, and making a treatment plan. Sprinkled among these activities are the sitting and waiting periods. We were taken to our usual closet-sized room, where we sat in adjoining, blue-green chairs. There was a desk to the left of us, a scale to the right of us, and the nurse, doctor, and resident took up all the remaining space in the room.

Andy's phone was on vibrate and in his pocket, as usual. It started vibrating to signify texts were coming through almost immediately after the team came into the room. We tried to ignore it, but the frequency of the vibrations kept on increasing. As soon as they left the room, I asked him who in the heck was texting him so much and held out my hand for his phone, thinking we would look at it together. The texts were from a number I did not recognize:

"Can we talk"

"I know u r tired of me, but I really need to see u"

"Hello, are u there"

"I won't bother u after today, I know u are tired of me."

I asked Andy who the texts were from and what it was about. He told me that he had no clue who it was, and that it must just be a wrong number. The team came back into the room, and I put the phone down on top of my purse as we spoke to the doctor. He told us the two options he was considering for treatment, and I said that I strongly supported trying the first option and gave my reasons why. The phone continued to vibrate. This time, the vibrations were more drawn out, signifying phone calls, then shorter ones. The team exited the room. I grabbed the phone to see three missed calls and some texts that read:

"I just tried to call u hun"

"My other phone is out of minutes"

"Why won't u say anything, babe"

I was starting to freak out a little. "Honey, this person seems pretty sure they have the right number. Is there anything you want to tell me?" I asked. He reassured me that he had no idea who it was and did not recognize the phone number. I told him I would just text her back and ask who it is. The nurse came back to confirm the pharmacy details while I texted the unknown phone number back asking, "Who is this?" The nurse left after several vibrations, and we looked at the phone together. I read the texts aloud:

"This is Carlie"

"My other phone is out of minutes, so I had to borrow someone's"

"Why are u treating me like this, babe"

The staff came in one more time. I have absolutely no idea what they talked about, as my head was spinning, and my vision was becoming blurry. Thoughts just kept coming one right after another.... Another woman is calling my husband hun and babe. Carlie wants to know why my husband is not treating her right. What does he do during his lunch breaks? My husband has a secret life. Who finds out they are being cheated on at their husband's oncologist appointment? I was actually in the middle of advocating for him to receive the best treatment.... What the heck??!!! I couldn't make this stuff up if I tried. This cannot be happening. It cannot be real. I will be waking up from a deep slumber in moments, for sure. This cannot be real.

After the appointment was over, I immediately snatched Andy's phone and walked out of the office. The soothing classical music playing in the background felt so incompatible with the frenzy of rage inside of me. I made it outside and called Carlie back, who answered and hung up when she heard my voice. Andy immediately went to the restroom, where he proceeded to have diarrhea for quite a while. Not surprisingly, as any type of stress causes him to have stomach issues now, and I'm sure he was stressed. Part of his secret life has been exposed. And something tells me this is only the tip of the iceberg.

He walked me back to my car, where we talked. I confronted him about having a relationship with Carlie. He said it wasn't like that, and he had just been helping out someone who was down on their luck. He was embarrassed that he had let it get this far, where she was asking him for help with things far too often and did not want to tell me because of this. I asked him how long this had been going on, and he hemmed and hawed, then admitted it had been a couple of years. I told him to not bother coming home and drove out of the parking garage.

Sobbing hysterically, I was trying my best to see the road through my tears as I drove. My volunteer duty started in an hour at Poplar Ridge Elementary School. I was supposed to be teaching about leaf identification to Booker and Amelia's classes. I didn't know how I would go through with it in my condition, but the kids love it when I volunteer at their school, especially for Explorer's Club. It would kill me to disappoint them after they've already told their friends I'm coming and Mrs. Davis was expecting me, so I decided right then that I could and would do this. I looked down to see that the car was on empty. I pulled into the gas station on fumes, but I was so distraught, I couldn't even figure out how to work the gas pump. Standing there looking toward the pump as I cried, I put my card in, but did not know what to do next. Too many thoughts were competing for my attention at the same time, I guess. Thankfully, an older man came and did it for me as I tried to stifle my whimpering long enough to tell him thanks.

Fourteen years of marriage: I just can't believe it. And I know there is more to the story. I remember discovering text messages between him and another woman years ago. Oh my gosh, he used the same explanation back then, and I bought it hook, line, and sinker. What a fool I am!! How far back does this go?

I always feel better if I have a plan. I called the church and set up an appointment with our minister for the next day. When I walked into the office and saw the first friendly face, the secretary, I almost crumbled into a pile. As soon as I made it into Pastor Brent's office and sat on the couch, I immediately blurted out, "Is it a sin to divorce if your husband is leading a double life?" I already have much guilt for my first divorce, feeling like I let God down. How can I do it again? What am I going to do? I admitted to him that I did not think I could be in the same house with Andy without becoming physically violent with him at this time. But is it sinful to kick my sick husband out of the house? He was very kind and supportive throughout our conversation. He told me that we will sort out what is a sin and what isn't later, but that the first priority is to make a plan so everyone is safe. We both agreed that I needed time to cool down and it would be best if we stayed separate until we had time to sort this out. After I shared what happened and recounted other times I felt Andy had inappropriate boundaries with women, our minister told me he thought it sounded like some kind of addiction. I hadn't even thought of that. He offered to meet with Andy and try to help, and I gave him Andy's number.

The days all blend together. How many days has it been since the infamous oncologist appointment? About a week, I think. I told the kids Daddy's going camping for a while because we need a little time-out from each other, similar to when they sometimes have to go to their rooms to get some space from each other. Reassuring them that they would still be spending time with Mommy and Daddy, they seemed okay with the fact that it would just be separate for right now. It was an awful feeling, knowing it was a strong possibility that our family would be breaking up. The littles are so in love with both of us and our family as a whole. I have to keep on reminding myself that this separation is for the sake of everyone's safety. I knew it would be more harmful for the kids to see me lose it or become violent with their daddy than knowing that we are in a timeout. The range of emotions I feel in a day is utterly exhausting.

Every minute that I am not caring for them is used to investigate what has been happening in my marriage. Every time I do this, I get more angry, because I shouldn't have to be an investigator. I started with Verizon records and looked at texts and calls as far back as I could go. Then, I cross-referenced those with the calendar to see when they were happening in relation to what Andy was supposedly doing at the time. Any number I did not recognize, or a call or text that came in at a suspicious time, I immediately called to find out who it was. Then, I logged it into my notebook.

I was a wreck. I AM a wreck. There is a pattern that I have noticed. He sometimes texted or called a number immediately after kissing me goodnight and heading to work at 10:50 P.M. He also would text or call a number after getting off work in the morning, before calling me to tell me he was on his way home. There were texting conversations that were 40 texts long in the middle of his work shift. There were phone calls immediately after I took the kids to Montana to visit my brother. We left Andy at home so he "could rest" because the medicines were making him tired. There was a 20-minute-long conversation when I took the kids ice skating and he stayed home due to "stomach problems."

My husband is having a double life. It is clear. To what extent, I do not know. I remember reading *Pilot's Wife* years ago and was so shocked by the man leading a double life. How could that happen? How could she not have seen all the red flags? And yet, all the evidence I am looking at points to exactly that in my own life…

*God, what am I going to do? What am I going to do? I need you.*

# Chapter 15

## The Admission

32 A.D.

There were times when they weren't sure little Hess would pull through, but as the months passed, both babies grew stronger. After he was able to nurse properly, he quickly put on much-needed weight. At nearly a year old now, his survival was no longer questioned, and it was an insurmountable relief.

Adinah felt herself exhausted in a way she never knew existed. Try as she might, she couldn't get the babies on the same sleeping schedule. As soon as she would get one of them to sleep and doze off herself, her eyes would barely close before the other would awaken. This was yet another reminder that, had she birthed them, she could nurse them back to sleep quickly before their cries woke everyone else. The way it was, she had to get back up and rock or feed them by hand, which was much more time-consuming. She knew her circumstance was different from most and presented its own challenges, but she couldn't help but compare her mothering skills to that of other women in her town. Things like getting the babies on a sleep schedule seemed to come easy to them, yet it was genuinely a struggle for her. Maybe it was all in her head, but she felt like all eyes were on her, waiting for her to mess up. No one had said anything to her directly, but sometimes when she was approaching the well with her children, the other women would suddenly grow quiet, as if they had been talking about her and didn't want her to hear. Most acted like they accepted her adopted children, but she knew she and Levik were judged by many others. In all honesty, she could not care less about their judgment. They had a beautiful family and saved the lives of two little ones in the process, so she knew God would be pleased with their decision. She wanted to be the best mother she possibly could and honor her vow to teach Drozah and Hess about God every day. However, part of her also wanted to prove the doubters wrong, so they could never have reason to say I told you so.

Levik helped get them back to sleep from time to time, but she tried to let him sleep as much as possible before he had to get up for work. Adinah was embarrassed to admit that sometimes she envied the fact that he could leave the house for most of the day, even if it was to do manual labor. She loved her babies, but she wasn't prepared for the exhaustion that brought her to the point of nearly passing out. She never thought it possible, but she actually fell asleep standing up a few days before. Parenting was definitely not for the faint of heart, but she promised herself that she would focus on what God had given them as adoptive parents and not on what she missed out on by not giving birth herself. A complaint about Drozah and Hess would never leave her lips, no matter how difficult or inconvenient. When she felt herself grumbling about daunting tasks, she would sing praises to God instead. That simple pleasure had seen her through many long days and nights.

It wasn't all difficult, though. Every so often, Adinah's mother would visit to help care for the children and give Adinah and Levik a few hours alone. They would usually take this opportunity to go on a walk and have a picnic or take care of things that were difficult to do with the babies in tow. On her *aima's* last visit, she brought along an outer garment for Drozah. It was handmade by her mother's *savta*, her grandmother, and it had been in their family for five generations. Adinah had once worn it herself, along with her younger sisters. Unlike anything else they owned, it had exquisite embroidery and beadwork. Adinah's *savta raba*, great grandmother, must have been quite a seamstress for it to have lasted all these years. She would always remember the look in her mother's eyes when she handed her the garment, wrapped and tied carefully. "Adinah, I have waited with great anticipation to bestow this to the first daughter of my daughters." Taking the package from her mother's hands, she carefully untied the strings that had been holding it together. When Adinah saw what it was, she threw her arms around her *aima* in an embrace that was tighter than she meant it to be. She was so grateful to her mother that she didn't want to let go. She knew this was more than a beautiful outer garment. It was acceptance. Her *aima* did not wait for her younger sister to give birth to a daughter. She gave the garment to Drozah, which meant she accepted Drozah and Hess just the same as if they were born into their family. That was an enormous gift in and of itself.

She often found herself missing sleep only because she couldn't take her eyes off of their sweet faces as they snuggled close to her chest. Their steady breathing was a mark of complete and total peace, and Adinah wished she could feel that much contentment. As much as she longed to drift off herself, she knew that every once in a while, they would giggle as they slumbered, and she didn't want to miss one single moment. The first time they saw Drozah smile was when she was suckling in her dreams. She wondered what they dreamed about, or if they realized they were the answer to her prayers. As she gazed in awe of them, she thought of how Hess's grasp around her finger got stronger, and his voice got more robust every day. She loved how he would reach up to her with his little arms, longing to be picked up and snuggled, which she was always happy to do. Drozah melted her heart when she started putting each of her chubby little hands on either side of Adinah's cheeks to turn her mother's gaze to meet her own. Then she would babble a string of nonsensical sounds, trying to form words that her mother would understand. It was so endearing, and Adinah couldn't help but notice how her daughter had already developed many facial expressions that mirrored her own. Perhaps Drozah studied her face as well.

Levik was such a proud father! She knew he would be from the moment he suggested they take that perilous trip to Jerusalem. Actually, maybe it was even as far back as when he began to mourn the fact that they couldn't conceive on their own. He didn't seem to think it was a threat to his manhood or that it brought dishonor to his family name, like other men were inclined to do. Levik cared little about all of that. He truly just wanted to be a father. He had a great relationship with his own *abba*, who always made it clear how much he cared about them. Unlike other fathers, he would take time to fish or play games with Levik and his siblings. Some of his fondest memories were when he was learning at his father's feet, both practically and intellectually. Everything he knew about his trade and about God came from his *abba*.

Long before Adinah and Levik realized they couldn't have children of their own, Levik would share how he couldn't wait to create those same memories when they had their own family. Her husband's yearnings were the source of both joy and pain for Adinah. She loved his sensitive heart, but her infertility made her feel like she was the reason it was breaking. Month after month, he would be so disappointed right along with her when it didn't happen.

Although it had only been just under a year ago, sometimes it seemed a world away. As she looked at Drozah and Hess, it was still hard to believe that they were theirs. Adinah loved to listen to Levik talk to his friends about their children. He would show them off to anyone who would take a moment to look, and it made Adinah's heart happy. She knew he would die for any one of them and loved his family with everything he had.

He was doing that very thing as they passed friends in the market one day, and an acquaintance overheard the conversation. He inserted himself into their circle and commented on how cute the children were and how much work it must be to have two so close in age. Then he said something that made Levik's eyes turn to steel. Casually, as if he were talking about the weather, he said, "It's a shame that your true bloodline ends with you. Hess and Drozah are cute, but in the end, they are still Roman."

Adinah had never seen her husband go from one extreme to the other so quickly. He was on cloud nine one minute, then close to physically harming another person the next. Their friends had to jump in and hold him back. She was sure Levik would put him on the ground, right there in front of God and everybody. To her surprise, the man wasn't even remorseful for what he had said. She realized it wasn't a mistaken insult. It was pointed. It was clear that even though they raised their children in their Jewish heritage, her family would always face this kind of unacceptance by some of the people who knew their story.

She and Levik were strong enough to handle it, but she feared what that might mean for Lazarus. He shared one evening that he had been planning the next rescue mission ever since they returned from the last trip to Jerusalem. It was killing him to know that with every day that passed, another child was likely to be thrown out like garbage. It didn't creep into his mind so much as he went about his day, but at night when everything got quiet, all he could hear were the cries of an infant who had been left to die. The most innocent of innocents: deceived by the one person in this world who was supposed to love and protect them the most. Is there a child out there now, being carried off by a wild animal? Left to scorch in the sun and be covered in insects? Slowly starve to death? His dreams would be haunted with visions of picked-over bones, and he would startle himself awake, drenched in sweat. The dreams carried the stench of guilt. He couldn't stomach the fact that he was lying in a warm bed with a full stomach while a defenseless child lay dying.

Lazarus knew he had to put his plan into action, but there were so many moving parts that he wasn't sure where to begin. The fewer people on the mission, the better chance they had of not being discovered by the Romans. Yet, he didn't know how to care for an infant, especially if it needed special care like Hess. It would be nice to have a woman go along for that reason, but it wasn't proper. He would have to enlist help from a man who could aid in defending them if they should come upon trouble. His mind rolled with possibilities, but he couldn't think of anyone who would be willing to risk their lives for this. When Levik and Adinah went, they were emotionally invested. They were different. But they couldn't take that risk again when they have their little ones to think of.

Until he got an orphanage up and running, there was still the question of what he would do with them. Would his sisters consider adopting a baby into their home? It would be difficult with neither of them married, but they could all help. If they did bring a baby into their home, would they raise it as a sibling or a child? There were so many fuzzy lines.

In true Lazarus fashion, he turned on his charm and had spoken to his *aima's* friends at the infirmary. Within days, they had agreed to designate a room for infant care as long as Lazarus would pay for a nursemaid if it was required. As it turned out, it wasn't even going to be necessary. At least not for a while. To their surprise, Levik had found another couple who wanted to adopt a child, and they wanted to accompany Lazarus on the next trip.

# *But*, Even Now

The plan was all coming together, and he could finally get some sleep knowing that he was doing God's will. He was careful not to give away any details to anyone who didn't need to know. There were still people who disagreed with what they were doing, and he didn't trust them not to turn them over to the guards. However, he knew he was fulfilling the life God wanted him to lead. He was so glad he listened to the voice that urged him to take on this mission.

Adinah was so caught up in taking care of the children that she barely noticed it was past suppertime. Levik should have long since been home. Now that she thought of it, this was not the first time it had happened this week. Being so happy to get some help when he walked through the door the last time, she didn't even think to ask. She just figured he had extra work to take care of, and frankly, was too tired to care. She just needed some sleep. But now, those feeling of insecurity and suspicion were creeping back in. She hadn't thought of the possibility of another woman in a long time. They had everything they wanted here at home, and Levik had been so loving to her and the children. Every Sabbath when they lit four candles, his eyes lit up with pride. She knew he loved her. Surely there was another explanation.

She dismissed the thought when she heard a knock at the door. It was Basharel, who offered to take both of the children into her home the following day so Adinah could get some rest while she nursed the babies. Adinah gladly took her up on her offer. They would never be able to repay her kindness.

It was almost dark before Levik walked in. He walked over to the babies, kissed Hess on his now chubby cheek, then picked up Drozah and held her up over his head. "Hello, my darling! Were you a good girl for *Aima*? Did you miss *Abba* today?" He kissed both of her cheeks and made silly sounds with his lips that made her eyes light up. He walked over to Adinah and kissed her cheek, then handed Drozah to her and sat at the table to eat his dinner as if he didn't notice that it had long since grown cold.

That's it? Is he not going to acknowledge that he is so late for the second time this week, with no explanation as to why? Although Adinah was angry, she wanted to give him the benefit of the doubt. As she poured him some water, she said, "Long day, huh?" Levik was a silversmith by trade, but silver had been scarce recently. When work was slow, he had been helping cut and clear nearby roads.

His reply was brief. "Yes, very long. Very hot."

"Did you stay busy at the shop?"

He was answering his wife but looking at Hess when he spoke, his voice high and overly enthusiastic, like people often do when speaking to a baby. "Yes, I was. So much work to be done at the shop. *Abba* finally got the shipment of silver he has been waiting for and has work piled up for days!"

So her worrying was for nothing after all. She felt guilty for letting those doubts creep in. Her husband was a good man. She decided that when the children were with Basharel the next day, and after a long nap, she would prepare a special lunch and surprise her hard-working man.

They talked as he finished his meal, and to their surprise, both of the children were asleep at the same time! That was such a rarity that they couldn't pass up the opportunity to go to bed early and lay in each other's arms. As she drifted off to sleep, Adinah lifted up a prayer of thanksgiving for all the blessings in her life.

The next day, she started making special preparations for lunch as soon as Levik left the house. Ever since he surprised her with the candlesticks, she could hardly wait to find the opportunity to return such a sweet gesture. She had made his favorite meal, tucked it carefully into a basket and covered it with her grandmother's embroidered kitchen cloth. Under the basket was a blanket big enough for them to spread out in a nice, shady area to enjoy their meal.

She carefully swaddled the babies and strapped them to herself for their walk to Basharel's house. Thankfully, they were content to be with her as she walked in the fresh air. She didn't want to leave her dear friend with grumpy babies. Lightheartedly, she walked back to her house to change into her best clothes and freshen up for their lunch.

Humming as she strolled along, she couldn't remember a time she was this happy. As she thought about the dates she had put in the lunch basket, she realized it was not that long ago when Mary held her as she cried over not having a family. My, how quickly things had changed! Who would have guessed that a few weeks later, she would have not only one, but two babies in her home? She wondered to herself if God knew it would play out this way. Was that His plan all along? He might have kept her barren for a reason. Maybe He knew that if she and Levik had children of their own, they would never have sought out the discarded babies in Jerusalem. Maybe He had big plans for Drozah and Hess. Maybe God chose them to be their parents because they were the only ones who could raise them in a way that would allow His plan for them to happen. Maybe God knew that was the only way to get Lazarus to start an orphanage and rescue the Roman outcasts. Maybe. She thanked God for knowing the bigger plan and allowing her to be a part of it.

As she approached the shop, she heard the familiar sounds of her husband's trade. Before she could even see him, she could tell what he was doing. Pulling off her head covering, she walked around the corner to surprise him. She was startled to see that it was not Levik standing there, but his apprentice. Embarrassed, she put her covering back on. "Forgive me, Josiah. I was hoping to surprise Levik."

"Nice to see you, Adinah! How are the little ones?"

"They aren't much for sleeping, but other than that, they are doing just fine." They both laughed. "When do you expect Levik back?"

Josiah looked uneasy. "I am not sure, Adinah. He has not been here in a few days. I thought he was home with you, helping with the babies."

Adinah's face grew flush, and she felt her heart begin to race with fear and panic. Not only was she angry with him for lying to her, but she was embarrassed to find that her husband had also deceived his faithful worker and friend. She didn't know what to say. She felt sick.

As Adinah backed away, Josiah put down his tools and tried to console her. "I'm sure there is an explanation, Adinah. He is a man of his word."

The basket suddenly felt heavy in her hands, and she knew she couldn't eat lunch now if she tried. She set it on a table. "Here, Josiah. Someone may as well enjoy this food." She removed her grandmother's kitchen cloth but then motioned to Josiah to help himself.

She wanted to bid him goodbye, but the words got stuck in her throat. Instead, she turned and ran all the way home. She threw herself across the bed where she and Levik had just laid the night before. It mocked her. She was glad the babies were with Basharel because she could think of nothing else but her husband in the arms of another woman.

Should she go try to find him? She wouldn't know the first place to look. Should she confront him? The thought sickened her because she was afraid of what she might hear. Should she pretend she knew nothing? That wouldn't work, as Josiah was sure to warn him about their conversation if he saw Levik first. She decided to pick up the children, make dinner as usual, and wait until he got home. She would casually bring it up in conversation.

That afternoon, he was actually home at his normal time, and again, he was in very cheerful spirits. He walked through the door and kissed her cheek and lifted Hess from her hip "Hello, my loves! How is my beautiful family today?"

Adinah wanted to smack him. Instead, she did her best

to act normal and remain calm. "Oh, you know. Some days are easier than others. How was your day?"

"Still very busy. I was lucky to get out of there at a decent hour today. We are so far behind from waiting on that shipment of silver."

Adinah was seething! How could he look her in the eye and lie to her face? Bethany is a small town. Did he really think she wouldn't put it together? Or that nobody else would? How could he disgrace their family like this, especially when everything was going so well? Throwing down the spoon in her hand, she hurried into the next room. She searched for her shawl and rushed to get away from him as quickly as possible. If not, she was sure she would do something she would regret.

Levik set the baby down and walked toward her, guarded. "Adinah, what's wrong?"

She spun around, and her eyes met his with fierce anger. She spoke through gritted teeth. "Don't you act like you have done nothing wrong. You know what you did!"

Levik looked confused. "What are you talking about?"

"I went to the shop to surprise you with lunch today, only to find that you have not been going there at all! Where have you been every day, Levik? Because you haven't been at work!"

"They needed my help on the roads."

"Nonsense! You have lied so many times you can't even remember what is a lie and what is the truth! That is not the man I married." She brushed past him to make her way out the door.

Levik tried to grab her arm, but she pulled away and stood facing him. She looked him dead in the eye. "Tell me the truth. Is there another woman?"

"Adinah..."

She interrupted. "No! No more lies. Is there another woman?"

"I was in the company of a woman today, but..."

That's all Adinah needed to hear. It didn't matter what he had to say. It didn't matter what his reasons were. She didn't care if it was because of bloodlines, or boredom, or if he simply fell in love with someone else. He betrayed her. She had braced herself for this before, but now, after the babies and the candlesticks and the night they just had together, this blindsided her. Their dream of having children had come true, and they had been so happy. Or so she thought. If he wasn't being unfaithful because she couldn't give him children, then her nightmare must be true. Maybe it wasn't about family at all. Maybe he simply didn't love her. She ran out of her house, unsure of what to even do next. Tears were streaming down her face, and she instinctually ran to find the comfort of Mary and Martha.

When the girls answered the knock at the door, they found Adinah slumped in a heap in the dirt.

# Chapter 16

## Trista's Journal Entry
## Shiny Wings

October 17, 2017

"Mommy, you won't believe this!"

Where do I even start? So much has happened in the last week. Most of it, nobody would believe if I tried to explain, but here goes. I found out more about the betrayal, but that's surprisingly not the biggest thing. An angel visited Bella in her dream! I will explain both, but first, the angel. I've gotta get this down on paper before I forget another one of the amazing ways my Heavenly Father has reached out to comfort me during my pain. How can someone feel grateful and yet bitter and broken at the same time?

The other day, I was brushing Bella's hair while she sat at the kitchen counter, getting ready to head out for school…

"Mommy, I had a really amazing dream last night!" she shared.

"Really, what was it about?" I asked.

"I was in this brown room with a man wearing a golden robe. He was wearing some gold sandals, and he had shiny wings. There was a bright light all around him. He told me not to be afraid and then told me that part in the Bible that you had us memorize. He said he knows the plans God has for me, plans to prosper me and not harm me, plans to give me a hope and a future. He was explaining things to me for a long time, and I was just sitting there speechless."

"Sounds interesting… what was he explaining to you?"

"Well, I heard you crying last night and was really worried for you. I prayed, and then I went to sleep. It was like he knew I was upset, because he kept saying to not worry, and that God will take care of things. He told me about two women in the Bible who were worried, and he showed me how God took care of them and there was no need to worry. One of them was Hannah, who was afraid she wasn't going to have a baby. He reminded me that God had a plan for her and kept saying not to worry. Then, he told me that God was going to bless our family. Then he went away just like that."

I was stunned. We had been doing some Bible studying together but not in that much detail. It could only have come from one place. I replied, "Wow! Honey, I think you were visited by an angel last night!"

I have no words. He has found yet another way to comfort me in a time of distress. As if speaking to me in the hospital was not enough to show me how loved I am by Him! He has now sent an angel to my daughter on the exact evening I found out unfathomable news about the man I love.

Which brings us to the backstory…. It has been about two weeks since I intercepted the text messages from Carlie to Andy. He is now living in the back barn to give each of us space. I have not seen him since the appointment, but I went out a couple times so that he could come and visit with the children. The focus has been on surviving and trying to be as normal as possible for the kids when they are home. During the day when they are at school, I am digging into accounts and cross-referencing with as many of my calendars as I can to find more answers. During the evenings when the kids are sleeping, I sometimes have texting conversations with him. This is the only way we can communicate at this time, so that I do not start screaming at him and throwing the phone across the room. The messages usually start out with me telling him how much I hate him and go from there.

The night Bella had her dream, I was questioning him. After buying a system to help recover deleted data, I recovered so many things that the file wouldn't open because of the size. There were emails, voicemails, and texts. I have no idea what I will find in these files. I explained that I would be going to my brother's (a computer expert) soon to have him open the files, but I would like to hear the truth from him first.

During the course of this texting conversation, I learned that this was not the only secret relationship he has had during our marriage. And we were finally in a place where I was asking questions, and he was trying to answer them truthfully. Up to this point, I truly believed that Andy may just have bad boundaries. At least I desperately wanted to believe this. Somehow, he must have got in over his head and then didn't want to bring up anything confrontational to me. God forbid there is ever any confrontation. Better to lie about even the dumbest thing than risk a small confrontation.... This has been his motto several times in the past. Yet, when it comes down to it, he is a good man, and he truly loves his family. I did not believe in my heart that he had really been unfaithful to me.

But I had to ask…. And so, I texted, "Did any of these relationships ever become sexual?" He typed for a long time. The three little dots kept on scrolling across the screen, and I just watched them and prayed that the answer was no. After a long time of seeing that he had been typing, I got the response of "no." I texted back, "It sure seems like you were typing for a long time, then you must have decided to delete it. I am going to find out the truth, eventually. Did it ever become sexual with these women?" The three little dots popped up again as I cried out to God, pleading with him for the answer to be no. I looked down at the screen and saw

"Yes, I'm so sorry."

I began wailing and couldn't stop. This had to be when Bella heard me and became worried. I called Andy and said some of the meanest things I could think to say and hung up. Then I called my sister, Abigail, and she had trouble even believing it. Everybody loves Andy. I just kept saying, "What am I going to do? What am I going to do?" I sat there, despondent, staring off into space for who knows how long. It seemed like everything around me was in slow motion, and it took every ounce of energy I had left in me to finish the conversation. The only thing I could manage to say was, "What am I going to do?" She told me I was strong and I am going to get through this and I am going to raise these three amazing kids God has blessed me with no matter what happens with my marriage.

*Dear God, what am I going to do?*

# Chapter 17

## Desperate Times

32 A.D.

Mary knelt on the ground, her mind racing with possibilities of what could be upsetting her friend. "Adinah, what is it? Are the babies okay?"

Adinah nodded her head that they were fine but could not compose herself enough for words to be formed. Martha stooped in the doorway with a hand on Adinah's shoulder.

The women simply sat beside her for a while, allowing her to feel whatever she was feeling. Sometimes you just need to know someone is there with you. When the sobs subsided, Mary spoke gently. "Is it the other?" Adinah nodded yes. Martha exchanged a confused glance with her sister, and Mary realized she had not yet shared about Levik. She didn't want anyone thinking badly of him for undue reason and had hoped the suspicion was proven false and forgotten about by now.

Martha motioned to them and said, "Let's get you inside. We will have privacy, as Lazarus is visiting with Avner and Judith to prepare for their trip to Jerusalem in the morning. I'll make a cup of tea."

Mary linked her arm through Adinah's, and the sisters helped her to her feet. As Martha filled the pot with water and stoked the fire, Adinah filled them in on what had just happened. How could he do this to her? Especially after all they had just gone through to create the family they always wanted. Looking in from the outside, they seemed overflowing with happiness, the way Levik would go on about the children to anyone who would listen. But the more Adinah spoke, the more flabbergasted Martha was with what she was hearing. It was as if Levik had been living a secret life. It made her wonder how many other men, and women for that matter, do the same? Although other men in their town had taken a mistress on the side without giving his wife a bill of divorce, she never would have suspected such behavior from Levik. She always thought of him as a righteous man.

"Shall we pray together?" Mary offered. She wasn't sure why she hadn't thought of this first. She was surprised when her suggestion was quickly shot down.

"Pray?" hissed Adinah. The word came from her mouth as if it were a curse, and it broke Mary's heart. "Why would I pray? I am so angry at God right now I cannot see straight! Why would He allow it to appear that my husband's heart was softened toward me, only to find that it had been turned to stone? I feel just as betrayed by God as I do by my husband!" The tears had passed, and now Adinah sat void of emotion. Although she had her suspicions of her husband's infidelity for a long time, she was still in shock that it actually happened. Question after question entered her mind, with no answers. How long had this been going on? Who was she? How did they meet? Did he seek her out, or had it just happened? Was he in love with this woman, or was he simply using her for pleasure? Was she even aware that he had a family? Would she even care?

A family.... Adinah's face suddenly went pale and broke out in a sweat. She felt sick to her stomach as the realization began to sink in. "He can take our children! Mary... Martha... If he chooses the process of a *get* and gives me a bill of divorcement, I would be required to leave our home and would have no choice in the matter. I could lose my babies! What am I going to do?" The sobs broke out again, and Mary and Martha simply rubbed her back and stroked back her hair as she cried. Adinah was right.

"I may or may not be able to forgive him for what he has done to me with this woman, but if he takes my children, I could never forgive him."

Martha finally spoke. "Perhaps that is not the course he will take. As devastating as this is, we must be careful not to indict him on an offense he has not yet committed."

Mary was sometimes astonished at the way her sister could keep a level head. She wasn't thinking that at all. Her mind was already going to how she would find a way to get Hess and Drozah back from Levik's woman of ill-repute who didn't deserve them.

They sat for a long time, and although Adinah was not yet ready to look at her husband, she realized she must go back to take care of the children. They would be hungry and Levik didn't know how to care for them properly. That may be the only thing in her favor in this situation. If she was served a *get* and he took this other woman into his home, it was unlikely she would be willing to take on what is required of raising two babies.

The three walked quietly together back to Adinah's home, where they could hear the babies before they saw them. As soon as their little cries hit her ears, Adinah's attention went straight to them and, at least momentarily, she couldn't care less if Levik was in the room or not. The women took turns embracing their friend and offered to help in any way possible as they bid her goodnight.

****

The next morning, Lazarus, Avner and Judith met at daylight to make their trip to Jerusalem. He had done this enough times now that Mary and Martha knew exactly how to help him prepare. His bag was packed and waiting by the door, and his meal was already waiting at the table when he awoke. His passion mixed with the excitement of hopeful parents made it easier for the girls to watch him walk away. They knew he was hearing God speak to his heart, and he was obeying the directive. Mary and Martha had many conversations about what their parents would think of his endeavors. They imagined that their father would go along with Lazarus, and their *aima* would probably be the one to organize the orphanage. Who knows? She would have probably even adopted a few herself. They couldn't wait to tell Jesus all about it.

Lazarus kissed the cheek of each of his sisters, and Avner and Judith hugged them each goodbye. The girls were so proud of their brother as they watched him walk away. As they had grown accustomed to doing, they joined hands and prayed for him until he was no longer in sight.

He had already warned his new friends of the potential dangers they could face from bandits along the road, or at the hands of the Romans if they were caught. However, as they walked the familiar path, Lazarus filled them in on the reality of the horrors that might lie ahead. As Judith listened to Lazarus' warnings, the scorching sun on their backs made her feel a bit nauseous. She didn't want to hear anymore, but knew Lazarus was only being blunt so they wouldn't be caught off guard like he had been.

Now that Lazarus knew where he was going, it didn't take them long to find the hiding place he had designated near where the infants were most often discarded. He got word that they were also thrown out with the garbage or at bathhouses, but he knew those areas were more heavily populated, and their chance of getting discovered was much higher. Those babies were also more likely to have already been killed or to have died from natural causes. The babies here were more likely to be left exposed to the elements, to die a natural death. It was considered an act of mercy to many Romans, but Lazurus viewed such as being worse than killing the children instantly. Here, they were left to succumb in unimaginable ways.

The first few days went by very slowly. They saw nothing at all except the passersby on the nearby roadway. Avner was starting to question whether or not they were in the right place. Lazarus was getting irritated at the fleas that kept biting his ankles but dared not pray that a baby would be discarded. If they were meant to leave with a baby, it would happen. If not, they would return another day.

Finally, on the fourth day, they heard the voices of the Romans. Lazarus recognized one of the guards. This must be his post. What a horrible job. He wondered if that man was bothered by it at all, or if his family knew what he did when he went to work every day? They watched as the guard with him tossed a bag toward a nearby rock. When the bag bounced off and hit the ground, they heard a baby start to wail. It must have either annoyed or disturbed the guard enough that he drew his sword to put the baby out of its misery.

The first guard grabbed his arm. "Stop. This was a sacrifice by the family to one of their gods."

"And?" asked the second. "I don't ascribe to that belief. What is it to me?"

"It is our practice to only use the sword on the ones who have not been used as a sacrifice or have been here far too long. Just walk away. The animals are used to coming to this place. It won't be here long."

The guards turned and one of them pulled a snack out of his pocket and began to eat as they sauntered back to their post. Lazarus could see the repulsion on Judith's face that they could so casually go about their normal day, as if this didn't just happen.

When the guards were out of sight, Avner began to get

up to run to the baby, whose cries were quivering in pain. It was so difficult to hear, but Lazarus stopped him. "Wait! I see someone coming."

Not far down the path was a caravan of people moving in their direction. They were carrying on and making a lot of noise, as if they had just come from a tavern. Lazarus heard Judith sniffle and realized she was wiping away tears. He understood her torment. Waves of intense emotion rolled over them. Judith was excited to finally get a child of her own but sat in agony upon hearing the baby cry in pain and being unable to comfort it.

The caravan moved closer. They hoped they would keep moving along, but one of them held up his hand and motioned for everyone to stop and listen. Oh no! They heard the baby! Two of them started walking in the direction of the cries, and Lazarus had to stop Avner from running towards it once again.

"Why do you keep stopping me?" Avner yelled at Lazarus in a whisper. "They are going to take our baby!"

"It's possible," Lazarus replied. "But is it better for Judith to return to Bethany minus a child, or minus her husband? You cannot take the chance! If they want the baby, as they see it, they saw it first. You would have to fight them for it, and they far outnumber us."

Avner gave a defeated sigh. He knew Lazarus was right, but he also knew his wife's heart must be breaking. He held his breath as they watched the men make their way through the trees until they came to the sack on the ground. One of them stooped over and peered in. He looked repulsed and jumped back. The second man, obviously drunk, kicked the bag.

The crying stopped.

Judith gasped and buried her face in her husband's chest as he tried to shield her from the atrocity she just witnessed. He wished he would have insisted she stay home so he could have spared her the visions that would never leave her head.

The men returned to their caravan and laughter and carrying on ensued as they made their way out of sight. At the nod from Lazarus, the three hurried over to the baby. Lazarus carefully lifted it out of the sack, only to realize it was covered in feces. He laid the naked baby down on top of the rock to get a better look. Upon a quick assessment, the baby appeared to be full term and healthy. It was a boy, but he didn't appear to be breathing.

"Is he alive?" asked Judith?

Lazarus put his finger under the baby's nose to see if he could feel any air moving. He could not. He put his ear to the baby's chest. "I can hear a heartbeat! It's faint, but it's there."

Tears were streaming down Judith's face as Avner put two fingers over the baby's heart. "I feel it! Maybe he passed out from the pain."

"We can assess him over there," Lazarus whispered, "but we have to hurry out of this spot."

Avner carefully picked up the newborn, and they hurried through the woods back to the cover of a fallen tree. They laid the little one on a blanket, and Judith began dipping a cloth into some water to clean him off. Who knows how long he had been laying in his own filth? He already had a swollen and bruised arm, and it was obvious that it was probably broken when the drunken man kicked him. Hard to tell if it had also shattered ribs. When Judith dribbled water over his head, the baby awoke and immediately began to cry.

"We have to go," warned Lazarus. "If they hear the baby, they will come after us."

The three quickly gathered their belongings and followed Lazarus as he zigzagged between rocks and trees. The baby was still crying, but Judith had him swaddled close to her chest. What a horrible feeling it was to know the pain the child must be feeling and be able to offer such little comfort! Avner had made arrangements with the town physician before they left, hoping to have their newly acquired child checked over upon their return. He was thankful he had the foresight to do so. This little one would need it sooner rather than later.

After a long while, they eventually made their way back to the commonly traveled path. It wouldn't be too much longer before they saw Bethany come into view, and Lazarus was glad of it. His skin felt clammy, and his head pounded. He couldn't remember the last time he took a drink of water, and they had used the last of it to wash the baby, which they had named Cheyim: *Life*.

The last half of the walk home all blurred in Lazarus' head. He was glad his friends were familiar with the road because his head was pounding so hard that he could barely think of anything else besides the pain. His sisters would know what to do. As they approached Bethany, Avner and Judith rushed the baby to the doctor and Lazarus made his way home. Mary was making her way back from the market and saw him coming from a distance. She ran over to him, eager to hear what had happened. As the distance between them got smaller, her expression changed from joyful to worrisome.

"Lazarus, are you okay? You don't look well."

"I don't feel well."

She touched his head with the back of her hand. "You are burning with fever! How long have you been like this?"

"It started sometime last night, but I didn't want to say anything to the others because we were so close. We rescued another baby, Mary! We did it." He smiled through tired, pain-filled eyes.

"I'm so happy to hear that, but you are going to have to tell me another time. Let's get you to bed." She took her brother's bag and put her arm through his as they walked the rest of the way. When they entered the door of their home, Martha was in the kitchen, preparing dinner.

"Mary, can you fetch me.... Lazarus! You're home!" She ran to his side and hugged his broad shoulders, and immediately knew something was wrong. "You are burning up!"

"He said it started last night, but he was afraid to say anything," explained Mary.

Martha knew exactly what to do. "Lazarus, dear, remove your travel clothes and sit on your bed. Mary, fetch water to wash his feet. I'll cut some cucumber to put on your head and boil some marigold and chamomile."

Everyone did as they were instructed. Lazarus, finally able to rest, closed his eyes and nearly fell asleep sitting up. By the time his sisters came back with the water and the medicine, he had slumped over in bed and dozed off.

Martha gently shook him. "Lazarus, you must drink some of this tea to help your fever."

"My head...." His voice was barely a whisper.

"I know, dear. The medicine will help your headache as well."

Mary unstrapped his sandals and gasped. "Martha! Look at his legs! They are covered in welts!" She looked up at her brother. "Lazarus, where did these come from? Are these spider bites?"

Lazarus uttered one last word before he lost consciousness.

"Fleas."

# Chapter 18

## Trista's Journal Entry
## One Sinner

October 21, 2017

"Hold on a minute. Is this even a real thing?"

The question of what I am going to do haunts me every waking minute. Out of our fourteen-year marriage, I don't even want to know how many secrets there have been, from erased histories on the computer to deleted text messages to outright lies and betrayals.... How many red flags have I overlooked? Until now, when we would cuddle on the couch, we would always get in a position where the phone in his pocket would be digging into me, and I would ask him to take it out. I would always say, "Why do you keep that thing in your pocket? It seems so uncomfortable!" Now I know why. He was always afraid one of his secrets would be exposed in some way during family time, which was supposedly off limits.

Well, Andy met with our minister, who prayed with him and referred him to a therapist who specializes in sex addiction. "Hold on a minute, is this even a real thing?" has been my initial thought about this topic since Brent mentioned it to me at the church. Isn't this just a politically correct or convenient way to cover for people who watch pornography or who choose to cheat on their spouses? I don't know. I want to totally call hogwash on this whole thing and run away except for this small voice that keeps reminding me about a testimony we heard a while back. In fact, the testimony was from a man who I really respect. He shared about his struggle with porn addiction and how God helped him to overcome it when we were at a Christian conference last year. He told us how it works like any other addiction, where the person eventually needs more and more of the "fill in the blank" to get the "high." With alcohol, they eventually need to drink more alcohol. If it's drugs, they eventually need higher doses or to switch to a harder drug. When it's pornography, if it isn't controlled, they can start acting out physically, which may look like serial cheating. Blah, blah, blah....

Well, I can't figure this all out right now. I have problems of my own I need to focus on. Whatever Andy's problem is, the fact is that since he has had relations with other women during our marriage, he has put me in harm's way. After all the love and support I have showed him over the years.... After all the struggles we've gone through to grow our family...and he has been putting my life in danger this whole time!! The life of the mother of his own children!! How do I wrap my brain around that? What if he has passed something on to me? I made an appointment to be tested for everything as soon as possible. I have to know.

After I found out the extent of Andy's betrayal, my parents came out to give me some support. I didn't even have to ask them to come. They just called and told me they were packing up and they would be in town later that evening. I'm so grateful. They come over and help me with the kids in the afternoons after school. In the evenings, when Andy comes over to visit with the kids, I meet them at the trailhead, and we walk and talk. They have been great listeners, although I've lost count of the number of times my dad has called Andy an ass. He just can't help himself, and I really can't blame him. And my mom just keeps saying, "I can't believe he did this....

He goes to church and everything.... You didn't deserve this...." She's so sweet. I try to explain to her that going to church does not make you immune to sin or addiction, but I really can't blame her for her shock, either. I think I've been in shock since I found out.

My mom also went to the doctor's appointment with me to get back on anti-depression medicine and get tested for all the sexually transmitted diseases. As I explained that I had recently found out my husband has been living a double life for most of our marriage, it was like I wasn't even in my own body. I felt like I was just a body walking around doing what I had to do, but I wasn't even in there. When I spoke, it sounded like it was someone else's story, not my own, but it is my own. I can't believe it.

I've stopped eating. I've become obsessed with investigating, and every new connection I make is like a knife in my heart again. He texted with another woman while he was eating a homemade dinner that I lovingly prepared for him. He texted with another woman while he was sitting on the couch with my son on his lap, and me three feet away one Saturday morning. I've also started researching divorce lawyers and how to proceed with this. Abigail and my bestie, Michelle, are praying for me as I don't even have the words right now.

****

October 23, 2017

Well, I got my test results back and I do not have any sexually transmitted diseases, praise the Lord! Now to focus on my mental health, I've checked out both online and in-person support groups. I'll update when I check one out. Am I really a partner of a sex addict? Is this really my life now? Lord, help me.

****

October 25, 2017

In one of our rare and short phone conversations, Andy told me that he went to his first appointment and shared with me that this therapist was a formerly betrayed partner of a sex addict. He will work on a program with Andy to get him to see how his thinking has gotten messed up over his life and how harmful his choices have been. He is going to begin an intense twelve-step program, meeting with his therapist weekly and doing homework from his workbook daily. The therapist recommended a book for me to read to help in my healing as well as understand the addiction. I agreed that I would read it. I'm also planning on going to a local church for betrayed partners. Guess I'm not the only wife who has had her world shattered because there are several of these kinds of groups within an hour's radius of here, in addition to many online choices. I don't know whether to be encouraged or saddened by this revelation....

Until yesterday, Andy and I were having limited communication via text, mostly. Mainly, our texts are how much I hated him for doing this to our family, how sorry he was, and arrangements for when he was going to come and see the kids or take somebody to a broomball game. After dropping the kids off at school, I came home and got into bed to rest as I haven't been sleeping well. I was so hurt and angry about some of my new realizations. Reaching for my phone, I wanted to hurt him back a little. I started to text him so many mean things, including that maybe life would have been better for all of us if he never would have come out of his coma. When I went to press the blue "send" arrow, the text was no longer there. It somehow just spontaneously got erased. Divine intervention? I was too exhausted to text that all again, so I just impulsively texted him a question about how apartment hunting was going. By the end of our texting conversation, we were both hot messes….

I went on. "I read about what Jesus said about divorce and feel I am totally justified in that, but I am afraid he's going to tell me to forgive u…. I started this morning with the meanest text I could think of to send u, and it was spontaneously erased."

He replied. "I think God may be answering my prayers, to have this guilt and shame lifted from me…. I want to be a better man for u, for our family, for God. I really feel confident for the first time that i can change my ways with the help of this therapist...can't stand the thought of hurting u again"

"I always wanted to be ur best friend and feel closer"

"I'm afraid that no one would ever want to be my best friend"

"I did"

"I'm so sorry I didn't believe that...I'm crying in a public place now"

"I am crying in what used to be our bed"

"I have to go to the car, trying to get a book at the store…. That was embarrassing"

"LOL I didn't think you ever cried"

"I'm crying now, I've been crying a lot lately...I was so glad to see your face again the other night, even if it was just a moment as you walked to the car"

"Can you believe an angel visited our daughter? What do you think the angel meant when he said God would bless our family?"

"I think he meant that we can have more peace in our family now that my secret life is over"

"btw, it really is time for another haircut"

"wow, you notice everything, I will cut it today"

"I love u so much, honey… I want you to be the man I know you can be, to live in the light and never return to the darkness again"

"I love u too, more than anything, u have dragged me out of despair more times than u know"

"u know God did this for you, right? He erased the meanest text ever so that we could have this conversation. He keeps on intervening for you, so he must have a good plan for u. don't let him down"

"I feel like this is a lifeline He is sending me, to encourage me to take this leap forward...I'm going to do the work with the therapist and get better. I want to be a mentally healthy person. U are so encouraging. It means the world to me"

****

Can I dare to hope to have a happy marriage after unspeakable betrayals? I have ordered the book his therapist suggested and started reading it. The experts typically recommend waiting 6 to 12 months in cases like these to determine if the addict is going to take his recovery from sex addiction seriously and truly change. There is supposedly hope that the addict can see the errors in their thinking, heal their brains from addiction, and be better people in recovery. Is God calling me to endure this for 6 to 12 months to try to save our marriage? Is that even possible?

*God, I will try to hold out for You to do Your work in him. Thank You for deleting my text so that we were able to have this breakthrough conversation. I know that the angels in heaven rejoice more over one sinner who is saved than 99 righteous people. I pray that You help Andy turn from his wicked ways and that the angels in heaven throw a spectacular party. I pray that You find a way to bless this broken, messy, hurtful marriage, even now. In Jesus' name, Amen.*

# Chapter 19

## But, Even Now

33 A.D.

Mary and Martha did not leave their brother's side. They took turns staying awake with him through the night and dipping a rag into some water to cool his body. It was to no avail. Regardless of daily visits from the town physician and trials of different medications, he had grown continually worse. Now, his throat and the areas around the flea bites were swollen and blistered. It had been two full days since he had last awoken, and his sisters were beginning to panic.

They had sent for Jesse, one of their father's good friends in Jerusalem, who was known to be the best doctor in all of Judea. He came right away, but despite his best efforts, he could tell that Lazarus was fading quickly.

He finally walked out to the front room and asked their visitors to please give them some privacy. He wanted to speak to Mary and Martha privately, so he sat them down at the kitchen table. "I have known the three of you since you were born. In fact, I even visited with your parents in Jerusalem at the dedication of Lazarus. It brings me great sorrow to tell you that I have seen this type of thing before. My best guess is that your brother has contracted a plague caused by the bites of infected fleas. The swelling in his body tells me that it has already advanced beyond anything I can do to help. I'm afraid it won't be long now."

Mary jumped from her chair so quickly that it fell backward and crashed to the floor. She ran to her brother's room and sank down beside his bed, burying her face in his chest. She could hear the beat of his heart and the sounds of his breath. What Jesse said couldn't possibly be true! They can't lose their baby brother. Had they made a mistake in encouraging him to make another trip to Jerusalem? They were supporting his dream, but she still felt the guilt of a protective mother creeping in. Could they have done anything to prevent this from happening? Each question brought a wave of new despair.

The sound of her sister's grief in her ears was too familiar. It brought Martha right back to the heart-wrenching pain each of them felt over the death of their parents. It seemed like only yesterday when the same sorrowful cries drifted through the air of their home. Only that time, she heard both Mary and Lazarus weeping. Now Lazarus was silent. She wasn't sure which way was better, but she knew it was more than she could bear. Martha sat in silence, staring with blank eyes back at their father's friend, knowing his heart must hurt as well. Her thoughts were interrupted when he reached across the table and took her hand. "Martha, I'm sorry."

As it had done many times before, her gaze caught the words her mother had written above their door. *The God who sees*. Even now, in this time of great hardship, Martha took comfort in the fact that their mother seemed to be speaking the love of God directly to her heart. If God really saw them, He would know Lazarus was in desperate need. She knew what she had to do. "Jesse, do you have any messengers that work for you who would be able to deliver a message as quickly as possible?"

"I have several. Are you in need of one?"

"Yes, please send him to find Jesus, the Nazarene. He is probably somewhere in Judea. Tell him that Martha and

Mary are sending for him, and that the one he loves is sick. Tell him it is urgent. He will come."

Jesse grunted without meaning to and shook his head. He knew his friends were desperate, but out of respect for their father, he couldn't let them make fools of themselves. "Martha, you can't be serious! I don't mean to sound arrogant, but I am the best physician in all of Judea. I know there have been rumors of Jesus healing the sick, but do you really think he will be able to do what medicine and I cannot?"

Martha looked him straight in the eye and said assuredly, "I know he can."

In any other situation, Jesse would have continued to prove his point, but his heart was moved with pity for her. "I will have my messenger leave tonight. Your message should get to Jesus in two days' time. I cannot guarantee anything faster, as it may take that long to find him." He didn't have the heart to tell her that her brother would likely already be dead. He would not make it long enough for the messenger to get to Jesus, and then for Jesus to make it all the way back to Bethany. His best guess was that Lazarus would be gone before the Sabbath. For the first time in his career, he was sad to say that his hunch was correct.

Lazarus passed quietly in his sleep two days later.

By that time, many had gathered at their home. Friends had gathered to give the sisters comfort and support, took care of all the chores, and had enough food prepared for anyone who entered their home. Despite the abundance of food, neither of the girls had much of an appetite.

During the days Lazarus was sick, Mary had not left his side. She continued to apply wet cloths and to fan him to try and bring his temperature down. He had remained unconscious and unable to drink the medication that was needed. Martha had paced from the bedroom to the doorway, watching for Jesus. Everyone who knew of their friendship was sure he would come rushing down the street at any time, so they gathered around the outside of the house. They had heard of Jesus healing the sick and performing miracles, so they were waiting to see one for themselves.

When Lazarus took his last breath before Jesus got back to them, Mary and Martha tore their clothing, and their sobs echoed through the windows. Those standing outside gathered together and began to recite the *Kaddish*, the mourner's prayer. "Exalted and hallowed be God's great name in the world which God created, according to plan. May God's majesty be revealed in the days of our lifetime and the life of all Israel…"

It didn't take long for the *chevra* to show up and help prepare the body for burial. The body of Lazarus was cleaned, anointed with oils, and wrapped in burial cloths, which consisted of a plain linen shroud, and a *tallit*, or prayer shawl. They respectfully laid him on the floor, lighting candles all around him. The *shomrim* had taken his post to guard Lazarus until burial, so the body would never be left alone.

Mary and Martha never expected to have to mourn the loss of their beloved little brother, but there was no question where they would have him buried. They would take him to the family tomb where their parents were already laid to rest. Down the steps and through the *antechamber*, there was another *arcosolia*, or arched cell, used for entombment. To the right of that was an empty tomb. That would be their brother's resting place.

It wasn't until the day of Lazarus' burial that Caleb, Jesse's messenger, finally arrived in Bethany to seek out the home of Mary and Martha. He had orders to confirm that the sisters' request had reached Jesus, as promised. As he looked for their house, he knew it was a good possibility that Jesus was already there. With other business to take care of between the time he spoke with Jesus and when he could make his way back to Bethany, Jesus had plenty of time to get there ahead of him. Aside from keeping up his good reputation, Caleb also had selfish intentions in his hopes that Jesus arrived ahead of him. Stories of miraculous healings were proclaimed in every town through which he traveled on business. If the claims were true, he wanted to see a miracle for himself..

As he approached what he thought was the house, he noticed people in mourning clothes and began to fill in the missing pieces. Either he or Jesus had been too late to make a difference. In light of this, Caleb wished he could simply walk away unnoticed. It was obvious that his mission did not change the outcome for their sick brother in the way the sisters had hoped. Even more, he did not want anyone to ask how Jesus had replied upon the delivery of Martha's urgent request. Now, it would feel like a slap in the face.

Still, Jesse had given him very specific instructions, and he had a reputation to uphold. He walked to the front door and introduced himself to those standing there but was hesitant and a little embarrassed to tell them of the conversation he had with the Nazarene.

He approached a woman standing outside the door. "*Shalom*. I am Caleb, the messenger of Jesse. Is this the home of Mary and Martha?"

Adinah, thankful that her visiting mother had volunteered to watch the children, was standing near and overheard his greeting. She quickly rushed over to speak with him. "*Shalom*, Caleb. Yes, this is their home. Can I help you?"

Normally, he would ask the sisters to come out so he could tell them directly, but in this circumstance he decided against it. "I've come to tell Mary and Martha that their message has been delivered to Jesus."

"Thank you for your services," replied Adinah, with resentment in her eyes. "As you can see, it is too late. Lazarus has already died."

"My deepest sympathy. After I delivered the message to Jesus, I had another message to deliver that was a day's walk in the other direction. I was hoping he would have been here ahead of me." He didn't want his reputation for being a reliable messenger to be tarnished in front of such a large crowd. He followed with, "The message to Jesus was delivered two days upon Jesse's instructions."

Adinah looked confused. Something didn't sound right. "If you don't mind my asking, what did Jesus say when you told him Lazarus was sick?"

Caleb cleared his throat and looked around at everyone waiting for his response. He looked at the ground when he answered, "Jesus said his sickness would not end in death, and that it is for God's glory."

"Did he know the urgency?" she asked. Perhaps something was lost in translation.

"Yes. I heard him tell those around him that they still had work to complete there before they returned to Judea, so I was sure to tell him the seriousness of Lazarus' illness."

Adinah's eyes glazed over with anger. She turned away and then turned back to anyone who was listening. "So, he performs miracles for strangers, but for those he loves, he chooses to wait? He left his friend to suffer and die? A true Messiah would not do this." Part of her was just saying out loud what she knew everyone there was thinking. But most of her words were spoken out of bitterness. Her family life was crumbling around her. All of this was just too much for her heart to take.

Mary and Martha were inconsolable for three solid days after Lazarus was placed in the tomb. They were surrounded by an outpouring of love from friends and were so appreciative of their love and support. Yet, they could not imagine why Jesus had not rushed to his side. He was like family to them. They would continue the *Kaddish* prayer for their beloved brother, but eventually came to terms with the fact that he was gone.

Finally, they got word that Jesus was not far from

Bethany. What would they even say to him now? Was it sinful to be angry with the Messiah, even if he was your friend? If Jesus had simply been too far away to make the journey, that was one thing, but that wasn't the case. He could have been here days ago and chose not to come. Even if Jesus would have come a day earlier, it could have made a difference. Lazarus had already been in the tomb for four days. Four! By this time, it was commonly believed that his soul had left his body. Now it was too late.

When Martha heard that he was coming, she urged her sister to walk with her to meet him on the road. She was unsure of how she would react when she met him, but felt the urge to go, nonetheless. Of course, Mary wanted to see Jesus, but she was not yet ready to be out of the house. The pain was still too great. People would want to stop her and give their condolences, and she was in no mood for socializing. Martha wouldn't be leaving herself for anybody else but Jesus. She kissed Mary gently on top of the head, understanding her sister's need for solitude. "I'll be back soon."

Martha hurried down the road until she could see Jesus coming from the other direction. Her feet felt heavy. Sorrow seemed to weigh her down. She wanted to cry out. *Why?* But even from a distance, when their eyes met, she could see that Jesus' heart was broken, too. With each step toward him, her heart softened, and her faith grew. Just being in his presence brought a wave a peace that she had never felt before. Her pace quickened to a run, and when she reached him, he swept her up in a warm embrace. Neither of them could hold back their tears. In the arms of her friend, Martha felt she finally had permission to weep in the way she deserved. She had been trying to be strong for her sister. Without their parents, she was the head of the household, the one who was supposed to have all the answers. Without being asked, she had become the glue that held their family and their faith together. But not now. Not in the arms of Jesus. She didn't have to put up fronts for him. Even in her anger and confusion, he was her strength.

She wept so deeply that Jesus could feel her body shake upon the release of emotions that had been pent up for so long. She loved Jesus and was in no place to question him, but she still didn't understand why he had not come when he got word from the messenger.

Martha broke the silence with words that came as more of a statement of belief than of accusation. "Lord, if you had been here, my brother would not have died." She could see his eyes welling up with tears, as his bottom lip rolled up and quivered with emotion. She continued. "But I know that *even now*, God will give you whatever you ask."

Jesus' heart overflowed with compassion. That one statement revealed the immensity of Martha's faith, even on the fourth day.

Awaiting his response, Martha saw a glimpse of eagerness in his eyes that didn't seem to fit the situation.

"Martha," Jesus said to her with complete sincerity, "your brother will rise again."

"I know he will," Martha answered. "He will rise again in the resurrection on the last day."

Jesus shook his head and clarified, "I am the resurrection and the life. The one who believes in me will live, even though they die. And whoever lives by believing in me will never die." He paused and looked into her eyes so deeply that she felt he could see into her very soul. "Martha," he asked, "do you believe this?"

She replied, "Yes, Lord. I believe that you are the Messiah, the Son of God, who is to come into the world."

Jesus smiled. This time, his eyes revealed tears of joy. "Go. Get Mary and bring her here with you."

"Yes, of course! I will bring her now." With that, Martha ran back to the house where her sister was sitting in the shadows. She spoke with a quiet urgency. "The Teacher is here and is asking for you."

Mary lifted her head from her knees. "He asked for me specifically? Is he upset that I didn't come with you to meet him on the road?"

"No," replied Martha, "but he wants you to come now." Mary got up without further hesitation and the two rushed out the door, with no explanation to the friends who had been there comforting them. The friends followed behind to see what was going on that would cause them to leave in such a hurry. Martha led her sister back to the place just outside the village where Jesus was waiting.

Mary was so moved with emotion at the sight of Jesus that she ran to him and fell at his feet, weeping. She was angry, but didn't want to be. She couldn't tell if it was truly the feelings of her heart or if it was her grief talking. She remained at his feet but raised her eyes to him. "Jesus, we sent for you. Why didn't you come sooner? If you had only been here, Lazarus would not have died."

He said nothing in response but helped Mary to her feet and wrapped her in his arms. As he held her, he noticed the moist eyes in the large crowd around them and realized how beloved Lazarus was. He was profoundly moved by how much loss Mary and Martha had suffered in such a short time. He knew his delayed appearance caused them more pain, but he couldn't tell them why he had purposely waited until after Lazarus had died. They wouldn't understand. But soon, they would see that it was an act of extraordinary love. The momentary heartache would bring them everlasting joy.

He drew back after a moment and tenderly released Mary from his embrace. He turned and asked Martha, "Where have you laid him?"

"Come and see, Lord," she replied.

As they walked down the lonely road to the tomb, Jesus wept.

By now, the crowd had grown. Not only were they

followed by the friends mourning with them but also with others who had heard of Jesus and wanted a chance to see him for themselves. Some were hoping they would find that he was, indeed, the true Messiah. Others, like Yokim, were only there to find something to hold against him.

Basharel and Adinah followed close to Mary and Martha. Basharel leaned over and whispered to Adinah, "Jesus has been weeping over Lazarus as we walk. See how he loved him!"

Adinah wanted to feel differently but was still bitter. She answered, "Yes, it appears so, but Jesus could have left as soon as he got word Lazarus was sick. If he loved him, why would he delay? He has performed many miracles, with many witnesses. He has even opened the eyes of a blind man. Could he not have kept Lazarus from dying?"

Basharel had the same initial reaction, but after seeing the way they had just interacted on the road, she felt differently. It was very evident that Jesus loved Lazarus and his sisters like family.

When they got to the tomb, Jesus paused, and a hush came over the crowd.

Martha pointed and spoke softly. "It's just down that stairway." Jesus nodded and motioned for them to follow him down the steps that led to the burial room carved in stone. Once they were standing in the *antechamber*, a small room that opened up to a larger one, Martha pointed to the *arcosolia*, the arched recess of the wall. There was the tomb where her beloved Lazarus had been buried days before. Martha's voice caught as she spoke. She still couldn't believe this was real. She stretched out her hand to the place where Lazarus lay. "It is there," she said to Jesus.

Instead of walking towards the tomb, Jesus stood in place and lifted his hands and eyes to heaven. For a long, quiet moment, his lips moved quietly as he spoke to his Father. It wasn't for anyone else to hear. It was a conversation between a father and a son. Mary noticed that his prayer did not end when he quit speaking. He kept his hands and eyes raised in silence, listening. She was sure he was hearing the voice of God speaking to him, and it was amazing to watch. Chills ran down Mary's spine.

After his prayer concluded, he motioned to the stone covering the tomb where Lazarus was laid to rest. He called over some of his disciples and said, "Take away the stone." Although a bit confused, the disciples had learned to obey anything Jesus commanded of them and immediately began to do as they were instructed. The crowd pressed in.

Watching what was unfolding, Martha was confused and a bit alarmed. She believed in Jesus wholeheartedly, but she thought they were merely coming here to pay their respects and pray. Why was he taking away the stone? Perhaps Jesus didn't realize how long it had been. She knew she was in no position to correct him, especially in front of such a large crow but felt she should say something.

She leaned in gently and with respect. She whispered, hoping only Jesus would hear. "But Lord, he has been here for four days. By this time, there is a bad odor."

Jesus looked at her in a way that calmed all her fears. "Martha," he said, "you told me on the road a few moments ago that *even now*, God would give me what I ask. Did I not tell you that if you believe, you will see the glory of God?"

"Yes, my Lord. I believe," she replied. And she did believe with her entire being.

Jesus did not answer her but looked up to the heavens. He lifted his arms and spoke for everyone to hear this time. "Father, I thank you that you have heard me. I know that you always hear me, but I say this for the benefit of the people standing here, that they may believe that you sent me."

The *antechamber* and stairs were full of watchers, and there were more waiting outside. As the men slowly pushed the vast stone to the side, Martha's warning came to fruition.

Everyone near the *arcosolia* began to cover their faces with their arms as the stench filled the air. All were silent as Jesus called out in a loud voice, "Lazarus, come out!"

The voice of Jesus sounded like thunder as it bounced around the stone walls before the echo faded away. Mary and Martha's eyes were huge, in bewilderment. Did he just tell Lazarus to come out? They clung to one another in disbelief, as the crowd looked on with a bit of fear intermingled with expectation.

Adinah recalled the words from the messenger. "Lazarus' sickness would not end in death." Is this what Jesus meant? Was this really happening?

You could hear a pin drop. All eyes were on the tomb. Martha thought she heard a rustle from somewhere in the darkness. Was she just imagining it? The people who had gathered were standing on toes and shifting their heads to get a closer look. Mary thought she saw something flicker in the light. Surely, her imagination was getting the better of her, because she thought she saw white linen cloths moving inside the tomb. Then, right before their eyes, Lazarus slowly stood before them! His hands and feet were still bound. The prayer shawl had fallen from his face, but his body was still wrapped in the burial linens. He was shuffling his feet, trying to walk towards them. Martha felt faint. Was Lazarus really alive after being four days dead? Everyone gasped in awe at the miracle they just witnessed.

The disciples who had removed the stone were standing closest to Lazarus. They slowly lowered the *tunic* sleeves from their faces; jaws dropped in amazement. As many times as they had witnessed the miraculous works of Jesus, it never ceased to stun them. Every work he did was more astonishing than the last, and it was baffling to them how everything he did fit together perfectly to fulfill God's larger purpose. Jesus instructed them once again. "Take off his grave clothes and let him go."

There were more gasps. Was this allowed? Touching a dead body would make one unclean. Yet Lazarus was no longer dead. There was no rule about touching a resurrected body! Jesus truly did change everything. Obediently, the men did as they were commanded and quickly removed the burial linens.

Lazarus slowly opened his eyes to a crowded room. Blinking several times, he struggled to get his eyes adjusted to the light. Through the haze before him, he stood for a moment, trying to put together what exactly he was looking at. His vision was blurry, and it took a minute for everything to come into focus. No one said a word. They watched in wonder as Lazarus gradually realized where they were standing, and his eyebrows wrinkled in confusion. Slowly looking around the room, he realized that they were in the burial tombs, but he had no idea why. He didn't remember anyone dying that he was close to. He saw familiar faces but wasn't sure why they were all looking at him. Why was no one speaking? He glanced behind him at the empty tomb, and then at the burial cloths around his feet, and he suddenly realized that he was not properly clothed. When he looked up and saw Jesus smiling at him, his mouth dropped open in disbelief as he put it all together. They were all there for him! He vaguely remembered feeling ill.

Martha covered her opened mouth with her hand, her chest heaving in joyous sobs, unable to process what she just saw. Tears ran down Mary's face, and she took a step to run to her brother, but hesitated, unsure of what to do.

Jesus smiled with tears of joy this time, as he watched the reaction of his treasured friends. A joyful celebration broke out among the crowd. Word of what just happened spread up the stairs and poured out to the gathering of people waiting outside. Yokim was among those trying to push their way in to see for themselves if what they heard was true. He wouldn't believe it until he saw it with his own eyes! And if he did, what then? Was there truth to what Chanoch and others had discussed?

Lazarus, now void of fever and swelling, was still trying to process what he thought had just happened. He scanned the room, putting names and faces together of those who stood gazing at him in anticipation. Then, his eyes locked with those of Jesus, and everyone else seemed to fade into the background. Captivated by the jovial tears on the beloved face of Jesus smiling back at him, Lazarus exclaimed, "You are the true Messiah!" The crowd erupted in jubilation once again, as Lazarus danced his way out of the burial cloths that had fallen around his feet. He and Jesus walked toward one another and laughed through joyful tears as they embraced in celebration.

Mary and Martha joined the embrace with Jesus and their brother as the crowd looked on. Martha stepped back and raised her hands and eyes to heaven. She whispered, "Thank you, Lord, for keeping your promise!"

Basharel and Adinah grabbed one another's arms and danced in delight. They never thought they would witness something so miraculous! Basharel was elated that so many others were there to witness that Jesus was who he said he was. It would be a story that would be told for generations, and she was part of it! She looked over at Adinah, whose expression suddenly changed from joyful to contemplative. Basharel knew her friend must be searching her conflicted heart to sort out her feelings about Jesus. Just moments before, Adinah had been angry with Jesus. But now? Basharel grew very serious as she gently took both of Adinah's hands. Facing her friend, she said firmly, "Do not stumble in your faith, Adinah. We shall both learn from this. The world told us that it was hopeless. But Martha's faith in Jesus was stronger than the ties that bound her brother's arms and feet. Even now, after being four days dead! If God can do that for her family, imagine what he can do for yours."

Adinah kissed Basharel's hand and leaned her head to rest on her shoulder. She thought of how she had been afraid to approach Basharel to be a nursemaid for her babies. Even though it was a desperate situation, would she have been brave enough to ask without the urging of Mary and Martha? She had been so wrong about Basharel's response to their inquiry. Instead of being accusing and full of judgment, she had rescued their entire family with her loving-kindness and understanding. Adinah was overwhelmed with the blessing of their friendship.

Adinah knew Basharel was right. Only a genuine friend would tell her words she needed to hear, even if they weren't necessarily the words she wanted to hear. Not only had her faith faltered when she was angry and doubted Jesus, but her heart had been growing more resentful toward her husband with each passing day. Even when she was physically cuddling and taking care of the babies, her mind wasn't there. She was contemplating how to make Levik hurt as much as she did, but feared her actions could trigger a divorce. It was not worth the risk of losing her babies. Nothing good could come of this behavior. If the roots of her heart remained this full of anger, it would choke out any love that tried to grow. She prayed at that very moment that she would forgive Levik and that their love for one another would be strengthened and renewed as they worked past his indiscretion. Yes, it would take a while for any of that to take hold, but it was a start. She was determined to do everything in her power to try. Immediately, she felt an indescribable peace.

# Chapter 20

## Trista's Journal Entry
## Car Ride

January 18, 2018

As I lay in bed, thinking about this crazy life I am living, I am loving my husband contemplating divorce at the same time…

DID I REALLY JUST WRITE THAT I LOVED HIM STILL? AFTER ALL THIS? HOW CAN THIS BE?!

Well, anyhoo, I realized that I had not even laid eyes on him since the oncologist appointment. I needed to see his face and confront him. I walked back to the barn using my cell phone light to see, and I found a place to sit down across from him. He sat up eventually, confused, as I had just woke him up. All I could get out was, "What in the **** were you thinking?"

He just looked at me and shook his head and said, "I don't know, I don't know…."

He proceeded to tell me the tip of the iceberg about what he was learning through his couple of therapy sessions and the workbook he had been assigned. I learned that he had exposure to pornographic material at a very early age. I did not know this previously, or at least I didn't remember him telling me. As hard as it was for him to admit it, his parents were neglectful, and his mom would probably be considered an emotionally abusive alcoholic. He learned at an early age not to ask for what he wanted or needed and to just take care of himself. Like when he ran out of shampoo, he just used bar soap on his hair, which was a total mess. Or, like when he needed comfort and he did not want to risk his mom's unpredictable demeanor, he found other ways to comfort himself with the newfound pornographic material in his garage. Then came the shame because he felt he was doing something he shouldn't be doing. Shame turned to resentment because his mother didn't know that he needed comfort and attention (and shampoo), and she should.

"Keep it a secret from everyone. You don't need anything from them. You can just take care of yourself," the devil whispered. And he obeyed.

Fast forward to our marriage. "Keeping secrets from the ones you love most won't hurt anybody. Porn is an easy way to get comfort, and I don't need to depend on anyone else to get it. Asking for what I want may get messy, and I may get a bad reaction from my loved one, so this is easier for everyone. My loved one should know what I need anyway, and I deserve this. It's their fault, and I resent them for not knowing that I need this or that." I had no inkling that I was walking into a disaster on the day of my wedding....

A couple of days after our first barn meeting, I got up early, as I was only sleeping a couple of hours a night. I took some cappuccinos out to the area he had set up to sleep in between the old, broken-down lawn mower and an ancient chicken coop. The old futon I was desperate to get rid of was coming in pretty handy for him now. The early morning was calm, and the kids were still sleeping. We talked more, we hugged, we cuddled, and we cried. He said he was committed to his recovery because the thought of hurting me one more time killed him. I told him he could come back home that night after he got off of work. The only thing I could promise was that I would read the book and try to give God and him some time to work a miracle. And having the same marriage, except him being faithful, was not going to be enough. I wanted to have a joyful, committed relationship built on trust. He promised to work to earn that trust back.

The next weeks were insane. He had a renewed love for me because he realized that his understanding of our marriage was full of thinking errors. Almost all the times he could think of that he got mad at me, I was actually trying to get us to be closer. He could never see that, though, because of all his baggage. And no one had ever known the whole true him and loved him. That was liberating for him.

I felt closer to him than I ever had. This was the first time in our relationship where there were no secrets. We couldn't wait to get the kids to bed so that we could just lie in bed and look into each other's eyes and kiss. For hours. Neither of us had ever experienced anything like this before.

Then I would wake up at about 3:30 in the morning in a trance. I would just lay there, inconsolable, and cry. I would just keep on repeating, "How could you do this to me?" This would go on for hours each morning, and he would hold me and say he is so sorry and attempt to comfort me. Although this was a wonderful time in some ways, it was also extremely painful. So many things triggered my feelings of shock and betrayal and anger all over again.

One night, when I came into the bedroom, he was texting Silly Lilly about her ice hockey game, and he put his phone down just as I entered. Seeing him do this brought back all the times that I saw him on his phone and trusted that he was doing something mundane, but sometimes he was texting his girlfriends about his schedule and when he could see them, and deleting said messages. Sometimes he was watching porn. I took the phone from him and threw it as hard as I could toward the wall. The pain of seeing him with the phone was so maddening.

One morning, he had brought me coffee after we got

the kids to school. We started talking about something that brought the pain back to me. All I remember is feeling intense heat go straight to my face and saying, "You better get out of here before I start throwing things." I flung my coffee at him and then launched the mug across the room as he was walking out the door to get his things for work. It hit the table and busted into a thousand pieces. I couldn't even deal with picking it up for hours. Looking at it reminded me of how my life felt, shattered…and it was never going to be the same no matter what I did, just like the mug. This isn't me! I need help to handle the rage that is inside of me because I do not want to feel this way. I have gone to God in prayer and asked for his forgiveness and his help. I don't want to behave this way.

Another night, the kids had gone to bed. The plan was for us to light a candle and sit down in our bedroom to work on our workbooks, our usual routine at this point. He was doing activities in his twelve-step workbook, and I was about 4 chapters deep into a workbook to help partners of sex addicts heal from their trauma. He took a shower beforehand. While he was in the shower, I was taken back to all the nights he had taken showers before going to work the night shift. I frequently teased him, saying, "Who are you taking a shower for? Do you have a crush on someone at work?" It hit me all at once that he could have possibly been taking showers to get ready for a meeting with another woman. I had been flirting with him and kissing him after he got out of the shower for all these years, and he could have been thinking about a future rendezvous with someone else. The pain was almost too much to bear. I felt like such an idiot. He got out of the shower, and it was like I was in a trance. I just sat there looking across the room and saying, "You really were getting ready for someone else. I can't believe it. How could you do this to me?"

This crazy in love feeling has since faded for me. Somewhere between Christmas Eve when he hurt my feelings by not sitting by me or holding my hand at church, and New Year's Eve when he hurt my feelings by just assuming I was going to spend the evening with him and taking me for granted, I literally "lost that loving feeling." I've been slighted for so long by him, it's hard to take anymore. I know they say love is a choice and not a feeling, but I sure do long for the feeling again. It just makes life happier, and I miss that.

Andy has made recovery a top priority, and I have been able to support him in that for the most part (when I'm not hurling mugs across the room). He sees his therapist and has joined a support group for people who struggle with sex addiction. He reads marriage books and does Bible devotionals on his own, things he has never done before. Amazingly, I am generally not angry with him anymore because I know it was not about me. He had this problem way before he ever met me. I am sad that I am no longer in love with him and holding out that God will resurrect my love for him.

****

February 14, 2018

"You should write a book."

I've had one of those lives where friends have said many times, "You should write a book." I usually just laughed it off, knowing that I found myself in many dramatic situations that would make for good reading, but I didn't really see why anyone would want to read a book about me and my problems.

Well, God has now told me it is time to write that book. A couple of months after D-Day, I sat down to do my Bible study homework. I have been doing Bible study with the same group of women for 19 years and have never done the wrong homework, but I did that morning. It was actually sixty pages off. I know now it was no mistake. The Word has never spoken to me like this before. God wanted me to hear the words of Martha, where I had "mistakenly" turned in John 11:22. "But I know that even now God will give you whatever you ask." (NIV) Her brother, Lazarus, had been dead for four days. He was buried and decomposing, and according to popular Jewish belief at that time, the soul had already left the body. How could Martha still have faith that Jesus could and would redeem their situation? Nobody else did! Her faith astounded me and permeated me. I was reading the story with fresh eyes.

Michelle and I were meeting later that day for a little snowshoeing. We were driving separately. During that drive, the idea came to me that I was to write a book about Martha's faith during her trial, and I should reframe my trials with that faith. By the time I got to the trail, God had already set up how I was to lay out the book, what the title was going to be, and written the chapters in my head. I was so excited to tell Michelle the minute we got out of our cars for the hike.

Little did I know that she had been praying out loud in her car for me during that 45-minute drive that God would reveal His plan for my life. We agreed that it was God's plan that I write this book. Now. Right in the middle of my mess. I have learned that having faith when everything is going well feels very different from having faith amid a seemingly unredeemable situation. After all, the situation with Lazarus probably seemed impossible, too. For everyone else. But not for Martha. Her faith was amazing!

Martha is my hero! To have the faith to KNOW that EVEN NOW, God would resurrect Lazarus when asked by Jesus, after four days!! I am holding out that God will do what I ask him to do in Jesus' name.... Let me fall back in love with my husband. Let us ride those donkeys in Yosemite with our family, on the trip we never got to plan. Let there be nothing but love and acceptance between us one day. I want to be crazy in love with each other, and faithful 'til death do us part.'

*Dear God, You are amazing! I truly love You from the bottom of my heart and can see that You have been with me through the trials of my life. I see where You have made bad things in my life actually work for good for me later. How do You do this?? You are amazing and faithful. You are a good, good Father! I come to You on this day in prayer. I ask that you resurrect my love for my husband in this impossible situation, just like You did for Lazarus, and I will fall madly and deeply back in love with him. You have done so many amazing things that I have been able to witness. You brought us amazing children, even though I was unable to have my own. You allowed me to hear Your loving voice when I was in need of comfort. You helped Andy turn from his wicked ways and find his peace in YOU! I come to You with the faith of Martha knowing You would help her brother. I ask in Jesus' name, that even now, You will resurrect my love and bless our marriage and our family. And, God, I will obey You. It is very clear that Your will is for me to write a book entitled (But) Even Now, and it is in the works. Anything to shine a light on Martha's faith in Jesus and possibly point other women to You who've gone through similar struggles! I will get to work on it right away, Father! In Jesus' name, Amen.*

# Chapter 21

## The Interrogation

33 A.D.

THE SYNAGOGUE IN BETHANY

Yokim could hear the crowd before the synagogue came into view. As he approached he could see that a large number of people were already gathered. There was to be a public meeting after prayer and worship. Were they here for that? As he got closer, he could easily see that a good number of them were outsiders. They were not meant to be at the synagogue already, and he was irritated with their lack of respect. But how could he blame them for searching for answers? There had been a resurrection. In their town. Right in front of their eyes. Everyone, including Yokim, wanted to hear what the rabbis had to say about this.

He stood near the front of the synagogue, watching people pour in. The Jewish faithful had slowly become more comfortable in the democratically run local synagogues than the temple in Jerusalem. Attendees here could worship without being under the eye of the Pharisees and scribes who made sure their strict Mosaic laws and traditions were carried out perfectly. Yokim rather preferred their traditional way of doing things, but others did not. It was not uncommon to see gatherings here three times a day, but there were never this many in attendance at once.

As usual, the men had taken their seats of prominence while the women stood on the balcony and lined the outer walls. For the first time in as long as he could remember, the inner walls of the synagogue were filling to capacity, with many more listening outside. Slowly gazing around the room, Yokim noticed that several different groups of people were standing together, talking in hushed voices, and it made Yokim uncomfortable. Their whispers didn't seem to be out of respect or reverence, so what were their intentions?

It was increasingly obvious that there were many unclean people using his beloved synagogue as nothing but a meeting hall. Before Jesus muddled things up, the lines were clearly drawn. People were either Jew or Gentile. Clean or unclean. Holy or sinner. Now it was a jumbled mess.

Jesus had perplexed many of the Jewish faithful, and the leaders of the synagogue weren't sure how to handle it. In truth, many leaders were confused themselves. Why wouldn't they be? Jesus, a devout Jew, just raised Lazarus straight out of the grave before their very eyes! Jesus was credited with a multitude of miracles that he claimed to perform in the name of God but then inadvertently ignored many of the sacred Mosaic laws that Yokim and his family had always meticulously followed. How could Jesus claim to be doing God's work and fail to comply with laws of the Torah at the same time?

Yet, there was no denying that Jesus honored God in everything he did. His message about the kingdom of heaven, repentance, and loving others was welcoming and sincere. Everything Jesus had done was in humble servitude. He obeyed Roman law, yet there were many reports that he was directly obstinate to religious law. He didn't even require his followers to do the ceremonial handwashing! That was a minimal task. He healed on the Sabbath, which was strictly forbidden, yet his healing changed lives and brought many stray hearts to be faithful to God for the first time. Good came from everything he did, even when it was breaking from time-honored traditions. So, although allegations grew, so did the faithful. The problem was that now, many were following his lead. Yokim feared that once the faithful started disregarding the importance of keeping the sacred laws, many would fall away.

The rabbis had questioned Jesus about this, and even they seemed torn at his reply. Jesus told the faithful to respect their rabbis, but to follow God's law, not man's. What does that even mean? Yokim always subscribed to the belief that their 613 sacred laws *were* God's laws. If Jesus implied that the scribes, Pharisees, rabbis, priests, and elders who dedicated their lives to following this law were being self-righteous, it was cause for alarm. Rage, even!

It was unmistakable that this new way of worship that Jesus taught created an unwelcome gap. Houses were divided. Friendships were strained. And now, there was a clear line being drawn between believers and skeptics.

The most powerful, yet minority, group represented here tonight were Pharisees from Jerusalem, who held a high degree of religious authority. At their request, Roman officers could place a person under arrest, even just for suspicion. Who had told them about this meeting? They must have an agenda because they thought it beneath them to be among such commoners. They believed Jesus was an insurrectionist and wanted him gone. He had already gained hundreds, if not thousands, of new followers after the death of John the Baptist. Now, the raising of Lazarus ushered in many more. Rome feared that a riot in Jerusalem was looming because the crowds that followed Jesus outnumbered their guards. If followers believed Jesus was going to save them, they would follow any instruction he gave. The question hanging in the balance was, how was he going to accomplish that? Would Jesus rescue them from Roman oppression? He didn't appear to be a warrior. His message was that of love and peace, not of revenge. He healed the sick, helped the poor, gave sight to the blind, cast out demons, and now raised dead men. It was almost Passover, and that is when Jews from near and far gathered in Jerusalem. There would be masses of them coming to worship and to offer animal sacrifices for atonement from their sins. Is that when Jesus would make his move?

Whispers of this rumor spread like wildfire, so Yokim guessed someone had reported such to the Pharisees in Jerusalem. His curiosity got the better of him, and he walked over to Chanoch to see if he knew what was going on.

Leaning towards Chanoch's ear, he asked, "Are the Pharisees hoping to run this meeting, or spy on it?"

Chanoch looked concerned. "I'm told that an emergency meeting was called with the chief priests at the Sanhedrin. There, they ordered anyone who found out where Jesus was to report him so they could have him arrested. They want to question him."

Yokim reflected on this new information. "An emergency meeting? Called by whom?"

Chanoch had no answers. Until now, he had thought it was probably called by Yokim. He still suspected that it might be. Maybe he's just saying this so he'll let down his guard.

With only a shrug from Chanoch, Yokim continued, "Jesus has certainly caught their attention, but surely he has no discretion serious enough to demand his death. Are they hoping Jesus will show up tonight so they can have him arrested?"

The thought of that made Chanoch feel anxious. Surely Jesus wouldn't come all the way back for this, but he has popped in unexpectedly to small town synagogues before. "Perhaps. They imprisoned and killed John the baptizer. When his followers went to Jesus, that made Jesus an even bigger threat. I'm sure they are hoping Jesus will succumb to the same fate."

Shaking his head slowly, Yokim replied, "They spent an exorbitant amount of time mounting a growing list of allegations against him but can never find enough to sentence him. Their allegations are always shot down upon review at the higher level when they can't get enough witnesses to press formal charges. I'm sure they are out for blood here tonight. It gives me an extreme uneasiness as to how this meeting will proceed."

Yokim nodded his head toward a new group standing together on one side of the room. "Especially with this group here."

Chanoch glanced in the direction Yokim was pointing to see who he was referring to. Both men knew it was the very group the Pharisees loathed. It was the former followers of John the baptizer, who were regarded as radicals by the religious elite. Their unruly beards and dirty clothes made them easy to recognize. After the raising of Lazarus, this group was growing uncontrollably. They told everyone who would bother to listen all about what Jesus had done and declared him the Messiah. The Messiah! To them, the coming of Jesus brought a new sense of comfort and hope that had been foreign to them until now. It was a breath of fresh air, and they would follow any command he gave them.

The two men listened intently, trying to pick up on bits of conversations happening around them. Yokim caught Chanoch's gaze and nodded his head slightly in another direction. "And what of this group?"

Near them stood a group of Gentiles who claimed to be converted only because of the miracles of Jesus. Yokim could hear them exchanging stories with the former followers of John while they waited. The Gentiles were even worse. They lived in ignorance of the laws of Moses, so they had no idea how many of the laws Jesus was breaking. They were now very vocal about proclaiming what they had seen, and people were paying attention, especially the Pharisees. The Gentiles were bringing *their* kind of people around. Sinful women. Tax collectors. Gamblers and drunks. In any other circumstance, people such as these would never be allowed in the temple or a synagogue. Yet, here they were because Jesus welcomed them all.

Then, showing no respect whatsoever for the holy ground in which they stood, there were the unbelievers who were just there to see a show. Yokim could feel his throat tighten and his face grow hot.

From his observation, the only group missing were those who considered themselves too well-educated to buy into the nonsense. They held to the fact that when people live in generational oppression and despair, they will cling to any whisper of hope. The meek wanted Jesus to be their savior and Messiah, even if they really knew he wasn't. Stories were sure to be exaggerated to make it sound the way they wanted it to sound. People would talk. Rumors would spread like wildfire. They didn't need to take any position at all because the ignorant would do what they always do, and the problem would eventually take care of itself.

Yokim almost envied them. With all the different groups intermingled at the synagogue this evening, it was sure to be abrasive. He had enough confrontation facing him without dealing with this. Each group would be adamant about making their side heard. If they had foreseen any of this happening tonight, Yokim would have hired security.

He found it ironic that, despite all of their differences, they all had one thing in common. Nobody really knew what to make of Jesus.

If nothing else, they could all agree that Jesus was a man of significant influence. Messiah or not, if the word on the street was correct and Jesus did have plans to conquer Rome, he was a threat. His followers were growing every day.

All of this whirred around Yokim's mind as he sat

waiting for things to get started. He used to know exactly where people stood, but now he even wondered which side his friends and close acquaintances were taking. So many were leaning toward leaving their sacred tradition and following Jesus but had not yet made it publicly known for fear of being kicked out of the synagogue. Would tonight be the night they declared it?

Yokim kept thinking of the confrontation he had months before with Chanoch, Lazarus, and the others. In fact, he wrestled with it daily. If all this hype about Jesus was correct, how did a young man like Lazarus see it so long ago but he had not? His entire life had been about learning the Torah. He first studied under his father, who was an outstanding scholar, then under some of the best rabbis in the region. Now, as an elder, he prided himself in upholding the sacred law to the highest standard. Although he would never admit it out loud, he knew the scrolls had many prophecies that pointed to the things Jesus was doing. Yet, he could not bring himself to come alongside those calling a simple man from Nazareth the Messiah. Surely the prophets had someone bigger in mind!

It was true that Jesus was credited with many signs and wonders, and before now, Yokim would argue that it could be chalked up to coincidence. Some sort of magic or illusion. But he saw Lazarus die and knew he had been in the tomb for four days. He was there to see firsthand how Jesus called him out of the tomb and how Lazarus walked out in burial clothes. As educated and cultured as Yokim claimed to be, how could he deny that he had witnessed a miracle when the resurrected body of his young friend had walked among them four days after his death? Jesus could not have done that by his own authority, so it had to either come from God or Satan. Which was it? If the authority did, indeed, come from God, as Jesus claimed, it would make sense to believe that he was who he claimed to be. The Son of God. The Messiah. He was afraid to admit that he was probably not the only elder entertaining such thoughts.

Now, the ground in which he had firmly stood was not as solid as it once had been. Yet, however shaky it may seem, he would continue to stand his ground until he had solid proof. He was sure the Jesus-followers didn't truly understand the enormity of such a claim. They didn't even seem to mind that Jesus referred to himself as the Good Shepherd and called them sheep. Sheep! The most simple-minded animal known to man, and Jesus convinced them to take it as a compliment!

Also absent from the gathering were Lazarus and his sisters. They now had a constant stream of people standing outside of their home, waiting for a glimpse of the young man who had been brought back from the dead. Since the day he had walked out of the tomb, the crowds had been pressing in so badly that the siblings didn't dare leave their house. Friends had been taking turns bringing them water, going to the market for food, and guarding their open windows. The outer walls of their home had become a makeshift altar of sorts, where pilgrims would leave flowers outside as their way of showing honor to Jesus. Every time they opened their door, people began pushing in and shouting questions. Many yelled at them, asking to touch the robe of Lazarus, as if doing so would heal them the way Jesus healed so many. It worried them that followers seemed to substitute faith with superstition. Lazarus did nothing to deserve a second chance, and he definitely could heal no one. All the glory was for God, through Jesus.

Without asking for it, everyone knew Lazarus' name. He was uncomfortable with that attention, but it was a welcome relief to be able to spread the message he once told his friends in secret. Now it could be proclaimed from the rooftops! He loved being even the smallest part of a greater plan that would bring more and more people to believe that Jesus was the Son of God.

For that very reason, it was rumored that the chief priests were pushing to have Lazarus killed as well. They didn't want it proclaimed from the rooftops. As a matter of fact, they were determined to stop it from being proclaimed at all. They would use every scare tactic and torture method they had in order to quench that fire, even if they had to kill Lazarus themselves to do so. If the man who had supposedly been resurrected from the dead was back in the tomb where he belonged, there would be nothing for people to see.

Yokim's thoughts were pulled back to the room when Chanoch said, "Well, it's time for evening worship to begin. I'm not sure how to tone down this crowd."

Yokim straightened his clothes. "Let's just take our places as usual. Hopefully, they will notice and respect that we will not begin until we have given God proper honor."

As elected members of the board of elders, Chanoch and Yokim took their places, facing one another in the synagogue, on opposite sides of the room. The other rabbis and leaders had agreed ahead of time that they would conduct the spiritual gathering as usual until the last psalm was sung, then they would open the floor to a communal discussion concerning the recent events. Chanoch would do the honor of reading the scroll that had been chosen from the Torah many weeks before. To Yokim's surprise, the synagogue grew silent as Chanoch took his place at the front of the room. He cleared his throat.

"A reading from Isaiah. 'The Spirit of the Sovereign Lord is on me because the Lord has anointed me to proclaim good news to the poor. He has sent me to bind up the brokenhearted, to proclaim freedom for the captives and release from darkness for the prisoners, to proclaim the year of the Lord's favor and the day of vengeance of our God, to comfort all who mourn, and provide for those who grieve in Zion — to bestow on them a crown of beauty instead of ashes, the oil of joy instead of mourning, and a garment of praise instead of a spirit of despair. They will be called oaks of righteousness, a planting of the Lord for the display of his splendor.'"

Yokim had heard that passage read hundreds of times, yet it made him uneasy hearing it tonight. Why?

When the service had ended, the scrolls were carefully put away and a Pharisee, who Yokim did not recognize, stepped up to the podium. Did he show up on his own, or was he invited? The Pharisee spoke with a twinge of arrogance. "It seems we have much to discuss. It has come to our attention in Jerusalem that a resurrection has been said to take place in Bethany. I am here to investigate. I'll say from the beginning that we fail to believe that this man, Lazarus, actually died. If Jesus was a family friend to Lazarus and his sisters, surely, they would orchestrate a plan to promote him as 'the Son of God.' For this unusual situation, we are taking extreme measures to prove this is all a hoax. I will call several different people to the podium to testify publicly."

The crowd whispered among themselves, wondering if any of them would be called with no advance notice.

The Pharisee continued. "I will first call the *chevra*, the volunteers who supposedly prepared the body." The sarcasm in his voice made some of the visiting rabbis laugh.

"Then we will hear from the *shomrim*, who claimed to guard the body until burial. Keep in mind that if any untruths are told by any person here tonight, I will place them under arrest and escort them to Jerusalem for trial." The Pharisee had personally 'encouraged' the witnesses ahead of time to say what he wanted them to say. He was confident they would do as instructed, and imagined the recognition he would get when the credit went to him for discounting the credibility of Jesus. With that, two Roman guards stepped in from the shadows behind him. How had Yokim not seen them?

Completely out of character for Yokim, he sat in astonished silence. He watched one person after another stand to be questioned. All refused to budge from the fact that Lazarus had been four days dead when Jesus brought him back to life. Their words were stated as facts, not opinions. Each one of them had been first-hand witnesses to the resurrection and had seen it with their own eyes. Even more to the chagrin of the Pharisees, all of them claimed Jesus to be the Messiah.

By the end of the night, the Pharisees were enraged. Everything they had come to do had backfired, and they were publicly humiliated. Not only had they not intimidated their witnesses, but their case against Jesus seemed to crumble. The guards had systematically taken one witness at a time into custody. They would be escorted to Jerusalem where they would face trial. Yokim counted twenty in all. He was quite certain that if they didn't back-pedal during the next questioning in Jerusalem, they would be taken to Rome, where they would surely all be martyred.

Yokim watched with both astonishment and desolation of spirit. He always thought himself to have a rock solid faith, but his seemed to pale in comparison next to what he just witnessed. These people were so adamant that Jesus was the Messiah that they were willing to give their lives before they would deny him. For the first time in his life, Yokim questioned his own path. Was his faith strong enough that he would die for it, as many of those witnesses probably would? That was another question in which he had no answer. All he knew for sure was that it was extremely difficult to believe one way when you have been believing another way for so long.

He wept on his walk home.

# Chapter 22

## Trista's Journal Entry
## Disclosure

February 26, 2018

Safe people, disclosures, polygraphs, boundaries, triggers... things I didn't think about at all before this. Now, this is my life. Gaslighting, trauma, betrayal, trust, forgiveness.... If you would have told me these terms would be a part of my regular vocabulary 5 months ago, I would have laughed and thought you were crazy. Now, they are what make up my thoughts, prayers, private conversations, group conversations, reading material, journaling activities, and therapy session topics....

I've now become a member of the secret club no one ever imagines they will join. Some call it "partners of sex addicts," and others call it "spouses of sexaholics" or "betrayed partners." No matter what you call it, I still can't believe I'm in it. Like I'm still in serious shock when I walk into the church where my group meets or log into my online support group or talk about what I've been through to someone. It seems like I'm playing a part in a movie and it's not really me at times. It can't really be me.

But yet it is, and the time has come for me to decide whether I want Andy to do his full disclosure. Telling all his secrets. Answering any questions I've prepared. Hooked up to a polygraph by a polygraph examiner I have to hire. Who

I have to pay. In a joint session with both of our therapists. Who I also have to pay. No, Diary, I'm not making this stuff up. I couldn't make this stuff up if I tried. This is the suggested plan our therapists have come up with so that I can know that I have gotten the full truth about Andy's betrayals. So that I know what I am forgiving him for if I choose to do so.

I would have loved to be able to do this back near D-Day, what the people in my new club call the "day of discovery." The months I wasted cross-referencing my calendar and his calendar and texts and call logs…but that period is over, and I feel satisfied that I know enough of the details. Do I really want to dredge these things back up and pull off scabs that have just begun to heal?

As soon as I could, I scheduled a double session with the therapist recommended by Andy's therapist. She supposedly has much experience in helping partners heal from betrayal. I went in hungry for guidance and support, and I came home with a bunch of book recommendations and information about this disclosure process. Yes, I wanted to know the truth and the whole truth! But, no, they recommend waiting at least six months so that the addict has some time to learn about the addiction and heal and prepare. Great for the addict… not so great for the spouse who desperately needs answers about the double life their husband has been living.

So, it's been close enough to six months that the therapists have asked if I still want to move forward with the disclosure. I was so certain I wanted to do it, but now I'm wavering. I have read about disclosures that have just confirmed what was already known, and that confirmation helped the woman to move on from the evidence-gathering stage and have some peace moving forward. Surprisingly, I've also read a story somewhere when the woman found out she had only been told a fraction of the truth and was devastated to learn about further betrayals. I am guessing the husband thinks he can trick the polygraph in these cases?? It is a relief to know this process is an option going forward, that I can request one in the future if I start doubting his sobriety. It is huge to know that there is a way I can get the undoubted and full truth if I need it.

Since we started talking about this process, I have invested so much time in healing in other ways. I've read books about addiction, trauma, and healing broken marriages. I've completed workbooks where I've set up boundaries, identified triggers, and learned about the addiction model. I've joined a group at a local church, an online support community, and attend Christian peer counseling. Wow! When I write it all down, it makes me realize just how much I have worked to heal from this. And I have come a long way. I know that I am not finished with my journey of healing, whether or not I choose to stay in the marriage, but I don't think I can go backwards. I just don't even want to at this point.

I think I've decided against doing the full disclosure, but I do want to take the time to jot down some things I've learned thus far in this bizarre part of my life.

Notes to self....

Never forget or minimize the dangers of exposure to pornographic material! Especially now that God has entrusted Booker, Amelia, and Bella to me! I found that 11 is the average age a child first watches pornography in the U.S., and 94% of children will view pornography by the time they are 14. It is a factor in most divorces in our country. We just accept that it is part of our culture and minimize all the damage to the victims in its wake! This is your daily reminder to protect your children from this epidemic any way you can!!!!! We don't need to hand over any more tools to Satan than he already has to destroy the innocence of our children and break up our families! Wake up!

Be amazing! Be like the women I've met who have chosen to conquer their plights, not stew in them. Never forget Judeline, who welcomed me to my first support group and used the very circumstances Satan wanted to destroy her to bless others instead. Never forget the brave women who have shared their embarrassing, tragic stories in support groups, online communities, and in books so that I felt like I wasn't alone in my misery. It was as if they were walking right beside me in my healing. Remember that being vulnerable and sharing what you have walked through can be powerful in your own and others' healing.

Do not let your difficulty in life define you; let it refine you instead. Where have I heard this? It is so relevant for what I learned from poor Debbie in one of my group meetings. Debbie and her husband had divorced years before and she was still coming to a group for partners of sex addicts. I couldn't help but picture her stuck in the mud and not being able to get out, ruminating in the past and in her traumatic pain. What good stuff she must be missing out on, still focusing on her ex-husband's addiction years later! Do not get stuck like Debbie. I believe God has something better than that for both of our lives!

If at all possible, do not marry someone who travels for work. Too. Many. Stories. To. Count.

As good as it feels to talk with someone who has experienced similar pain, do not forget that God is always available to talk to, and He has "been there, done that" with pretty much any problem we face. Loss of a child, check. Betrayal by someone you love, check. I remember how it felt to finally talk to another person who was grieving the loss of her foster child. Someone else finally understands my pain, I thought. And then going to these groups and meeting other women who were also lied to and cheated on by their husbands for years. I thought at least I'm not alone in this…. But I never was alone! God has never left my side through these trials, and He is always available to talk to. Remember this!! Joshua 1:9 tells us: "Have I not commanded you? Be strong and courageous. Do not be afraid, do not be discouraged, for the Lord your God will be with you wherever you go."

****

February 28, 2018

Well, I was on fire with my homework assignment from God until there was an actual fire in part of our house and my laptop turned into a melted mess. Thank the Lord for Google Docs so that none of my progress was lost!

Recently, I began homeschooling the kids. Because of this, we are almost always home, but I guess it doesn't take long for fire to spread. Evidently, Bella decided (without permission) to enjoy a candle-lit bath in the morning and she left the candle burning. Then, the whole family went out for some fun in the snow. We made snow angels, built a snow dog, and had a couple of snowball fights, then we all headed in for some hot chocolate and our daily reading time.

As we trekked through the snow, from way back by the barn to the house and rounded the corner, we saw flames and smoke. By the time we called 911 and the volunteer firefighters arrived, our bedroom and bathroom were pretty much destroyed. When the fire marshal gave us the okay to enter and assess the damage, we were inundated with the overpowering smoky odor. Ash and sticky soot replaced or covered almost all items in the adjoining bedroom and bathroom. Three items were able to be salvaged, found under where the bed used to be: Booker's Pokemon book, a sweet letter from Amelia about how sorry she was for being mean to me one day, and my Bible.

*Dear God, when it rains, it really does pour! Thank You for protecting all of us, including our cherished pets, during the fire. What am I supposed to learn from this? I already know things do not matter, but I'm so grateful to You for sparing my Bible. One day, I hope to pass it down to a family member who would appreciate all the underlining and random notes in the margins. Giving You all the glory on this day! Hopefully, we can get all the insurance quotes and rebuilding decisions taken care of so I can fully focus on this book You want me to write, Father. I will share about the faith of Martha and open up about my life's struggles so that You may use it as you see fit. I will do my best to honor You as I write this book You have asked me to write. In Jesus' name, Amen.*

# Chapter 23

## The Celebration

33 A.D.

When it was time for the Jewish Passover, thousands journeyed to Jerusalem for the ceremonial cleansing. Those who wanted to kill Jesus knew it was his custom to return to Jerusalem each year, so they made plans to stand in the temple courts and look for him. They had many others keeping watch for him and offered rewards for anyone who would turn him in. The disciples of Jesus suspected this would be the case, so when Jesus announced that they would still go to Jerusalem for Passover, they tried to discourage him.

"Rabbi, these Jews were just trying to stone you, and you want to go back?"

Jesus replied, "Are there not twelve hours in a day? If one walks during the day, he does not stumble, because he walks in the light of this world. But if one walks at night, he stumbles, because the light is not in him."

The disciples weren't exactly sure what that meant, but they could tell his mind was made up. Jesus added, "I would like one of you to go ahead of me to Bethany to bring word to Mary, Martha, and Lazarus that I will visit them before Passover. I do not fear what man will do to me, but I want to be sure my visit won't make them fear their own safety. I have celebrated Passover this way every year since I was a young boy, and I don't intend to stop now."

As Jesus had done many times before, he once again assured his followers that he did not come to conquer the Roman kingdom, but the heavenly one. He did not come armed with swords but with forgiveness. He was not asking them to fight their enemies but to love them. His disciples could not understand why the chief priests and Pharisees didn't hear this message and back off, but Jesus knew. Soon, everyone would know. This is the cup he was meant to drink. The reason he came into the world was to die for it, as a living sacrifice, so that the sins of any believers could be forgiven. His death would give them everlasting life. He could not make them understand now, but soon he would be resurrected in a glory that was far beyond even what happened to Lazarus. Then they would know.

****

Home of Mary, Martha, and Lazarus

The siblings were so excited to receive the message from Jesus that they planned a dinner party in his honor. This would have been impossible just a few weeks before, but the crowds that had been gathering outside their home had slowly faded away. Word had spread about the arrests of so many during the synagogue meeting, and now many feared the same would happen to them if their intentions were on public display. Those arrested on the night of the meeting were still being held. Their fate lay in the hands of those wanting revenge, and it didn't look hopeful that they would be released anytime soon, if at all. Yet, they refused to change their story or their belief, thus solidifying their claims to those watching from the outside. So many would never risk their lives for a lie.

## *But*, Even Now

It was six days before Passover when Jesus arrived, and it was a bittersweet visit, full of tears, laughter, and storytelling of days gone by. Much like before, Lazarus reclined at the dinner table with Jesus. The guests took turns making lighthearted jokes about Lazarus stinking up the place. As usual, Martha served. Mary was at Jesus' feet.

It was customary to give visiting guests a means to wash their feet, but Jesus was no ordinary guest. With a full and humble heart, Mary took out an expensive pint of pure nard perfume. With tears of love and gratitude in her eyes, she poured it on Jesus' tired feet and wiped them with her hair. At first, nobody noticed, for she didn't do it to draw attention to herself. She simply wanted to honor Jesus the best way she knew how. However, when the house filled with the fragrant perfume, the attention of the guests turned to Mary.

As the room grew silent, some looked at her, confused. Jesus knew a few would question, but he also knew the heart and devotion of his sweet friend. He spoke to her as she continued to wash his feet but said it loud enough for everyone in the room to hear. "Ah, Mary. Such a humble act. You have become a loving servant, after all."

There was a chuckle in the room from those who remembered the rift between the sisters the last time Mary was sitting at his feet while Martha did the serving. Yet, there was one disciple who didn't seem to appreciate the humor. Perhaps the joke went over his head because he was a newer disciple and wasn't there the first time. The siblings had not met him before. His name was Judas Iscariot, and it was rumored that he was formerly a money-hungry thief. Nobody really thought anything of it because hearts were changed and sins were forgiven in the presence of Jesus. People were made new and given a fresh start. After all, he wasn't much different from Matthew, who had been a tax collector and got rich from over-taxing his own people. Yet, now Matthew was among the most loyal, faithful, and devoted.

Judas grew agitated, and it seemed to escalate when he recognized the fragrance Mary used to anoint Jesus' feet. He knew that perfume was one of the most expensive on the market. How could Jesus allow Mary to pour such an enormous amount of money onto his feet? What a waste! Ever since he had known Jesus, he heard it preached time and again how they were supposed to sell what they had to give to the poor. What a hypocrite! He could feel the anger move from his chest to the pit of his stomach. He sat in wait for the gaze of Jesus to catch his own, but when he was ignored, he lashed out at Mary. "Why wasn't this perfume sold and the money given to the poor? It was worth at least a year's wages!"

All eyes were on Mary now, and the tension in the room was thick. She was worried she had done something wrong. Not sure, she immediately looked to Jesus for guidance. However, Jesus didn't speak to her, but to Judas.

"Leave her alone," Jesus replied. "It was intended that she should save this perfume for the day of my burial. What's it to you if she uses it now?" The others in the room were caught a bit off guard by his comment. His burial? Why would they be preparing for his burial? But Jesus knew the time of his death was near. He continued, "You will always have the poor among you, but you will not always have me."

His guests couldn't even contemplate the weight of that statement. Many of the disciples had given up everything they knew to follow him for the last three years. They could no longer fathom their lives without him.

That is, everyone except Judas. The reprimand in front of everyone sent him into a rage. How dare Jesus embarrass him like that after he had left everything behind to follow him! Judas got up and left them, pushing his way through the guests he had no intention of getting to know. He headed toward Jerusalem, intent on turning Jesus over to the authorities. He would find whatever reward was being offered and claim it for himself.

Everyone watched him walk through the door, but nobody seemed disappointed to see him go except Jesus. Awkwardly, they waited for Jesus to break the silence. He lifted his glass and said, "Well, we better finish our meal while this pleasant fragrance is covering up the stench from Lazarus." The room exploded in laughter, and the lively conversation picked up right where it had left off.

Avner, watching Judith attend to their own rescued and adopted child, had been holding a great deal of guilt in his heart about Lazarus' death. He couldn't help but think that Lazarus probably contracted the illness while they were looking for their dear little Cheyim. He would have never forgiven himself for the sacrifice his friend made for him. Now, looking around the room at the joy in each face, he was at total peace. It felt as if they were all living in a dream. Adinah and Levik, once barren, now with two children. He and Judith, cherishing every day with their sweet child. Lazarus, once four days dead, now eating and drinking and telling stories with everyone else, as if the rot of death never touched him. Mary and Martha, serving and anointing the feet of the Messiah. Fishermen, tax collectors, trade workers, and sinners were now disciples of the Messiah and had the incredible privilege of witnessing mighty miracles. If he were to write the story of their lives in a book for future generations to read, many would not believe it. Yet, every person at that table could testify to the truth. All of their lives had been changed because of Jesus.

One guest spoke to Lazarus from across the table, asking the very question that had been burning in Avner's mind, but he had not been bold enough to ask. "Lazarus, I cannot speak for everyone in this town but know that you have the admiration of everyone in this room for your courageous endeavors. Repeated trips into the unknown of Jerusalem to save the lives of innocents is nothing short of remarkable. Nonetheless, you likely contracted the flea bites that contained the plague during one of these rescues. I can't help but wonder if this experience will put an end to any future trips. I think we all want to know. What are your plans?"

The room fell silent, apart from the babbles of the children who were never asked to leave a room in the presence of Jesus. Everyone did, indeed, want to hear his plans.

Mary and Martha exchanged glances and looked at their brother, waiting for an answer, along with everyone else. It was a subject they had not brought up and a question they were afraid to ask. There was a time that Martha would have never stood for him to take such a risk again. Her selfishness of keeping him safe at all costs would have held him back from following his heart. Not anymore. For the first time, she didn't worry about her brother. Through tragedy, her faith grew. And through the triumphant resurrection of her beloved brother by her beloved Messiah, there was no doubt in her mind that with God, all things really are possible.

Lazarus didn't even hesitate in his reply, as if he was waiting for the right time to announce his plan to the group. "I will go back. In fact, I plan to make another trip soon after Passover."

Avner so admired the bravery and faith of Lazarus. "Are you not afraid of more flea bites?"

"It may happen, yes. I am not naïve enough to think that it could not. But I was not given a second chance at life to live it in fear." He hesitated, wondering how much he should share. There was a time that everyone would think he was out of his mind for telling this story, but after all that they had witnessed through his resurrection, he felt his secret was safe. "When I was walking back from Jerusalem with Levik and Adinah, God spoke to me."

The room, once again, was completely silent. Jesus and Lazarus locked eyes, and Jesus almost laughed out loud, beaming in approval. A thought occurred to Lazarus, and he started laughing as he asked Jesus, "You already know, don't you?"

Both men laughed as Jesus said, "Yes, but I'll let you tell it."

Guests chuckled as Lazarus went on. "It was almost morning, and we were exhausted from the rescue, caring for the babies, and the walk home. I heard an audible voice, and at first I thought it was Levik, but he was so enthralled with the baby that he was nearly tripping over his own feet already."

Levik laughed. "He is not wrong."

"I heard the voice again," he continued, "and realized that I was the only one who heard it. It was made clear to me that my purpose was to continue with these rescue missions and that I was supposed to start an orphanage."

Avner spoke again. "Even now, after what you have gone through?"

"Especially now," Lazarus answered.

"Then I will help you," said Avner. Judith, his wife, instantly looked to Mary and Martha for their reaction. Mary simply answered with a shrug of her shoulders. How could they disagree?

Levik was sitting at the table with the men, and Adinah watched him from across the room. Even amid so much going on around them, her mind kept wandering to the conversation she had with Basharel at the tomb. Martha's faith really had changed her. With God, all things really are possible. Was Adinah's faith strong enough to believe that God could help salvage their marriage and bring back the romantic love for her husband? At this point, it would take another miracle because that emotion seemed foreign to her now. She thought of the irony of her own heart. She was infuriated with him for destroying the good thing they once had, yet wanted to protect him from public scrutiny at the same time. Only a couple of people knew what he had done, and they were loyal friends who would tell no one. As far as anyone there could tell, he was the same man he had always been: handsome, charming, educated, interesting to talk with. He was an honest businessman to everyone who knew him. Conversely, the human side of her found it extremely irritating at the same time. Why could he not have been honest with her? He was faithful to God and had sworn his allegiance to Jesus. Why could he not have been faithful to their marriage?

She watched how his attention was so easily pulled from the conversation at the table to gaze at their beautiful children, Hess and Drozah. He would smile in their direction and then jump back in the conversation as if he heard every word, but she knew he hadn't. He really was a wonderful father. Was it still possible for him to still be a wonderful husband? Was it possible for her to forgive him completely and allow him to try? Could she ever forget what he had done, or trust him at his word again?

He seemed to be able to push the whole thing from his mind when he didn't want to think about it, but she couldn't. There were so many unanswered questions. Had he fallen in love with that woman, or was he just using her? How long had it really been going on? If they had been able to conceive early in their marriage, would he still have done this? Did he secretly hope that this other woman would give him children in his own bloodline? Did he think of that woman when they were together? Would he stray again? She couldn't push these lingering questions out of her mind, and sometimes she wanted to just rip off the bandage and let it all bleed out. It would be difficult to hear, but maybe then the emotional infection could begin to heal. Yet she wasn't entirely sure she really wanted to know the answers to her own questions. Sometimes the truth just hurts too much.

They had talked at length about what happened, but she dodged many of the questions in her mind because her heart could only take so much. He explained that he met that woman when he was out working on the road, and she kept making a point to come back down the same path so she would run into him. Afraid that Adinah would seek her out, he would not tell her the woman's name, or what part of the road she came from. He said it was over, so she could lay her worries to rest. There was no intention of seeking a *get*, a divorce, as long as she could find it in her heart to forgive him and look at him with the same eyes that she did before all of this happened. Was that even possible? She had known women who got through this sort of thing before, but she didn't know if true forgiveness would ever come. She didn't want to be weighed down with suspicion every time her husband went to work.

As if he knew her thoughts, Levik's gaze went from the children to his wife. He caught her watching him and smiled at her in the same loving way he did with the children. Adinah wondered if he meant it, or if it was for show. Then he winked at her in that intriguing and seductive way that only he could. That's the wink that won her heart years ago. Just when she felt a tug at her heartstrings, she wondered if he winked like that at the woman on the road. Would these questions ever stop tormenting her?

She excused herself and walked outside for some fresh air. As the sun was beginning to set, she noticed the first sign of stars taking over the sky. Birds were chirping nearby, and she could hear a soft breeze rustling through the treetops. Seconds later, the breeze blew across her face, and it brought to mind something Jesus had told them. He said a Comforter would soon be with them. One they could not see but could feel. Like the wind. She wasn't sure what that even meant, but in that moment, she felt like it was a whisper from God himself. When she really needed to feel God's presence, she often surrounded herself with the beauty of his nature. For her, finding solitude in these moments had proven to be a salve for her soul.

The music from their celebration floated in the air. There were so many reasons to be joyful, but her heart just hadn't yet caught up with her mind. Sometimes she doubted if she would ever feel genuine joy again, or if it would always remain masked with underlying sorrow. When she felt the breeze again, she knew that living in constant sorrow was not what God wanted for her.

It was suddenly clear that she had two choices. She could continue to be angry and grow further from her husband, or she could find a way to forgive him and love him again. She couldn't stand in limbo. How could she forgive if she couldn't let go of the anger? She didn't want their children to remember her as a bitter old woman. She would have to find a way to change her expectations. Or her heart.

Adinah felt the need to pray, but none of the memorized prayers she had learned seemed to fit these circumstances. When Jesus prayed, he often just spoke from his heart, like he would speak to a friend. He said they could do the same, but she had never tried. Standing here now, she felt a sudden need to be as close to God as possible. She stretched out her arms to the sky and lifted her face to the heavens. "El Shaddai, Creator of all the universe, Jesus said that we could talk to you just like we talk to a friend. He said we do not have to be at the temple to pray. Lord, I am not worthy. Is it okay to talk with you this way? Humbly, I come to you now and ask that you remove anything that stands between you and me. Please remove anything that stands between my pride and the love I know you want me to have for my husband. I cannot get Levik's sin against me out of my mind, but I do know that I, too, am sinful. I beg your forgiveness. Please remove the heart of stone that is growing within me. I want to love my husband, but all I feel right now is a betrayal that brings out the desire in me to seek vengeance. I do not want that kind of spirit."

She paused, deep in thought, then continued. "We are such sinful people! And until now, I didn't see our wickedness with such clarity. You continue to love us, even when we have betrayed you over and over. Even when we have been unfaithful to you, your faithfulness to us still stands. How does your heart not harden towards us altogether? God, I love you with all I have! Yet, there are not enough sacrificial lambs in all of Jerusalem to forgive us for all the sin we have committed against you."

Her eyes filled with tears as she paused to gather her thoughts. With a quivering lip, she pleaded, "Help me forgive. Please. I can't do it on my own. Show me how. How do you do it?"

She heard a voice come from behind her. "One word will answer all of those questions, Adinah. It is *love*."

Adinah turned to see Jesus walking towards her. "*Shalom*, Jesus. I was just...." She wiped her eyes, embarrassed. How much had he heard?

"You are carrying a heavy burden, Adinah. Give it to me."

"What do you mean, Lord?" she asked.

He thought for a moment, then said, "Let me put it another way. I heard you ask for your sins to be forgiven."

Adinah looked into Jesus' eyes and could see her own reflection. "I'm so unworthy!"

"Everyone is unworthy. Why do you think I was sent?"

Adinah's eyes widened. "So, it is true? You really are the Messiah, the Son of God?"

There was a look of assurance in his eyes when he answered. "I am." Jesus paused, giving her time to soak it in.

"Lord," Adinah said, with downcast eyes, "please forgive me for doubting you."

Jesus gently lifted her chin. "Look up, dear one." Adinah's eyes met his. "You have already been forgiven. And you were right in asking God to help you forgive Levik. That is difficult in itself, but let me challenge you even further."

What could be more difficult than that? Adinah braced herself for whatever he was about to say.

Jesus looked deep into her eyes and said, "Forgive the other woman."

Adinah stepped back in surprise, but Jesus stopped her before she could balk. "I know it is difficult, Adinah. But remember that you must forgive in order to be forgiven."

"I'm trying," she said honestly. "It just hurts so much."

"I know. I'm sorry." He was so genuine when he spoke. "It won't always be easy to do, but you must love your enemies. Do good to those who hate you. Bless those who curse you. Pray for those who hurt you. Love each other as I have loved you. That is how others will know you are mine." In just a few days, he thought, they would all know how deep his love was for them.

They were interrupted by a guest who had seen her walk out and yelled back to Levik, "There she is!"

In a moment, Levik was walking out the door towards them with Hess crying in his arms. He yelled to Adinah, "Someone is missing his *aima*!"

Jesus and Adinah laughed together, and he gave her a smile. "There is the little one you had been praying about," he said. With that, he took Hess from Levik's arms, and Hess immediately stopped crying and studied the face of the one who held him.

"Well, Jesus, you have the touch!" said Levik. "If I knew you were this good with babies, we would have sent for you weeks ago so we could get some sleep!"

Jesus kissed Hess on top of the head and said, "I will leave you two alone. You have much to discuss." He walked off, cradling Hess in his arms.

They heard Jesus say, "Whew! Someone is stinky! How can such a big smell come from such a little guy? You give Lazarus some stiff competition!"

Adinah and Levik laughed together for the first time since their fight. It had been weeks, and the laughter felt good. The sun was almost gone, and dusk was setting in. They both looked up to see the stars getting brighter in the sky, then stood facing one another, not sure where to begin.

Adinah felt the breeze across her face once again, and it gave her the strength she needed. God was with her. She broke the silence. "I came out for some fresh air, and it appears that Jesus did the same. I didn't see him come behind me, but he heard me praying."

"Oh, yeah?" said Levik. "What were you praying about?"

"You," she said. "Us." She looked away, afraid that she could not hold back her emotions if she looked him in the eye. "Levik, I trusted you with my whole heart and you broke it."

"I am so sorry I hurt you, Adinah" he said, and this time, she could tell he meant it. His shame was heavy. He didn't even look like the same light-hearted man she was just watching from across the table moments ago. The guilt changed him. For a split second, she felt sorry for him, but it diminished quickly. The fact remained that he would have to work hard to earn back her trust.

He must have been thinking the same thing. "A decision has been made that I think you will support. I have told the men on the road that I will no longer be available to help them. That will remove the temptation altogether. I will seek other work if I have to, but our marriage and our family are more important to me than a comfortable job. "

This took Adinah by surprise. She couldn't believe he took that initiative on his own but was so glad to hear it.

"And," he added, "I told Josiah what I have done. He already suspected, and I could tell that he was disappointed, which brings me more shame. He looks up to me, both spiritually and professionally, and I have been a terrible example. I apologized for my pathetic behavior and asked for his forgiveness as well. Being the upstanding man that he is, he not only forgave me, but he has agreed to pray with me each day before and after work at the shop. He will help hold me accountable to you and to God."

Even with a trusted friend like Josiah, she knew that would have been very difficult for her husband to do. She felt her heart softening toward him.

"In addition, I will come home to eat the noon meal with you and Hess and Drozah each day. When Josiah told me how you showed up with a meal to surprise me, and then how devastated you were when you found out I had been lying, it almost brought me to my knees." Levik stopped and turned away, trying to gain his composure before he could speak again. "I…." He couldn't get the words out without crying. "I know what lengths it must have taken you to arrange that for me. To prepare and pack the meal, to make arrangements for the children, to walk to my shop instead of getting much-needed sleep. You did that for me. You love me so well, and I missed it. Adinah, you three are my world. You all deserve the best version of me. I vow to you now that you will never have to worry about another indiscretion."

With all her heart, Adinah wanted to believe him. She felt a tear slip down her cheek, unaware that she was even crying. It seemed that's all she had been capable of doing lately, but this time, the tears felt different. They didn't sting. They cleansed.

Levik took one of her hands in his and gently lifted her chin with the other. For the first time in weeks, she didn't cringe at the touch of his hand. Their eyes met. "Adinah, do you believe me?"

She looked deep into his eyes before she answered. "Yes," she said, and meant it.

Cautiously, he spoke again. "My beloved, can you forgive me?"

She had hoped he would never ask that question, because before today, she didn't know if she ever could. But somehow, the resentment was gone. Maybe it was her prayer, or the words of Jesus. Perhaps she would feel differently tomorrow, but right now she saw the remorse and regret in her husband's eyes and knew that he was sincere. She wanted no more lies between them, so she answered as honestly as she could. "I pray about it every day. That's what I was praying about when Jesus walked out."

"Thank you for your honesty and for your prayers. I hope it will come in time." Still holding her hand, Levik looked up at the sky, trying to gather courage enough to ask his last question. Looking back at his wife, he asked, "Do you still love me, even now?"

Adinah's heart was full, and she meant it when she answered, "Yes. Even now."

# Chapter 24

## Trista's Homework for God
## (But) Even Now, Chapter 1

May 4, 2018

Here it is, God… My very personal journals, combined with the lesson you taught me through Martha. I hope I will make you proud! I never set out to write a book, but I'm almost 100 percent sure this idea was from you, so I ran with it! It is my hope that the trials you have brought our family through will help others going through the same thing, EVEN NOW! Thank you for leading me to John 11 that day. I will do my best to tell the redemptive story of Mary, Martha, and Lazarus the way you intended us to know it, through the characters of Adinah, Levik, and others that I have created.

Date: 33 A.D.

Setting: On the way to the tomb of Lazarus in Bethany of Judea, four days after Lazarus had died

Conversation:

Martha: "Lord, if you had been here, my brother would not have died. But I know that even now God will give you whatever you ask." (John 11:21-22, NIV)

Jesus: "Your brother will rise again." (John 11:23, NIV)

Background Story:

Martha, Mary, and Lazarus were siblings. Their family

was close friends with the family of Jesus. We will get into the details of this a little later, but you're probably familiar with the most well-known story of these three, that of Jesus raising Lazarus from the dead. We often hear the great Bible stories about Mary washing the feet of Jesus with her hair, being present at the crucifixion, and at the empty tomb. Yet, often, the most quoted verse about her older sister Martha is when she is whining about Mary not helping her prepare a meal. However, we will see how Martha's faith was not only rock solid, but amazing!

One day, when Jesus was teaching in another village, Lazarus fell ill. Martha and Mary sent a message to Jesus, saying "Lord, the one you love is sick." (John 11:3, NIV) Jesus did not rush to get back to Bethany. In fact, when he finally got there, Lazarus had been dead for four days. Martha rushed out to meet him, and this is where their conversation occurred. After she acknowledged her disappointment that Jesus was not there earlier to heal Lazarus, she made a statement which just rocked my world. "But I know that even now God will give you whatever you ask." (John 11: 22, NIV) Even now? These words jumped off the page and into my soul. Even then, when the situation was so bleak and the writing was already on the wall, she knew God would give Jesus whatever he asked. How did she know that? And how does this relate to me today?

I get so excited about these two little words said around 1,985 years ago because as I write this, I am in an "even now" moment in my life. As a matter of fact, I have been in many "even now" situations in my life. It made me wonder. If Martha knew that even then, God would give Jesus whatever he asked, do I believe God will also give me whatever I ask in Jesus' name? Even now?

Do I truly believe this? Do you?

Martha must have been holding out for a miracle as she reminded Jesus that God would do whatever He asked, and she had no doubt that Jesus could deliver on that miracle. Why else would she send a messenger to him in these extreme and seemingly hopeless circumstances? In order to understand what this says about Martha's faith, we need to understand the story in its entirety.

I've always just accepted the popular belief that Mary was the sister with the greater faith, choosing to sit at Jesus' feet at their home during an earlier dinner party. Maybe this is because Jesus gave a gentle correction to Martha when she complained that she was doing all the work to serve their guests, while Mary was listening to Jesus and not helping her. (Luke 10:38-42) This scene may make Martha look like she was focused on trivial and worldly details, where Mary was more mature, and knew the importance of making the most of every second they had with Jesus. I just kind of accepted these generalizations about the sisters until I reread John 11.

Let's take a deeper look at the situation. When Mary and Martha sent the message to Jesus that the one He loves is sick, they were hoping and expecting that He would come right away and heal their brother's sickness, preventing his death. That did not happen.

By the time Martha heard Jesus was near and ran out to meet him, Lazarus had already died. His body had been wrapped in linens and burial cloth and put into the tomb. The funeral had already taken place. The gathering with loved ones and mourning together was in full swing, as we read in John 11:19 (NIV), "and many Jews had come to Martha and Mary to comfort them in the loss of their brother." Lazarus had already been in the tomb, which was a cave with a stone rolled across the entrance, for four days. Martha knew at least a little about what shape her brother's body was in because she warned Jesus that there would be a foul odor by this time when He said to remove the stone. Doug Greenwold explains the situation like this:

> "The Mishnah seems to suggest evidence of a Rabbinic belief that the soul (nephesh in Hebrew) hovered near the corpse of the dead person for three days, hoping to be able to re-enter the body. But by the fourth day, there began a process of (smelly) decomposition that prompts the soul to depart. Thus, if we had a Richter scale (1-10) of miracles like we do for earthquakes, bringing someone back to life on the day of death—like Jarius' daughter and the widow of Nain's son—might be a 9.9 reading. But bringing someone back to life on the fourth day would be off the scale, unthinkable, a virtual impossibility!"[1]

I think this is why her statement moved me like it did. Martha had already seen her brother through his sickness. Knowing how much Jesus loved Lazarus and His ability and willingness to perform miracles for strangers, I'm sure that Mary and Martha's hopes were high. Jesus was going to come and save their brother before it was too late! What other outcome could they picture?

Can you imagine the despair and hurt they must have felt knowing that Jesus could have made a difference but ignored their urgent request? He didn't get there in time. Now, it was too late. Their brother was dead.

At the very least, I'm sure they held out one last hope that Jesus could still redeem the situation if, as Greenwold stated, they believed the soul was still near his body. Were they still hoping that the seemingly impossible could still be possible if Jesus responded to their message within the first three days?

However, the fourth day came. Even if there was any last shred of hope in the sisters' minds, it would have surely been squashed by this time, right?

Nathan Jones explains the difference between a body on day three and day four like this:

> "The upshot is for the first three days you're just dead, but from the fourth day on, you're totally dead-dead."[2]

Lazarus was "totally dead-dead." (Jones) The situation for Martha and her sister, Mary, could not have been bleaker. This was an "even now" situation if there ever was one! The fourth day came. The body was decaying in the tomb, and the soul was no longer near. Martha said it herself in John 11:39 (NIV) after Jesus asked for the stone to be removed. "By this time there is a bad odor, for he has been there four days."

And yet, even after day four, Martha's faith was strong enough to know the most important thing. Even now, God would give Jesus whatever he asked for.... AND HE DID!!!

Sometimes, we are also tempted to analyze and overthink when our prayers are not answered in the manner or time frame we think is best. As we read John 11:17 and go through this difficult time with Mary and Martha, Dr. Eli Lizorkin-Eyzenberg explains the intentions of Jesus like this:

> "Jesus clarifies for his disciples that his close friend Lazarus had died. What is important in vs.17 is John's statement that when Jesus arrived in Bethany, it was already the fourth day. This explains why, after hearing the news that Lazarus was very sick, "he stayed two days longer in the place where he was." (John 11:6) Jesus knew how long it would take to travel to Bethany. He was determined to arrive, not only after Lazarus' death, but when, according to popular Jewish belief, resurrection was no longer possible–on the fourth day!"[3]

When Jesus received the message about Lazarus from the sisters, He declared that his sickness will not end in death. (John 11:4, NIV) Everyone who heard Him say that must have thought Jesus got it wrong this time when they eventually realized that Lazarus did die. But here's the cool thing… Jesus already knew that He was going to raise Lazarus from the dead, and that it would bring more glory to God if it was done on day four. Although His dear friends asked Him to heal Lazarus and prevent his death, Jesus knew that would just be chalked up as one more miracle under His belt, as He had been performing in other regions. No, He was going to do something even better for His friends. But in order for the big picture to come together, Lazarus was going to have to die. His family and friends were going to have to mourn. And He was not going to raise him on day one, day two, or day three. Nope. He knew that resurrecting him on day four, after it seemed utterly hopeless, was better because it would point to God. Jesus was always pointing to God in everything He did.

Mary and Martha probably felt betrayed, just as I have felt betrayed by my husband, but they only felt this way for a little while. Jesus knew this miracle would not only strengthen the faith of His friends, but that it would also help fulfill the purpose of His mission. Raising Lazarus after day four would foreshadow His own death and resurrection that would take place in just a short time. If they already saw it happen once, they would be more likely to believe what was about to happen to Him. Betrayal from friends. False accusations. Painful scourgings. Death on a cross. Mourning by friends. But then, over and beyond what happened with Lazarus, His glorified resurrection would bring forgiveness to all believers and usher in the Holy Spirit and eternal life with God the Father. Talk about a day four moment!

Isn't that often the way of it? So many times, we just see the pain. The loss. The betrayals. We see unanswered prayers.

Exhausted from our trials, we cry out to God, just like Mary and Martha. We just want the pain to subside, and when it doesn't happen right away, we feel like He doesn't hear us.

Yet, I can almost hear Jesus whisper back, "Sometimes, it's not about you. Sometimes it is about a higher purpose that you don't yet understand."

We have tunnel vision. Just like Mary and Martha, that vision often leads right through a burial tunnel to a dead body in a tomb. We see hopelessness, but God sees a jubilant celebration. He knows that if we stay faithful and love Him through our pain like Martha did, our hurts will only be temporary. The tunnel will open up to something much bigger and better than we ever could have imagined!

So, where are you in your "even now" moment in life? Is the situation just starting to get bad, and you don't know how or if things can be restored? Has the situation gotten to the point where it feels more hopeless with every day that passes? I don't know about you, but I sometimes still feel pretty 'day four' with my broken marriage. As I sit here 7 months after D-day, I feel unsure about the future. The shock and anger and rage have subsided for the most part, but, sadly, that "in love" feeling has also faded. He told me he loved me when I was leaving for a trip the other day, and my response was, "I'm trying really hard to get back to that place with you." I do try, every day. Sometimes I feel successful, and sometimes I don't. But I continue to take it to God in prayer because I know there are no hopeless situations where God is concerned.

Whatever you are walking through, my friends, ask yourself this question. Is it worse than a body four days dead on the cusp of stench and decay? Is it worse than the defeating feeling that the soul is nowhere near? Worse than knowing your best friend could have helped and chose not to respond to your message?

Now you know why I need hope and faith in the Lord

more now than ever. Many of you have been there before or may be there now. Let us hold out for a miracle from God, just as Martha did. So many lives depended on God redeeming their situation, just as they do in my current situation. Martha is my hero. In that one short verse of John 11:22, she reminded us all that God can redeem any situation. Yes, ANY. We can go to Him, asking and expecting Him to do a miracle.

And for some reason, in the midst of this current storm, I now find unexplainable peace while trying to salvage a marriage that almost every person I have trusted with my story would have left. (That peace did not come from me!) I am finding patience while trying to home-school three young ones, something I never planned on doing. That patience surely did not come from me. Just for kicks, throw in a hyperactive dog who's always into something, a cat who needs insulin twice a day, and a crazy neighbor who likes to yell at us when she goes on her daily walk by our house. That is just the stuff of life right now, in the middle of my mess. I have been sharing a home with a husband who I can't even look at some days because of things we will get into later. Yet, I have somehow been able to forgive. I know this is because God is redeeming my heart! God got me all excited about having faith in my "even now" moment and has convicted me to sit down and write a book about my life and Martha's faith.

As I sit at my computer in our renovated bedroom, with stop signs and "keep out" messages posted on the closed door, I obey God and I start typing. Trust me, it's not because I need something else to do! My platter seems full enough at the moment. Currently, Andy is out in the living room teaching the kids about the United Kingdom. I can hear the faint background noise of the European geography song from YouTube as I type. The first hour of the day was devoted to total chaos as we saw four bison strolling along and grazing in our side yard. Yes, bison! Evidently, they escaped from our neighbors' fence up the way and a rescue mission has been launched. Since they went on their way, I have gone out and loudly redirected the kids three times already, threatening no Star Wars shows tonight even though it is May fourth. (Evidently a day to celebrate Star Wars??? LOL May the force be with me now!) And if this was not enough excitement for the week, our dog, Lulu, is reluctantly laying by my side as she is on strict orders from the vet to rest today. She broke a hole in the front porch screen last night, escaped into the back forty, and received fifty-six quills from a scrap with a porcupine. Yes, life is crazy around here on our eighty-acre piece of Wisconsin paradise, and I wouldn't have it any other way. There's no way I would have chosen this timing to add something new.

However, I begin this book now because God has made his instructions clear to me. I am not sure if it is for my therapeutic benefit or for God's purpose. I believe maybe it is for both. Or, maybe, it is because you are going through an "even now" moment in your own life and need this encouragement from someone who has been there. Maybe I'm just the instrument God is using for you to hear this message sent through me and straight to you from Martha, 1,985 years ago. Your situation is not as hopeless as it may seem to our human eyes. If God was able to resurrect Lazarus after day four, then God is able to resurrect my love and trust for my husband. And guess what? God is also able to redeem your seemingly hopeless situation too.

Friends, our Lord is amazing! Martha knew it! I know it! You know it! So, sit down with a good cup of coffee and let me tell you about how God answered so many of my prayers. Prayers that I offered when the situation looked and smelled and felt like a "totally dead-dead body." (Jones) Each of these requests made to my Father in Heaven might have seemed ridiculous to someone looking at the situation with tunnel vision.

Maybe, just maybe, there is a higher purpose in what we are going through. It may seem to keep lingering like a soul around a dead body on days 1, 2, and 3, but God can turn it all around on your day 4, in a beautiful way that brings glory to our Father. Maybe our dead, smelly corpse can stand up and take the grave clothes off and start dancing!

I am praying for whoever reads this book as I am writing it. I pray that God resurrects both of our situations! Let's go through our storms together, with the faith that Martha has shown us in her storm. The body was dead. Smelly. Decomposing. The soul had left. God can make any situation beautiful! Martha believed it. I believe it. I hope you believe it, too.

## Chapter 1
## Adinah's Tears
## 31 AD

Mary almost didn't hear the distant sobs…

# *Epilogue*

## Bella

Date: 2036

Andy kissed Trista and whispered, "Good luck," as she hurriedly tried to catch up with the nurse leading her down the hall to the delivery suite. He sat down with a smile from ear to ear, filled with gratitude that he and Trista had the privilege of becoming grandparents. He began to pray as he watched his wife hurry down the hall.

In the delivery room, Bella looked up at her mother, who stood holding one of her hands. Her husband Paul held the other. Bella knew that tidal waves of emotion must be ripping through her mother's mind. After the stories Andy and Trista had told them of how they became a family, Bella knew her mother never thought in her wildest imagination that she would find herself in a labor and delivery room. Yet, true to form, there she was. She was always by her daughter's side. Bella could see Trista's lips move in prayer every time she would yell out in pain. She knew her mother hurt right along with her as she tried to bring her baby girl into the world.

Bella squeezed the hands of two of the people she loved most, as she gave one final push and felt her baby slip from her body. She was exhausted from hours of labor, and everything blurred momentarily before she could focus on the sight in front of her. She watched as the doctor held their baby up for everyone to see, and tears of joy slid down her mother's cheeks.

"Hello, our faithful Martha," Bella declared as she beamed at her beautiful baby girl.

These words were an echo of the exact greeting spoken to another baby girl 2,000 years earlier, in a town called Bethany, by a mother named Drozah.

## Glossary of Terms

**Abba** — father
**Aima** — mother
**Antechamber** — a small room that leads to a larger one
**Arcosolia** — an arched recess in a wall that is used for the purpose of entombment
**Caligae** — heavy-soled sandals with hobnails, worn by Roman soldiers
**Chevra** — volunteers who prepare the body for a sacred Jewish burial
**Get** — Jewish divorce process
**Kaddish** — a mourner's prayer, said to honor the deceased
**Kiddush** — a prayer recited in times of thanksgiving, praise, and celebration
**Palus** — elegant, embroidered robe
**Savta** — Grandmother
**Savta raba** — Great Grandmother
**Shabbat** — the Jewish Sabbath
**Shalom** — a Jewish term for peace, said at greeting or parting
**Shomrim** — one who would guard the body until burial, while the soul was still lingering
**Stola** — elegant garment worn by Roman women that was usually sleeveless and worn under a tunic. The female version of a toga.
**Tallit** — Jewish prayer shawl
**Tunic** — a layered garment that went from the shoulder to the hip or knee, worn by men and women

And now, a sneak peek at the next book in this series...

# The Two Marthas

A NOVEL

## *Prologue*

### The Birth

51 A.D.

Drozah looked up at her mother, who stroked back her hair as the midwife put wine with hyssop to her lips. She sipped it, but the pain was so great that she didn't see the point. Only the delivery of her child would make the pain subside. As she looked up at her mother's face, she knew Adinah must be feeling a mix of emotions. After the stories her parents had told them of how they became a family, she knew it couldn't be easy for Adinah to watch her daughter struggle to bring her own baby into the world when she had been unable to do this herself. Yet, true to form, there she was. She was always by her daughter's side. Drozah could see Adinah's lips move in prayer every time she would yell out in pain, as each contraction grew longer and felt stronger.

Drozah squeezed tighter to the birthing rope as she gave one final push and felt her baby slip from her body. She was exhausted from hours of labor, and the hyssop made everything blur momentarily. She watched as the midwife tied the cord and handed her beautiful baby girl to Adinah, who held her up for everyone to see.

Tears of joy slid down Drozah's cheeks as they handed her the baby. Everything else going on in the room faded away as she cradled her daughter against her chest. In an instant, she understood the fierceness of a mother's love.

"What shall you name her?" asked Adinah, trying to absorb every second of this moment.

Drozah wiped her eyes as she answered her mother. "Amnon and I have already decided. Above all else, we want our child to know and love God. We will name her after the one who showed you how anything is possible if we stay faithful to our Lord." Adinah's eyes met those of her beautiful daughter, as she spoke to her for the first time. "Hello, our faithful Martha!"

# *Chapter 1*

## Bella's Journal Entry

December 10, 2040

Well, today is the day I'm going to start keeping a journal! I found this beautiful one on my last trip into town and it has inspired me with its combination of muted green background and vibrant pink flowers. Writing about the happenings in my life and reflecting on my feelings has been on my mind ever since Mom shared her pretty, but tattered, journal with me. It was around the time Paul and I got engaged. On one of our regular walks on the trails across from Mom's, she told me she would like me to read her journal, that it was important to her I saw and understood how God has worked in her and Dad's lives. She explained that although I knew much of their story, there was much that was not age appropriate until now.

Wow, that ended up being a long evening.... Dad was on a men's fishing outing with the church, so it was just her and I. We made hot tea and got set up in the living room, me on one recliner and her on the other. She worked on her crossword puzzle book as I read. I now know all of their story; the good, the bad, and the ugly. God showed up for her in so many ways, and she stayed faithful to both Him and Dad through it all. Amazing!

Since then, Mom has really stressed how helpful it has been for her to journal through her ups and downs, and she has been encouraging me to do so in my current funk, so here goes....

I am desperate to feel some of that Christmas joy I used to feel growing up! Poor Martha deserves all the Christmas glee and special memories my mom made for me through the years. I remembered the ultimate Christmas mood enhancer used to be shopping at the little stores in town for homemade gifts and candles and such. The best time to go was in the evening on a weekend, so you'd be sure the lights would be twinkling and the local choir would be singing their annual performance of Christmas favorites. I decided we would all bundle up and go on Saturday night and even remembered to take our Santa hats out of storage for the event.

It has been a couple of years since we got to experience the town during Christmas. Grandma passed away two years ago, and Grandpa passed away last year. So this was going to be Martha's first time to experience it since she was a baby! Paul and I were so excited! I couldn't wait for Martha to taste that famous creamy hot chocolate with a candy cane stirrer from Java Joe's, too.

We parked on the street a little way down from town so that we could walk by the heavenly nativity scene on the corner. This one has always been my favorite of all that I have seen because Jesus is looking right into Mary's eyes with his hands held up toward her. Mary is looking so lovingly down at him with her hands in a prayer position. We walked by the corner and no nativity scene was there. I then recalled a news story about them having to take it down last year, something to do with the property it was on belonging to the post office or something like that. How sad!

As we walked toward town, we saw glimmers of the gold and green Christmas lights wrapped around the trees lining the street. How perfect!! Martha's favorite color is gold. But something was different. The music coming down the street was classical music with no words. Hmmm… Maybe the Christmas tunes would come on later. Nope. They never did.

We finally arrived at Joe's and ordered our three Christmas Cocoas. Joe topped them off with candies and as he handed them to us carefully, he made it a point to say, "Here are your three Holiday Cocoas." They were just as creamy and chocolate-y as I remembered, and Paul and I took turns blowing on Martha's drink so that she could eventually drink it without burning herself. She was laughing at us as we were puffing our cheeks up really big before we blew the steam away for her. We finished our drinks as we shopped in a couple more stores, making our way to where the choir usually sings. As good as they were, it just wasn't the same without the Christmas tunes playing in the background, though.

Finally, we made it to the spot where the beautifully

decorated Christmas tree usually stands... where the choir from Pine Ridge Elementary school sings their hearts out for the entire city to hear...and the scene was very different from what I expected. No tree. No kids. Instead, a large sign that read:

> 'A Million Americans know MYTHS when they see them. What myths do you see? American Atheists. Since 1963. Athiests.org.'

Under the writing were photographs showing King Neptune, Jesus Christ, Santa Claus, and Satan.

What in the heck?? I guess this is the new normal now. Christmas Cocoa, the town's Christmas tree, playing "Little Drummer Boy" in the town square, children singing Christmas hymns.... All of these things have been deemed to be offensive by the powers that be.

Paul and I just looked at each other and made the sleeping signal with our hands on our cheek to indicate we would talk about it later in bed. We explained to Martha that if we wanted Christmas carols tonight, the three of us were going to have to sing them ourselves. That is still allowed, isn't it?

So we skipped all the way to our car singing, "Oh Christmas tree, Oh Christmas tree, how lovely are your branches!"

*Dear Father in Heaven, what is happening? Why do people feel the need to take You out of everything? I wanted to share the wonderful traditions and memories that Mom and Dad made for me with Martha. But the world is different now. They will tolerate less and less of You, but I want more of You. As disappointed as I am about the loss of my favorite nativity scene and our town's Christmas traditions fading, help me focus on You and the true meaning of Christmas.*

*Help restore my joy in You and let our little family make new traditions that do not depend on the world's swinging pendulum of ideas. Let us sing joyful noises unto You even if the Christmas tree has been replaced and the choir's performance is canceled. Thank You for being You. Please bless our marriage and help us raise our precious Martha to be Godly in an ungodly world. In Jesus' name, Amen.*

# Chapter 2

## The Jar

57 A.D.

Drozah's hands jumped from her mending when she heard something crash to the floor. The sound came from the kitchen. Since they had few possessions, she knew it could only be one of two things. She closed her eyes and took a deep breath before making her way into the next room to see what had been broken this time. *Please don't be my aima's jar, please don't be my aima's jar.* As she scanned the room, her heart sank. It was, indeed, her mother's jar, which had been handed down from her mother before her. Now it was in several large pieces around the heels of six-year-old Martha, who was staring up at her with dark brown eyes.

Martha knew how special this jar was to her mother. She had told her the story of its significance many times. Her grandmother, Adinah, had once fetched water in this jar for her friends Mary and Martha, after whom she was named. That doesn't sound special in and of itself, but the water was for a very special person. Jesus himself had been a guest at their home that day, and he drank water from this very jar. Ironically, it was so special that her mother no longer used it to go back and forth from the well, in fear that she would drop and break it. She now used it to store grain. Martha looked from the pieces on the ground back up at her mother, with eyes full of worry and a heart full of sorrow at what she had just done. Not only had she broken something that was irreplaceable, but the jar contained some of the only remaining grain their family had, which was just enough for dinner. Now, it was scattered in the dirt. She had no idea when they would be able to get more.

"Darling, what happened?" Drozah asked, bending to pick up the pieces. She didn't want to make eye contact and let her daughter see the same emotions reflected back in her own eyes.

"I'm sorry, *Aima*. I was just trying to reach a cup for these." She pulled a handful of wildflowers from behind her back and extended them out towards her mother.

As Drozah took the butterfly weed and yarrow from her daughter's hands, she wrapped her in a hug. She could feel Martha's little hands clinging to the back of her *tunic* as she pressed her cheek against her belly. Little did Martha know she was also embracing the baby in her mother's womb. Drozah chuckled to herself, anticipating what it would be like to tell her family the news. Martha was such a loving child, and was doted over by her grandparents, Adinah and Levik. Under most circumstances, Drozah knew it would be glorious news, but after the great famine that had spread throughout Judea, everyone was cautious. When the ground got dry, they were always afraid another drought and famine was just around the corner. In fact, when Martha was born, there were times that Drozah was so close to malnutrition that she feared she wouldn't even produce enough milk to care for her. The midwife had concocted teas for her to drink with fennel, thistle, and fenugreek to help her lactate more productively. For the last several years, she and Amon had been very careful not to conceive. It was difficult enough to find food for those already in their home without bringing new life into it.

Drozah had a love/hate relationship with Rome. They were the cruelest, most dominating and unforgiving people she knew. Yet, if it wasn't for the young Roman girl who birthed her and left her to die in the woods, Adinah and Levik would never have claimed her as their own. Sometimes Drozah wondered how different her life would have been if she and her brother Hess had been raised by Romans. The thought sent shivers down her spine.

The economical tide was turning, but it was happening quite slowly. Rains began to come more often, which produced better harvests, but starving passersby on their way to Jerusalem seemed to help themselves during the night. When it got really bad, Paul and Barnabas, who were friends and disciples of Jesus, came from Antioch with supplies. They did what they could to help the people in their area and as far across Judah as they had supplies to reach. The kindness of Paul and Silas got their family through the lean months, but just when they seemed to get back on their feet, something else would happen to cut off their means of making a living.

Just during Drozah's lifetime, their little town of Bethany had suffered a great deal. Being only a short distance outside of Jerusalem, oppression at the hands of the Romans was heavy. There were so many moving pieces at the root. The three biggest pieces were the Romans, the Jews, and the followers of Jesus, who were now referring to themselves as Christians. They had coexisted smoothly for a while, but they were all beginning to twist, splinter, and crash together.

Even though the famine had ended years before, food was often still difficult to come by. For Drozah's family, now was one of those times. As she stood comforting her daughter, the grain scattered across the floor reminded her of the feasts they once had. Roasted lamb with mint sauce. Salads with lettuce, parsley, chives, cole root, and celery. Lintels, beans, artichoke. Dried apples and pears with honey. Fresh bread dipped in olive oil. Just the thought of it made Drozah's belly growl. She realized her daughter had experienced nothing like that, and she desperately wished she could provide such a meal for her family now. Some day.

Her husband, Amnon, walked through the door and saw his wife and daughter embracing. He was on a break from helping his father-in-law, Levik, work in the silversmith shop. Silver had been more difficult to come by than food, but they were very skilled. The rich from Jerusalem often sought them out to have certain items melted down and made into something else. Many would willingly pay a higher fee if Levik and Amnon were willing to make the trip to and from Jerusalem to gather and deliver the items, so they traveled quite often. Today, they were working in their shop just down the street. Drozah knew that meant there was little work.

Amnon understood what was going on when his gaze fell from his wife and daughter to the jar and grain scattered in the dirt. "Oh, no, what happened here?" He held out his arms to Martha, who left her mother's side and leaped into her father's arms.

"*Abba*, I broke the special jar!" Her sobs were those of true remorse.

He looked to Drozah, who explained, "It was an accident, of course. She was reaching for a cup to surprise me with these magnificent flowers."

"Well," he said, "those flowers are magnificent, but not nearly as stunning as both of you." He leaned back so he could look Martha in the eye. "It is a very special jar, but it's just a jar. Nothing is as special as you."

Martha's smile beamed through damp eyes.

"And," he continued, "I will find a way to fix it. Don't

you worry." He set his daughter down, and she immediately picked up the pieces to hand to him.

As she put each piece in his hands, he said in an exaggerated voice, "Oh, how heavy is this jar? I don't know if I am able to carry it all by myself. What strong arms you must have, Martha!"

She giggled, and Drozah's heart was so full as she watched the interaction between father and daughter. She couldn't wait to tell her husband about the child on the way, but for now, it was a secret just between her and God. Something about that made her feel especially close to the Creator, and she wanted to keep it that way for a little while longer. She would tell Amnon when the time was right.

Drozah grabbed the cup from the shelf and filled it half full of water. "Let's get these flowers into some water, shall we?" She set them on the table and said, "Look how lovely! Thank you, my darling."

To her husband, she said, "I set aside some salted fish for your lunch. I will come up with something for dinner. When you go back to the shop, I'll go see if anyone is in need of some goat's cheese. I made some fresh this morning."

****

Nobody came to the door when Drozah knocked, but she could hear them inside. They bought cheese from her every week. She and Martha were a day earlier than usual, but that shouldn't be a problem. Perhaps they didn't hear her. Martha helped her knock again, louder this time. Finally, the door opened, but not wide and welcoming, like usual. She feared someone inside must have an illness and was being careful not so spread it.

"*Shalom*," Drozah said in greeting when Gelleh, the mother of the house, peered out at her. "Is everything alright?"

"That's an interesting greeting, coming from you," said

Gelleh.

Drozah was confused. Gelleh had always been so pleasant to do business with. "Whatever do you mean?"

"*Shalom* is a Jewish greeting of peace. You are no longer Jewish, and I do not wish you peace." With that, Gelleh slammed the door.

Martha looked up at her mother, who stood in stunned silence. As they turned to walk away, one of Gelleh's sons yelled from the window. "We don't buy cheese from Christians!" Drozah took her daughter's hand. As they walked away, she could feel the stares from neighbors. She wondered if this was what it was like for her mother after she and Levik had taken Roman babies in as their own.

Martha looked up at her, also confused. "Mother?" she said, looking for some guidance or explanation that Drozah did not have. Gelleh's children had often played with her, and she didn't understand the source of their hatred.

Drozah simply squeezed her daughter's hand and said, "They must not be in need of any cheese today. Let's pay a visit to Basharel!" She tried to sound cheery but was sure her daughter knew better.

Martha played with Basharel's grandchildren while the women talked. Drozah explained what just happened with Gelleh, and found that Gelleh's husband, a Jewish rabbi, was instructed from the Pharisees in Jerusalem to cut off all connections to anyone claiming to be a Christian. That explained it. Adinah had been warned that this day would come, but she was hoping they could still find a way to live together in harmony, despite their differences.

After visiting for a while, Drozah and Martha headed to the market. She could use the coins Basharel had given her for cheese to buy more wheat. She was disappointed to find that there was no wheat left, but she did find some barley. That would have to do. Arriving home, she prepared a meager dinner and tidied up while she waited for her husband to arrive. Her stomach was in knots, thinking of the events of her day, and she wondered what his reaction would be when she told him what happened.

Amnon finally came into view but did not come through the door. Instead, he peeked his head in and said, "Close your eyes!" Drozah did as she was instructed, anticipating what her husband was up to this time. He was always doing little things to surprise them.

"Are they closed?" he asked.

"Yes, they are," answered Drozah. By now, Martha had also come into the room and echoed, "Yes, they are!"

"Ahh, you must close your eyes as well, little one," Amnon said.

"They are closed!" Martha replied, as she squeezed her eyelids until her nose crinkled up.

"Keep them closed until I tell you to open them," he said, and they could hear him shuffle into the room and set something on the table. "Okay, open!" he said.

Martha squealed in delight and Drozah gasped as their opened eyes revealed Amon's gift. The jar was not only put back together, but it was sealed together with shining silver. It was strange how the silver highlighted the broken cracks yet made it even more beautiful. It was exquisite!

"Amnon! This is amazing! How did you…? Where did you…?" She knew how expensive silver was and how hard it was to come by. She figured her husband was either in debt to someone or had spent everything they had.

"Your father has a jar where he has been collecting silver dust left over from projects for many years. Then, we had a customer pay us with an extra silver spoon. We melted it all down to put this together for you." He was beaming, so proud that he was able to make his wife smile. Drozah ran to her husband and threw her arms around his neck, kissing him on the cheek.

Martha ran and threw her arms around him as well.

"Thank you, *Abba*!" Her voice was muffled against his legs.

"I told you I would fix it for you," he said, as he stooped to look his daughter in the eyes. "Martha, every time you look at this jar, I want you to remember that God can take broken things and make them into something beautiful."

Drozah loved the way Amnon was always pointing his family to God. She was so lucky to have a man who loved his family so fiercely. She would wait to tell him about what happened with Gelleh, so the joy wasn't sucked out of this day. Yes, the jar had been broken, but only through an accident when her sweet daughter was trying to surprise her with flowers. An act of love. And it was put back together by her husband and father in a way that was nothing short of a work of art. An act of love and sacrifice. She couldn't wait to tell her mother the story of what happened and show her the jar. It would surely be a family legacy.

Just then, she felt something hit her foot. Scanning the floor, she realized what it was and instantly felt like she would vomit.

Blood.

## Meet the Authors

***DENAE JONES*** and her husband Darrin are the parents to six children, ages 12-22, who love spending time fishing, 4-wheeling and hiking together. She currently teaches middle school and writes for local newspapers. Through her passion to share the love of God with others, she has authored Love, Joy, Peace, and co-authored Everyday Grace for Teens and Everyday Grace for Mothers. Her writing has also been in Chicken Soup for the Teacher's Soul, and A Second Chicken Soup for the Woman's Soul.

***JENNIFER THOMAS*** and her husband are the parents of five children, ages 11-27. A former elementary school teacher, she now homeschools her three young ones. The family enjoys hiking and skiing together, along with just hanging at home with their dogs, chickens, and ducks. She believes strongly that the Bible is still relevant to us today and is passionate about sharing this message.

## The Message of But, Even Now

The characters and hardships of Adinah and Trista were created to show that even the most faithful are met with trials, but none of them are new. Someone, somewhere has done it and come out stronger on the other side. Sharing powerful stories helps others know that they are not alone and there is no shame in voicing doubts or in seeking help. Most importantly, we see how God is at work in all of it. There is nothing we can do to diminish his love for us - even now.

# *Reader's Discussion Guide*

## FOR THOSE WHO ARE SEARCHING

Trista and Adinah were both searching. For explanations. For family security. For a deeper relationship with God. Think of a time in your past when you were searching and eventually got what you were looking for. (For example, were you ever searching for a job and finally landed something better than what you were expecting?)

What circumstances led up to that playing out the way it did?

Is there anything you are still searching for?

Have you asked God for guidance? Listen for His answer.

***Scripture reflection:***

Psalm 139:23-24 NIV
"Search me, God, and know my heart. Test me and know my anxious thoughts. See if there is any offensive way in me and lead me in the way everlasting."

Matthew 6:33 NIV
"But seek first his kingdom and his righteousness, and all these things will be given to you as well."

## FOR THOSE WHO ARE STRUGGLING WITH DOUBT

Trista and Adinah both struggled with doubt at different times. How did doubt affect their relationships with their husbands?

How did doubt affect their faith?

What was the turning point for each of them?

Did they seek God, or did God seek them?

Have you experienced anything similar? Consider sharing your story.

Did you also reach a turning point? If so, what led up to that? If not, how can you continue to seek God?

***Scripture reflection:***

Mark 9:24 NIV
"Immediately the boy's father exclaimed, "I do believe; help me overcome my unbelief!"

Psalm 50:15 NIV
"And call on me in the day of trouble; I will deliver you, and you will honor me."

## WHEN WE ARE BARELY HANGING ON

Both Trista and Adinah were met with crushing circumstances that were out of their control, but they each had a support system. Who were the people they could count on?

What did they do to help?

Was there a time when they could have leaned on God for support, but chose to try and handle it on their own?

How did that work out for them?

Was there a time when they sought God first, instead of leaving prayer as a last resort?

What was the turning point?

Addiction. Unfaithfulness. Infertility. Illness. Trista and Adinah's situations seemed hopeless on more than one occasion. How did God show up for them?

How would their outcomes have been different if they would have given up?

Have you struggled with a circumstance in the past that seemed hopeless, but turned into a praise? How did you persevere?

Are you or someone you love in a seemingly hopeless situation now? Have a talk with God. Let him know your fears, your worries, and even things that anger you. He already knows your heart ... share it with Him.

***Scripture reflection:***

Matthew 19:26 NIV
Jesus looked at them and said, "With man this is impossible, but with God all things are possible."

Romans 12:12 NIV
"Rejoice in hope, be patient in tribulation, be constant in prayer."

**Check us out at:**
***www.facebook.com/LivingLifeOnTheBrightSide***

Endnotes

1) preservingbibletimes.org/wp-content/uploads/2014/ The Rest of the Story, A Closer Look at Familiar Passages, pages 86-87, by Doug Greenwold

2) Deeper Insights Into the Resurrection of Lazarus (Part 1 of 2) March 27, 2018 Nathan Jones.

3) Resurrection Of Lazarus, Jews And Jewish Tradition (John 11:1-44) By Dr. Eli Lizorkin-Eyzenberg, November 28, 2013

CPSIA information can be obtained
at www.ICGtesting.com
Printed in the USA
JSHW020455170323
39064JS00001B/6

9 798985 520095